Playing Matchmaker

Constance listened to the verbal exchange between the two but more interesting by half was the silent communication of flicking glances, long looks, and the lowered eyes whenever one or the other became conscious that he or she was staring.

Constance had promised her mother she'd do all she could to help her father. And then, curious, she'd asked how she would know if he was falling in love. Lady Cranston had chuckled weakly and then smiled mistily at her daughter. "You will know by how he looks at the woman. There will be a stunned look about his eyes. He will stare rudely and be unaware he does so. And he will find it difficult to look away. Oh, yes, you will know when he has met a woman he may wed—once he thinks of it!"

"Wed?" whispered Constance too softly to break into the others' conversation. "My Annabelle?"

Her gaze went from her father to her companion and back again. A barely repressed giggle rose up inside her at the thought of her grandmother's reaction to such a connection. *But why not? I'd not lose my beloved Annabelle if they were to marry,* she thought.

She watched them, careful not to disturb the discussion between the other two. . . .

—from "A Father's Duty" by Jeanne Savery

A KISS
FOR PAPA

Jo Ann Ferguson
Valerie King
Jeanne Savery

ZEBRA BOOKS
Kensington Publishing Corp.
http://www.kensingtonbooks.com

ZEBRA BOOKS are published by

Kensington Publishing Corp.
850 Third Avenue
New York, NY 10022

All Kensington titles, imprints, and distributed lines are
available at special quantity discounts for bulk purchases for
sales promotion, premiums, fund-raising, educational or in-
stitutional use.

Special book excerpts or customized printings can also be
created to fit specific needs. For details, write or phone the
office of the Kensington Special Sales Manager: Kensington
Publishing Corp., 850 Third Avenue, New York, NY 10022.
Attn. Special Sales Department. Phone: 1-800-221-2647.

Zebra and the Z logo Reg. U.S. Pat. & TM Off.

First Printing: May 2002
10 9 8 7 6 5 4 3 2 1

Printed in the United States of America

CONTENTS

THE BEST
FATHER
IN ENGLAND

Jo Ann Ferguson

One

"Now here is just what you need, Elzanne."

Looking up from the papers she was grading, Elzanne Corbett smiled at her brother Orson, who was a teacher at the private boys' school. No one had any idea that Elzanne helped him with his work. The rest of the staff at the small school believed that Elzanne did nothing more than keep house for her brother. Only Orson knew of her longing to teach in a classroom and appreciated how much she helped him with his work.

Orson was sitting in his favorite chair by the hearth of their parlor with his feet propped on a petit point stool. A calico cat was perched on his knees, snoring softly. The flickering fire reflected on his hair, turning it a shade nearly as red as hers, and glittered in his dark eyes. He held out a page, his freckles connecting as he grinned.

"I recognize that expression," she said with a laugh. "What is wrong with that essay that you don't want to read it yourself?"

"Now, now, Sister dear, I do not give you *all* of the most difficult papers to read."

"Just most of them."

He chuckled and picked up his pipe. Sending a bluish cloud aloft around him, he said, "Do me a favor and read this one, Elzanne."

"From which class?"

"The twelve-year-olds."

Elzanne wondered what her brother was up to now. She was certain that he had teased her, nonstop, from the very day she was born. And she had jested back. This small cottage on the grounds of Lindenmere School was often filled with laughter. She had heard the same sound coming from his classroom, and she knew his students were fond of him, for they often called even after they had gone off to university or to London for the Season.

She took the page he had held out and frowned. "What a mess this is!" She shook the paper to be certain the thick spots of ink were well dried. "Is this the boy's customary work?"

"Actually it is better in appearance than most of his work. I suspect he enjoyed this assignment more than most of the ones given to him. Do read it aloud, Elzanne, if you can pick your way through the poor writing skills."

Tilting the page, so the lamp's light flowed across it, she gasped. "The spelling is atrocious. He is twelve, you said?"

"Yes. The spelling is why I want you to read it aloud. It's easier than trying to figure out the words by just reading it to yourself."

She looked over the page at him. "Aha!"

"Aha?"

"Now I understand why you want me to read it. You cannot navigate your way through it, and you are too vain to put on your barnacles."

"Eyeglasses will do little good with that jumble."

Leaning back in her chair, Elzanne stretched out her legs to prop them, too, on the stool. " 'The Best Father in England by the Honorable Mr. Rudyard Trowbridge,' " she began, then chuckled. "The young man looks upon himself with great admiration, I see."

"Read on, Elzanne."

"Very well. 'The Best Father in England by the Honorable Mr. Rudyard Trowbridge. My father, Lord Trowbridge, is the best father in all of England or any of her colonies.' " She paused with a frown. "I think that word is supposed to be 'colonies,' although the spelling is not close." She tilted the page toward her brother. "What do you think?"

He peered at it. "I suspect you are right. Spelling is not, as I told you, a strong suit for the boy."

"So I can see." She ran her finger along the page, trying to follow the line of handwriting that seemed to go in every direction but the one it should. " 'My father always has time to play a game with me or to listen to my—' " She shook her head. "I suspect he was going to write something like troubles, but the word is lost in a blotch of ink. 'My father is proud of what I have learned at school, and he cannot wait until I come home for the holidays to brag about me to his friends. My father spends hours with me doing fun and interesting things like making a kite or reading a book. My father has introduced me to many important peoples . . .' *Peoples* is what he wrote." She frowned at her brother. "Really, Orson, this boy has no more writing skills than a child half his age."

"Trudge on and finish it."

Elzanne did, and her voice grew soft with amazement as she read, " 'My father has introduced me to many important *people,* and he is teaching me all I need to learn to oversee his estates when I follow him as viscount. My father never tires of my company. During the last holidays, my father spent all of one afternoon fishing with me in the pond and then postponed a meeting with the local mayor so we could eat what we had caught. My father has taken me for a sail on a ship from London to Penzance and let me steer the ship. My father is teaching me to drive his coach-and-four and does not care if I drive it as fast as the wind. My father refuses to be away from home at night, so he can tuck me into bed and always read me a story. My father is the best father in England.' " She lowered the page to her lap and smiled at her brother. "What a paragon! I doubt if any living man can be so perfect."

"Well, you shall find out for yourself." He smiled and took another puff on his pipe as the smoke swirled up to the rafters on the low ceiling.

She set the essay on the table beside her. "Is Lord Trowbridge calling here at the school?"

Orson set down his pipe. Looking at her, he propped his chin on his palm and his elbow on the arm of his chair. With a chuckle, he said, "He is not coming here, but you will be meeting him soon."

"You are speaking in riddles, Orson."

"Quite to the contrary, I am being very clear. You are not listening."

"I heard you say that I shall be meeting this apparent paragon named Lord Trowbridge soon, but he is not coming here." She frowned. "Really, Orson, are you suggesting that I shall be encountering him elsewhere? Mayhap when the Honorable Mr. Trowbridge drives his father in a coach-and-four through the school's front gate?"

"Now, now, Elzanne. Sarcasm is not a pretty trait in a woman."

"Withholding information is not a *handsome* trait in a man."

"Touché."

Elzanne could not help laughing. Her brother could prattle on endlessly in circles and enjoy every minute of it. Usually she challenged him, word for word, but she was too curious about why and where Orson believed she would be encountering "the best father in England." Her nose wrinkled at the very thought. If the father was even half as self-satisfied as the son, he would surely be an obnoxious bore.

"Do tell me, Orson. If I am not about to encounter Lord Trowbridge here at Lindenmere, then where?"

"In Sussex. At Trowbridge House, to be completely accurate."

"We are calling on him there?"

"We? No." He chuckled again. *"You* will be meeting him when you take the Honorable Mr. Rudyard Trowbridge there tomorrow so he may spend the early summer holidays with his father."

"Me?"

"It would not be the first time you escorted a student to his home."

She set the other papers on the table and stood. "No, it would not be, but you have always traveled with me as a representative of Lindenmere School. What would Lord Trowbridge think if I show up with only young Rudyard—"

"Elzanne, remember yourself. He is the Honorable Mr. Rudyard Trowbridge."

She ignored his hoaxing as she asked, "What would his father and mother—"

"Lord Trowbridge is a widower."

"So what would his *father* think if I showed up with only the boy as my escort on such a journey?"

"He will have no choice but to think that you are the very best tutor the boy could have for his holidays."

"Tutor?" She wished her heart did not leap in anticipation at the very idea of teaching. She so longed to be in a classroom where she could instruct on something more interesting than embroidery, as she had at a neighboring girls' school until she had been overwhelmed with *ennui*. More than once, she had considered cutting her hair, binding her breasts, and donning men's clothing to present herself to the headmaster as a prospective teacher of composition or mathematics. Orson acknowledged that she had a true talent for helping hapless students, but nobody else would. Her excitement abated as she said, "Orson, I doubt if Lord Trowbridge will be pleased to have his son tutored by a woman for the summer holidays."

"Quite to the contrary. I have received correspondence from the viscount which informs me that he is grateful that I am sending my assistant to serve as a tutor for the Honorable Mr. Rudyard Trowbridge."

"Did you, perchance, remember to mention that your assistant was your *sister?*"

He picked up his pipe and puffed on it before saying, "I do not recall."

Grabbing a small pillow from the settee, she tossed it at him. He laughed as he caught it before it struck his head.

"Elzanne, it is all arranged. The lad is in dire need of tutoring, as you can see from his work. You possess more patience than I could ever hope to have, so you are the most obvious tutor for the lad."

"Patience?" She gave him a scowl.

"The lad is somewhat of a trial."

"Somewhat?"

He laughed again. "I shall be honest with you. He is an intolerable imp, always looking for ways to avoid doing his work and is very high and mighty."

"That I saw in his writing." She folded her arms in front of her and tapped her toe in her most furious pose. And it was just a pose because she was thrilled with the idea of teaching during the early summer holidays. "You might have had the decency to mention your machinations to me."

He pointed at her with his pipe. "Then you would have given me all the reasons why you thought it would not work. Just as you are now." He abruptly became serious as he set himself on his feet and put his hand on her shoulder. "Elzanne, I know how much you long to teach something substantive. This is your chance."

"I don't know whether to thank you or ask if you are out of your mind."

"You should thank me, I believe, for you have already suggested that I took an early knock in the cradle."

Elzanne flung her arms around his shoulders and gave him a quick embrace. "I do thank you for devising this chance for me and convincing me to give it a try."

"So you will go with the boy tomorrow?"

"It appears I shall. I do hope I can be as persuasive with Lord Trowbridge as you have been with me." She pointed to the page she had read from. "But a paragon like that should be eager to have help for his son."

"Yes . . ." He bent and picked up the page. "Elzanne, you should know—"

"Mr. Corbett," came their housekeeper's voice from the door to the front hall, "one of your students wishes to speak with you." Agatha Marlowe came into the parlor. She was not much older than Orson and a pretty blonde. In Elzanne's opinion, Agatha hoped for a match that would promote her from Orson's housekeeper to his wife.

"Which one?" he asked.

"Mr. Wells."

Orson rolled his eyes as he said under his breath, "Who is a match for the lad you'll be tutoring, Elzanne." He raised his voice and said, "Tell him to wait in my office, Agatha. I shall be there soon."

"I will be glad to, Mr. Corbett." She flashed him a come-hither smile as she walked out, her hips swaying in an obvious invitation to watch.

Elzanne smiled when she saw that Orson was doing just that. Mayhap her brother had another reason for wanting to send Elzanne with his student to Trowbridge

House. Orson and Agatha would be a nice match, and Elzanne would never own that she had hired Agatha with just that thought in mind.

"You were saying . . . ?" she asked when Orson continued to stare even after Agatha had disappeared from sight.

"Oh . . . I don't recall."

"You said something about something I should know."

He picked up his pipe and drew deeply on it. "I am sure I did, but the thought is quite gone."

"Agatha does that to you, doesn't she?" She laughed when he blushed. "Oh, Orson, do not think you are hiding anything from either me or her."

"I didn't." Squaring his shoulders, he said, "I did ask Lurline if she wanted to go with you. I thought you would want your abigail with you."

"And leave you and Agatha without a watchdog?" She wagged a finger at him. "Take care, Orson, that you do nothing to damage *your* reputation."

"I shan't, because I will be visiting a friend during the holidays."

She was tempted to ask if he was going to visit that friend alone, but only said, "I should go and oversee the packing so I can journey to Trowbridge House."

"With the Honorable Mr. Trowbridge."

"I hope *you* are not going to regret this," she replied as he walked toward the door.

He turned and faced her. "I shan't. Do you think you will?"

"No," she said honestly. She looked forward to teaching this recalcitrant lad . . . and to see how accurately he had portrayed his father. Her curiosity had never gotten her into trouble before. She hoped it would not now.

Two

Bradley Trowbridge pushed aside the reports his estate manager had given him to read nearly a fortnight ago. He had promised Quinlan that the reports would be read before the midsummer quarter day. That was only a few weeks hence, and Bradley had not read past the first page.

Standing, he crossed the navy blue carpet in his office, a room that was uncluttered with anything but his desk and a pair of chairs, and went to the tall windows that overlooked the avenue leading from the gate to the front door of Trowbridge House. He peered through the diamond-shaped mullions, but saw nothing through the rain and mist that had rolled up off the sea.

Lurking here was a useless exercise. A footman would come to alert him as soon as the carriage he had dispatched to Lindenmere School returned bringing Rudyard and his tutor.

He rubbed his brow, which had had a tendency to begin to ache each time he thought about his heir and only child coming to Trowbridge House for this holiday. Other holidays had been spent in London or visiting with friends. This was the first time that Rudyard had come back to Trowbridge House since the death of his mother two years ago. If this holiday had not coincided with the quarter day ceremonies, which Bradley needed to attend, the boy would not be coming here now.

"How much longer are you going to hide yourself in here?" asked a familiar voice from the doorway.

Bradley did not look over his shoulder as he said, "Good afternoon to you, too, Mother."

He heard the soft swish of her gown against the carpet. He did turn when he heard a chair move. His mother had shifted the chair so she had a good view of his face. Her blond hair showed little gray, and most of the lines in her face had been imprinted by smiles and laughter. However, she was not smiling now. With her hands on the arms of the chair, a single finger tapped. He chuckled, in spite of his grim thoughts, for his mother never had been able to hide her opinions. Nor did she wish to, he honestly believed.

"Would you please sit so that I may look at you with some modicum of comfort?" she asked. "The boy is coming here, and there is nothing that you can do to rush it." Her voice gentled. "Or stop it."

"Rudyard is my son, and I want to welcome him home upon his arrival."

"Nonsense! You dread his visit with every inch of your bones. And why not? He is a bratchet of the first degree. You have allowed him to have his way too often in the past two years, Bradley."

"We have discussed this before, Mother."

"True, but not when Rudyard is coming *here*." She took his hand and gave him a sorrowful smile. "I know how difficult it is for you when the boy looks more like his mother with every passing day."

Bradley did not have to answer because a footman came to the door and said, "Lord Trowbridge, the carriage has passed through the gate."

"Thank you," he replied, then offered his arm to his mother. "Shall we go and greet the sprig?"

"Most happily." She paused. "Can you say the same, Bradley?"

"I hope so."

"I hate this place," mumbled the towhead sitting beside Elzanne. The lad was rocking his feet back and forth, striking the seat in an ever-increasing rhythm.

"You hate your home?" she asked, glancing at Lurline, who was scowling. Her gray-haired abigail seldom wore a frown, but she had since the first mile past Lindenmere School. Elzanne was unsure if Lurline disapproved of the actions of just the Honorable Mr. Rudyard Trowbridge, or if Lurline disapproved of Elzanne's, too.

"I want to go to Town." The boy affixed her with a fearsome glare as he continued to rock his feet.

"You will have to discuss that matter with your father."

"I want to go there now."

Elzanne resisted rolling her eyes. Master Rudyard had found fault with every inch of this journey. He did not like having to sit facing forward; then when he switched, he did not like sitting facing backward. The food at the coaching inn when they rested the horses was not fit for a sow, he had announced in such a loud voice that the innkeeper had lost his jovial smile. The trip was taking too long. Now he wanted to lengthen it by turning about and going up to London.

No wonder Orson had mentioned the need for patience. This child could try the patience of a martyr.

Reaching over, Elzanne put her hand on his knee to halt him from kicking the seat. He scowled at her and thudded his other foot harder against the seat. She grasped his other knee through his gray breeches and held it still.

"Release me at once!" he ordered imperiously.

"I see no reason to, for you will only begin that incessant thumping again," she said, earning a relieved smile from her abigail.

"Release me! You cannot tell me what to do!"

"I believe I just did."

He let out a screech that suggested he was being slain by slow torture, but she did not shift her hands. He drew in a deep breath to scream again.

"Making such a hullabaloo will gain you nothing from me," she said.

He regarded her with every bit of his twelve-year-old dignity, which, in Elzanne's opinion, was not much. She did not look away from his narrowed blue eyes. Something flickered through them. It was her only warning before he leaned toward her ear and shrieked again.

Elzanne pressed her hand over her bonnet and her ringing ear as he gave her a snide smile.

"What is going on in there?" asked a man's voice. "Rudyard, are you all right?"

She looked over her shoulder and saw that not only had the carriage stopped, but a man had thrown open the door. She could not see much of his face, for it was shadowed by the porte cochere that the carriage now stood beneath.

The lad clambered over her toward the door, managing to step on both her feet in the progress. She doubted if it had been an accident when he gave her another triumphant smile before jumping out of the carriage, almost plowing down the man who had opened the door. He ran toward a woman who was waiting on the steps to the front door of the house, which must be grand if this entrance was any example. Busy with trying to remind that unlicked cub of his proper manners, she had not stolen even a moment to glance at Trowbridge House.

"Who are you?" asked the man as Elzanne stepped from the carriage with the assistance of the tiger. Pain riveted her left foot, but she ignored it as she moved aside to let Lurline get out of the carriage as well.

She turned and realized what she should have immediately. This man must be Lord Trowbridge. Like his son, he was tall, although he possessed a mature, easy grace instead of the boy's gangly limbs. His son's pale blond hair was several shades lighter than that of the viscount who had a single curl on his forehead. Was that a sign that he was as stubborn and self-centered as his son?

Impossible! After all, he was the best father in England, if she was to believe Rudyard's essay. Any father who endured that child's tempers must be exemplary.

"Miss Elzanne Corbett." She wondered why in his essay Rudyard had failed to mention his father's incredible eyes, which were the exact color of the rain clouds overhead. He was not wearing a coat, but his dark blue vest and breeches were the perfect foil for his white shirt, which closed with an informal cravat beneath his strong chin. "My brother wrote to you about me."

"Brother? Mr. Corbett?" His eyes narrowed. "Mr. Corbett, the composition teacher at Lindenmere School?"

"Yes, Lord Trowbridge," she said, even though he had not given her the courtesy of introducing himself. So much for the paragon young Rudyard had written about! "Because my brother was unable to make himself available to tutor Master Rudyard this holiday, he wrote to you that he was sending a substitute tutor."

"He did write, but are you suggesting that *you* are the tutor he has sent?"

"Yes, Lord Trowbridge."

Those gray eyes grew even more stormy. "If this is someone's idea of a jest, Miss Corbett, it is not an amusing one."

"It is no jest. I can assure you that, as my brother's assistant, I am well familiar with the facets of the schoolwork. I can help Master Rudyard focus on his lessons during his holidays so he will find himself catching up with the other students."

"Catching up?"

She took a step back at his furious question. Before she could come up with an answer, the blond woman who had greeted Rudyard walked down the steps and held out her hand.

"Miss Corbett, is it?" she asked.

"Yes."

"I am Lady Trowbridge, Rudyard's grandmother. *I* am delighted to have someone who is obviously concerned with correcting Rudyard's shortcomings here at Trowbridge House." She flashed her son a challenging glance. "I am certain that, once he overcomes his shock, Bradley will be delighted as well."

Elzanne almost asked who Bradley was, then realized Lady Trowbridge was speaking of her son.

"Mayhap, Mother," Lord Trowbridge said quietly, "you might inquire as to her qualifications to tutor Rudyard."

"Zounds, Bradley! What qualifications are you looking for? Her brother is an experienced teacher, and I do believe Mr. Corbett, whom you have spoken of with the greatest respect, wrote that Miss Corbett often assists him with his work. More importantly, she is willing to teach the boy during the holidays." She smiled as she turned back to Elzanne. "Do come in. The weather is very chilly today. Mayhap your young bones are immune to it, but my older ones dislike the damp."

"Thank you." She took a step and winced.

"What is amiss, Miss Corbett?" Lord Trowbridge asked as he paused on the step beside her.

She was tempted to tell him what his vexing son had done, but she could not accuse the child when it truly might have been an accident. She doubted that because

Rudyard's shoe had come down hard on her right toes, and he had tread even more heavily on her left instep, which now ached as if it were broken.

"My foot hurts," she answered.

He put his hand under her right elbow, and she jerked it away, startled.

"Miss Corbett, do you need assistance or no?" the viscount asked, obviously irritated at her reaction. Apparently he had not felt the sudden shock that raced through her when his fingers grazed her arm.

"You surprised me. Forgive me."

"Allow me to help you up the steps." He put his hand under her elbow again.

Biting her lower lip was more to hold in her gasp of unexpected pleasure at his kind touch than to silence the pain that was even worse as she put her foot on the first riser. His broad fingers curved gently up her arm, but his expression remained cool as he assisted her up the quartet of steps.

As she reached the top, she saw Rudyard standing by the door. He was smiling broadly before he slipped into the house.

It was, she decided, going to be a long holiday.

Three

Elzanne slowly turned about and stared at every inch of the bedroom that would be for her use while she was at Trowbridge House. Calling this incredible building a house was like describing a thunderstorm as light and sound. It was an accurate portrayal, but did not do it justice.

The bedchamber was a pink so creamy that it was almost the white of the coverlet on the high bed. She guessed the paintings hanging on the wall depicted Trowbridge House from many different angles. The French windows opened onto a balcony that would, on a sunny day, offer wondrous views of the gardens, which were an ecstasy of color. She was tempted to look in the glass by the small desk and make certain it was really Elzanne Corbett in this amazing place.

The dream shattered when pain clamped onto her leg as she turned at a knock on the outer door of the ante-chamber. That room also served as the schoolroom for Rudyard. She had been astonished to discover there was no nursery in this massive house. Although she wanted to ask how long it had been since the viscount resided here, she had not. She could not forget how distressed Rudyard had been to come here. Mayhap he had not been just spiteful. Mayhap he had a reason for his complaints.

Elzanne limped to the door, wanting to answer it before Lurline could be awakened by the knocking. Her abigail had been exhausted by the trip and *"that child."*

A very correct footman in dark blue livery stood on the other side. Bowing his head slightly, he said, "Miss Corbett, Lady Trowbridge wishes to know if you find your rooms satisfactory."

"Tell her that they are more than satisfactory."

"Further she sends her request that you join the family for dinner."

"Me?" When she heard her voice squeak, she put her hand over her mouth. She saw the twinkle in the austere footman's eyes as she added, "Please tell Lady Trowbridge that I would be honored to join the family for dinner."

"I shall, Miss Corbett."

"Before you go," she said as he started to turn from the door, "I would appreciate directions to the dining room."

"A maid shall be sent to escort you there, Miss Corbett."

"Thank you." She closed the door. Her fingers lingered on the latch as she wondered if everyone in this huge house, save for Lady Trowbridge, found it difficult to smile.

The door opened, bumping into her. She jumped out of the way as Lurline began to apologize.

"I thought you were asleep," Elzanne said. "And no need to ask pardon. I should not have been lingering behind the door."

"A wise servant meets her counterparts wherever she goes." Her brow furrowed. "You should be sitting and resting your foot."

"I shall now, but I needed to explore these rooms and prepare for the boy's first lessons."

"You look distressed, Miss Corbett."

"I must erase that expression before I join Lord Trowbridge and his family for dinner this evening."

"You?" Lurline hurried to add, "Forgive me, Miss Corbett. I did not mean to suggest—"

Elzanne waved aside her apology. "I know what you mean, for I share your amazement. I have never heard of it being common practice to invite a tutor to sit at the family's table for a meal."

"Whatever shall you wear?"

"Oh, I did not consider that." She sighed. "My best dress will have to do, although I doubt it is good enough for such company."

Lurline hesitated, then asked, "May I speak my mind, Miss Corbett, and offer you some advice?"

"Please do." She laughed uneasily. "I can use any guidance you might have."

"I spoke with both the housekeeper and Rouse, the butler. They are surprised that Lord Trowbridge allowed his son to come here."

"It is the boy's home, isn't it?"

"This is the place where his mother died."

Elzanne sat on a tufted green chair and looked up at her abigail. "No wonder he was so resistant to coming here. The poor child."

"It will make him more difficult for you, I fear."

"Lurline, you fret too much."

"Your brother has given you a huge challenge, Miss Corbett."

"And I must not let him down. I intend to persuade that young man to enjoy learning, so he can do better at Lindenmere School."

Lurline took a deep breath and sighed. "I hope you can." Doubt filled her voice. "I hope you can."

* * *

Bradley took a deep breath as he walked into the smaller of the two dining rooms in Trowbridge House. This one, decorated with dark wood paneling that was lightened with the fading sunshine, could seat no more than twenty people. The other was a vast chamber that had a ceiling so high that a word spoken only a few chairs along the table was lost.

Why was he so dashed uneasy? Rudyard had arrived without putting the whole household at sixes and sevens. In fact, after Bradley had asked his son about that screech from the carriage, Rudyard had been so quiet that Bradley wondered if the lad had forgotten how to speak.

Rudyard was now standing on the window seat set within the bay windows, which had several variations of the family crest set into stained glass along the top. The rain was still falling, and Rudyard was tracing a single drop down the length of the glass. When it vanished out of sight, he reached up as high as he could and began to follow another.

Bradley sighed. This was a game Rudyard had often played with his mother on a day when both of them were bored. The sight made him sad, but his son was not what made him uneasy. Then it must be someone else causing his consternation.

"My dear Miss Corbett," he heard his mother saying from the opposite corner, "that is simply intolerable."

He recognized her tone. His mother was about to take on a new crusade, which was certain to upset the household even more than Rudyard ever had. Mayhap he could persuade her to postpone her zeal until after Rudyard had returned to school.

As his mother and Miss Corbett emerged from the shadows, he found himself staring at this most unexpected tutor. She had a sassy shade of red hair and green eyes that revealed every emotion. The few freckles scattered across her nose and cheeks gave even her frown a cheerful warmth. In her cream gown she added light to the dark room. No one had done that since . . .

He walked to the sideboard and poured himself a glass of wine. Dash it! He did not want to think of Nola. He could keep his memories of his late wife quiet when he was far from Trowbridge House. Here they pounced on him when he let his thoughts wander freely for only a second. Dash this quarter day that required each Lord Trowbridge to be present! Some traditions should be banished back into antiquity.

"Bradley, do come and be hospitable to our guest," his mother called.

Guest? Miss Corbett was here as Rudyard's tutor, not to pay a call. He silenced that thought. Mayhap his mother was as anxious as he was for any diversion to keep from thinking of Nola's death, and Miss Corbett could provide that diversion.

"Good evening, Miss Corbett," he said when his mother frowned at him. He must speak to Lady Trowbridge privately at the first opportunity. If Miss Corbett was involved in his mother's latest project, the house was sure to be put into a huge flutter.

"Good evening, my lord." She met his eyes squarely, startling him.

Most women he had encountered among the *ton* were demure and flirtatious, not straightforward. This tutor seemed determined to meet the world on her own terms. That was a most disconcerting thought, and he knew Miss Corbett was the source of his disquiet. And *that* was another perturbing thought.

His mother tapped him on the arm, and Bradley realized he had been staring at Miss Corbett far longer than propriety allowed. He tore his gaze from her intriguing green eyes to face his mother.

"I do hope you have set aside your prejudices, Bradley," his mother said.

"Prejudices?"

"That Miss Corbett is not fit to tutor your son." She glanced at where Rudyard still stood chasing raindrops, and Bradley guessed his mother had not used Rudyard's name because she did not want the boy intruding to discover why they were talking about him. "I have been speaking with her, and I find her answers to my questions more than satisfactory."

"That is good to hear." He could not say anything else, for he did not want to embarrass Miss Corbett.

"She has satisfied *me* with her answers. Now it is your turn." Lady Trowbridge strode toward her grandson, calling for him to let her show him the very best way to follow raindrops down the glass.

He hoped that Miss Corbett would say something that would allow him to end this conversation without delay. She did not as she continued to regard him with that polite, yet direct expression. No woman had the right to be so attractive and so businesslike at the same time.

"I trust," he began, hoping he would not stutter over his words like a schoolboy, "my mother has interrogated you about your credentials."

"She has graciously asked me, yes."

Her answer astonished him anew. He decided the only option was to be as blunt, so he said, "I stand corrected."

"You are welcome to ask me any questions as well."

"Any questions?"

"Any questions about my credentials to be your son's tutor."

Was she daring him to try to undermine her cool serenity, or was she attempting to see what it would take to disintegrate his?

Glancing at where his mother was chatting with Rudyard, who was excitedly pointing at one section of glass, he saw Lady Trowbridge lift a single blond eyebrow. A hint of a smile curved along her lips. He was tempted to say that he was glad that one of them was enjoying this uncomfortable gathering.

"Do you have any questions, my lord?" Miss Corbett asked, bringing his attention—quite willingly—back to her.

"One."

"Please ask it."

"Why do *you* wish to teach such subjects as arithmetic?"

"You say that as if you believe I should not wish to teach such subjects."

He smiled. "You are a woman, and it has not been my experience that arithmetic is a subject that appeals to the fairer sex."

"That is because we have not had the chance to meet before this. I assure you that I find that subject most interesting, and I hope to share my enthusiasm for it with your son."

He frowned. "That answer sounds as if you have practiced it often."

"All the way from Lindenmere School."

"You are determined to keep this serious, I see."

Those incredible green eyes did not lower. "I find the matter of your son's education something that should be taken seriously."

"And what do you not take seriously?"

"Myself."

He laughed, surprising himself and his mother, who turned to stare. The sound was raspy. He clamped his lips together. Had he forgotten how to laugh? Mayhap, for he could not remember the last time he had.

Rudyard rushed up to him. "Are you ill, Papa?"

"No, I am quite well." He took a drink of his wine, but could not pull his gaze from Miss Corbett's. She wore an expression that suggested she was as perplexed as he was at his strange reaction.

"Papa, come and see the rain."

"In a moment, Son."

Rudyard stamped his foot. "Now, Papa."

"In a moment." He mussed his son's hair.

"Now!"

"Rudyard—"

"Now!" Rudyard's voice rose shrilly.

Bradley saw Miss Corbett was struggling not to frown. He was tempted to tell her she was wasting her time trying to hide her reaction, for it was displayed vividly in those emerald eyes.

His mother came around the table and said, "I think we have left the kitchen waiting long enough. Shall we enjoy our dinner?"

"Papa, come and see the rain!" Rudyard tugged on his hand.

"On our way to the table." With his hand on his son's shoulder, he turned Rudyard toward the window.

Bradley did not look away quickly enough, however, for he saw Miss Corbett's frown. A disappointed frown, he realized. Disappointed in him? She need not waste her disappointment on him, for, during the past two years, he had lived with his own regrets and disillusionment at learning he was not the man he had thought he was.

Four

"I don't want to do this." Rudyard sat stiffly in his chair with his arms folded in front of his narrow chest.

"You need to practice your sums so you will be able to do them as well as the other students." Elzanne wondered how many times she had repeated this admonition during the past week. Too many times, but the boy had not listened once.

She might have believed that he was trying to make her sorry for coming to Trowbridge House, but she had witnessed him being as stubborn with his grandmother and father. Although she did not want to go to them with her concerns, for she had wanted to prove that she could be equal to the task of tutoring this difficult child, she might have no choice.

"I don't want to do them." He scowled, jutting his chin toward her. "And you cannot force me to. You are not a real teacher. You are just a woman."

"Just a . . . ?" She stopped before she could say something that would create even more trouble. If that was possible. "Master Rudyard, you need to complete these sums before you do anything else."

He scowled, then bent over the paper.

Elzanne was amazed. Not once in the past week had he been so earnest about his work. She stood and walked around to check on his work. When he drew his arm forward so she could not see his paper, she smiled. Mayhap somehow, and she had no idea how, she had inspired him to do his best.

Going to the closest window, she looked out at the sunlit garden. She hoped to have time after this session of schoolwork to spend some time exploring the gardens. She enjoyed tending the small patch of flowers she had in the tiny garden behind the cottage at Lindenmere School, and she had been daydreaming of a walk among these flowers. This was the first day since her arrival at Trowbridge House that rain had not fallen.

She turned when she heard Rudyard's chair being pushed back. Walking to the table, she asked, "Are you finished already?"

"I am finished." He smiled broadly as he bounced to his feet.

Elzanne tensed. She did not have to look at his paper to know that he had not done the work she had assigned him. Picking it up, she gasped and dropped it, because it was soaked with ink. In dismay, she realized some of it had dripped onto her gown.

"Master Rudyard, this is not acceptable." She fought to hold on to her temper, for she suspected he hoped to make her fly up to the boughs. "You will have to begin from the beginning."

"I don't want to do it again."

"You do not have to."

He stared at her in amazement. "I don't?"

"No, you do not have to do it again. In fact, you cannot do it again, for you have not done it yet." She took another piece of paper and tried to wipe the ink off her hands. "While you clean up this mess, I shall prepare another page of sums for you to calculate."

"I don't want to."

She sighed. The boy, who was so charming to his

grandmother, sought every way to misbehave in the schoolroom. Sitting in her chair across the table from him, she gave him a stern look and said, "It is not a matter of what you want or don't want to do. It is a matter of what you *do* need to learn. Please be seated and prepare yourself to do your sums."

"I don't want to."

"So you have said. I have listened to you, and now it is time for—"

The door from the hallway opened, and Lord Trowbridge walked in with a jaunty smile. When Rudyard almost threw himself at his father, Elzanne saw the viscount's puzzlement. She understood his confusion, because his son had refused to speak to him at breakfast this morning.

"Papa," Rudyard whined, "I have been working so hard. Can't I go outside now?"

"I brought a footman along, assuming that you would be eager to take a break from your work."

"A footman?" The boy's voice became even more petulant. "Why do you need to send a footman with me?"

"Go along, Son. The fresh air will do you good."

Rudyard, apparently deciding to get out before his father changed his mind, flashed her a triumphant smile and rushed from the room.

Elzanne came slowly to her feet. "That was unwise, my lord."

"The boy is on his holidays, after all."

"The boy is far behind his fellow students and is falling further behind every day. I thought you wished for me to help him prepare for the next term. I cannot do that if you give him *carte blanche* to avoid his lessons whenever he wishes."

"There are other lessons he can learn away from the classroom."

"Mayhap, but, my lord, the lesson he learned today was that he can run to you to override my requests for him to calculate the sums we have been working on." She did not hesitate, even though she knew her words might guarantee her *congé,* as she added, "Surely you understand the importance of Master Rudyard's being able to do the simplest computations. One day, he will be the one overseeing this estate and its tenants. If he is not able to understand how to ascertain the rents due and read reports sent to him of the harvest and requests for repairs, how is he to do this estate or your family any good?"

Lord Trowbridge regarded her in silence for so long that she could not guess if he was too furious or too shocked to speak. Just when she was about to plead with him to say something—anything—he said, "I trust you are not always so outspoken, Miss Corbett."

"You are correct. I only speak my mind so plainly when I am talking about something that matters deeply to me."

"Helping my son matters deeply to you?"

"I would not be here otherwise."

He picked up the paper his son had been working on and an expression close to pain crossed his face as he dropped it back to the table. "Is this his?"

"It was." She pointed to one corner where the ink had not obliterated the neat column of sums she had written and the boy's careless answers. "He spilled ink on it."

"And over you, too."

"Yes."

"I trust he told you that he was sorry for the accident that ruined your dress."

She raised her chin. "No, for it was not an accident." She pointed to the blackened page. "He wished to avoid doing his work this afternoon."

"When he gets in a stubborn mood, Rudyard can be resistant to doing his best," the viscount said.

"*This* is his best, my lord."

"You are jesting, I hope."

She shook her head. "I wish I could say that I was. Master Rudyard is not bacon-brained. To the contrary, he could do quite well on his work if he concentrated on it. Today, he did not get a single answer correct. He seemed to be willing to work, but you can see the result."

"When he is on his holidays—"

"Excuse me." She reached for a bag under the table. Relief filled her when she saw the ink had not splattered onto it. Setting it on the table, she drew out a sheaf of papers. "My brother suspected you might be concerned that Master Rudyard's effort was less focused during his holidays, so he sent with me some of Master Rudyard's work from the end of the most recent term."

Lord Trowbridge paged through them quickly, his pained expression deepening with each one. Setting them down on the table with such speed that she knew he was eager to be rid of them, he said, "I had no idea."

"When you requested a tutor for him—"

"I thought it would be best for Rudyard to continue to be challenged. The reports I received from the headmaster at Lindenmere School suggested he was doing well."

"The headmaster does not wish to offend the parents of any of his students."

"Or lose the tuition they provide for their sons?" A surprising smile spread across his face.

"Yes." Had she seen him wear a genuine smile before this? She could not recall anything but that strained smile he had worn at dinner her first night here.

"Do you think you can change the course of Rudyard's poor work?"

"I believe I can make a start." She knew that she

might be again treading on dangerous ground, but she would be doing neither Rudyard nor his father any favor by remaining silent. "I also believe, my lord, that if he knew how disappointed you are in his efforts, he might improve."

"I hope you are more accurate with your first assumption than your second." He motioned for her to sit and drew up another chair to the table. "Miss Corbett, since his mother's death, Rudyard has tried with every fiber of his being to be as outrageous as possible."

She remained on her feet. "So I have seen." She hesitated, then asked, "May I be honest, my lord?"

"Can you be any other way?"

His cool tone annoyed her, and her own voice became waspish. "I can fill your head with fabrications, if that is your choice, my lord, but I had guessed you would prefer to hear the truth."

"About my son's education, yes."

"But not about his behavior beyond the schoolroom?"

"Does that concern you as well?"

She was in too deep now to stop, so she replied, "He is a very unhappy child. That concerns me."

He came around the table, and she realized how she had appreciated that barrier between them. She knew she should step back, but she could not move as she stared up into his eyes.

His finger rose to glide along her cheek. He pulled it back, his startled countenance easing the taut lines in his forehead.

"Miss Corbett, I should not have done that."

"No, you should not have." She held her breath, hoping he would be so bold again. Every chaste brush of his fingers against her, each polite touch, even an unintended moment like this sent that incredible, exhilarating sensation hurtling through her.

"I do not take advantage of my household. I owe you an apology."

"None is necessary, my lord." She finally forced her feet to move her a pace back from him. Turning away, she gathered up the papers on the table. "If you will excuse me, I will clean up this mess."

"A mess I assume you believe Rudyard should have cleaned before running off."

She glanced back at him. "Yes."

"You are wrong, Miss Corbett."

"My lord, I assure you that you are not helping your son by allowing him to avoid facing the consequences of his actions."

He chuckled, astounding her anew. "I meant that you were wrong about me not owing you an apology. It appears I owe you more than one."

"What you owe me, my lord, is the chance to teach your son without intrusion."

"Point taken. In the future, I shall arrange with you in advance any time I plan to come to this makeshift schoolroom."

"I would appreciate that." Pausing, Elzanne asked, "Why did you come in today?"

"To see how Rudyard is faring, and you have shown me quite clearly." His smile vanished as he picked up another page and, looking at it, shook his head. "I was assured that Lindenmere School was an exemplary place to send my son to prepare for his life ahead."

She put the papers back into her bag. "It is. My brother spends much time working with any of his students who have a hunger to learn."

"With you assisting?"

"Behind the scenes, if you will. You are more open-minded than many of the parents would be if they learned I was helping my brother's students even anonymously."

"Anonymity must be distasteful for you."

She set the bag beneath the table. "Until this holiday, my lord, it has been my sole venue for teaching something other than embroidery or the rituals for pouring tea."

"So you prefer a challenge?"

"Yes."

He edged closer to her again. She would have moved if her feet had not abruptly become a part of the carpet. He did not touch her again, but she quivered as if he had. Looking up into his eyes, she wondered what would happen if she did not resist the temptation to lose herself in those enigmatic gray depths.

His voice was hushed. "Something we have in common, for I find I cannot disregard any challenge."

"I shall remember that."

A slow smile spread across his face, and she longed to close her eyes and have him touch her cheek again. Quietly, he said, "I thought you would."

The sound of footfalls beyond the door must have penetrated his head more quickly than it had hers, because he stepped away just as the door opened to reveal Lurline. The abigail stared at them, and Elzanne knew something had betrayed them.

Betrayed them? They had not, save for Lord Trowbridge's one brazen caress, overstepped the boundaries of propriety.

Bowing his head toward her, Lord Trowbridge said, "I bid you *adieu* until the evening meal, Miss Corbett. I trust you will be joining us."

"Yes . . . Yes, I will be there."

"Good, for I believe that you will find my conversation with young Rudyard most interesting."

"Mayhap I should not be there if you are going to scold him."

"It would be better to have you present, so you hear for yourself what I have to say."

"As you wish."

He sighed. "If it was as I wished, this discussion with my son would not be necessary." He went to the door, acting as if he did not see Lurline scurrying quickly aside. He paused and turned. "Oh, Miss Corbett, may I make a suggestion?"

"Of course."

"You might want to wipe that charming smudge of ink from your cheek before you come to the table." He walked out and closed the door.

She put her hand to her cheek. Until now, she had been certain Rudyard was her biggest problem. Now, as she recalled Lord Trowbridge's mesmerizing touch, she was no longer sure.

Five

Bradley finished reading the last page of the estate manager's report and put it atop the others on the table beside where he was sitting. He heard another page rattling and looked across the room to where his mother sat. She wore a light blue gown and a very somber frown.

Setting himself on his feet, he poured two glasses of lemonade. He handed one to his mother as he leaned a shoulder against the bookcase beside her chair. "You look pensive, Mother."

"I am."

"Why?" He looked down at the low stack of papers she was reading. "Or should I ask who is causing that expression?"

"Your son."

"What has Rudyard done to cause you to be so lost in thought on such a lovely day?"

"His work. His sums."

"Ah, yes. I have spoken with his tutor about that." He let his mind drift to the pretty Miss Corbett. If his son were a few years older, Bradley would have understood why Rudyard found it difficult to concentrate on his schoolwork. Certainly Bradley had had trouble thinking of anything but Miss Corbett's soft skin and sparkling green eyes since their first conversation in the school-room two days ago.

"So I understand."

"You do?"

"Really, Bradley, you should know by now that what one servant sees or hears is soon known by all of them. Rouse was quick to tell me that you have been checking often on the boy."

Bradley smiled. "Rouse seems to believe a butler's duties include being the first to spread any news, whether it is true or not."

"So you have not been there often?"

"I didn't say that."

"I noticed." Lady Trowbridge chuckled, then said, "This is the work Rudyard did this morning." She handed him the page. "As you can see, in spite of his reluctance to offer Elzanne the least respect, he is showing improvement in calculating his sums."

"Elzanne?"

"It *is* her name, Bradley." She smiled as she picked up her embroidery hoop. "She is very accomplished at this as well, I have learned, for she has taught me several stitches I never had seen before."

"I did not realize you were in such good *pax* with my son's tutor."

Lady Trowbridge laughed. "Jealous?"

"What sort of question is that?"

"An honest one. Why don't you give me an honest answer?"

Bradley tossed the page back onto the table by his mother's chair. "If I did not know better, Mother, I would say you have matchmaking on the mind."

"She is a charming young lady. I am not saying you should marry Elzanne. I am simply saying you should enjoy her company. She is witty and enjoys laughing.

There has been a dearth of laughter here in Trowbridge House since—"

"Nola died."

She shook her head. "Since before then. You may have canonized Nola since the accident, Bradley, but I recall her with clear eyes. Nola was not without her faults, and one was that she had no sense of humor."

"I must agree."

"She sucked the laughter out of this house—and out of you—because nobody wished to put her into an uncomfortable position by telling a jest that she would not comprehend." She sighed. "Do not misunderstand me, son. Nola was a fine woman and a devoted wife, but she was a bit too serious."

"She was."

"And now *you* are too serious."

"Yes." He had not expected the conversation to take such a turn, for his mother had not mentioned Nola's name in months.

Jabbing her needle through the linen within her hoop, Lady Trowbridge said, "It is time for laughter and bonhomie to return to Trowbridge House. For both you and Rudyard."

"And you?"

She smiled. "You should have taken note that I have forgotten neither how to laugh nor how to smile."

"Nor how to tell a joke. I heard the bawdy one that you were sharing with Rouse this morning."

With another chuckle, she said, "He seems to be coming about as well. If Elzanne is the cause of this lightening of spirits within this house, she will have done far more than teach the boy to do arithmetic." She met his eyes sternly. "It is *your* task, Son, to keep that laughter alive after she leaves."

"A most difficult task."

"To keep the laughter alive or to let her leave?"

He considered circumventing the truth, but he did not want falsehoods to become as common in Trowbridge House as frowns. "I suspect the answer is both." When he began to discuss the upcoming quarter day, he guessed his mother was not done with the subject of Elzanne Corbett.

Neither, he suspected, was he.

Elzanne held her dress up out of the dew-washed grass as she wandered past moonlit bushes. Beside her, Rudyard was chattering like a jay. He had been in this uncustomary good mood since she had told him that they would skip his lessons today and explore the gardens. This afternoon, they had visited the water garden with its pool that sparkled in the bright sunshine. Tonight, she had brought him to the formal garden where the box-wood was cut into a geometric design that urged her to wander about, tracing it from one end to the other. Tall trees edged the garden and blocked the stars that were sprinkled across the sky beyond the milky orb hanging low near the eastern horizon.

"So how many stars do you believe you can count up there, Master Rudyard?" she asked, as if it were an aimless question. If the boy had any inkling that he was part of a mathematical problem that she had developed with him all day, he would become intractable again.

"There must be a thousand." He spun slowly to look at the sky from every angle. "Do you think there are a thousand stars up there?"

"Mayhap more, but let's say there are exactly one thousand up there." She did not pause as she added, "And you told me this afternoon that you believe there are one hundred fish that you have yet to catch in the pond within the water garden."

"What do the fish have to do with stars?"

"If you had to name an equal number of stars for

every fish you caught, how many would you have to name each time you hooked one?"

"Ten."

She hid her astonishment at how readily he gave her the correct answer. It confirmed what she had guessed from the onset. Rudyard Trowbridge was capable of doing all the problems she had given him and probably much more complicated work as well.

"That is right," said Lord Trowbridge as he walked out of the deeper shadows beneath the trees. "I had no idea you had become so skilled with your arithmetic, Son."

"You are proud of me?" Rudyard asked.

"How could I not be proud of you?"

Rudyard started to smile, then said, "Because you never trust me to let me do anything on my own." He whirled and ran back toward the house. They could hear the door slam from where they stood.

Lord Trowbridge looked down at his hand, which was still poised to rest on his son's shoulder. His puzzlement was visible even through the darkness.

"I thought he would be pleased with my praise," he said. "Why did he run away like that?"

"I don't know." She forced herself to look directly at him instead of lowering her eyes. In the darkness, he would not be able to see her uneasiness, which might reveal how her dreams of the past few nights had persuaded her to continue Rudyard's lessons tonight instead of seeking her own bed in a futile effort to sleep. Lord Trowbridge must not guess that he was the hero of all those dreams, and she had been the heroine he held in his strong arms.

"Did he think I was hoaxing him when I told him that I am proud of him?" asked Lord Trowbridge.

Elzanne shook away her frivolous thoughts as she

heard the pain sharpening his voice. "You may have overmastered him with your acclamation."

He frowned at her. "Do not attempt to soothe my feelings with platitudes. His reaction just now was not unique. He seems eager to spend time with me and to avoid me at the same time."

"He is twelve years old, my lord."

"Which means?"

"He sees himself as not quite a child, but not yet a man. It is a difficult time for a boy." She smiled as they continued to stroll along the path of crushed seashells edging the boxwood design. "I recall my brother being most intolerable when he was that age. Of course, as his younger sister, I bore the brunt of his outbursts."

"As I am with Rudyard."

"I am afraid so."

He sighed so loudly that she could hear it over the gentle rustle of the breeze through the leaves. "So do I tolerate it or confront him on it?"

"You are asking me about things I cannot help him— or you—with, my lord."

"After what I heard here, I would have guessed you capable of just about any miracle."

Elzanne smiled. "I knew he could do much more than he had led any of us to believe."

"Your faith in him is commendable."

"You must have the same faith in him. He is a mischievous boy, that is true, but it may be because he is curious about everything and everyone around him."

He paused, facing her. In the dim moonlight, his face was a map of dark, hidden valleys and bright plains, all waiting to be explored. Her fingers started to rise, but she clasped them tightly in front of her.

"He is a most fortunate boy to have you here as his tutor . . . Elzanne."

Her heart fluttered when she heard her given name in

his voice. Just the act of his speaking it seemed to add zest to her name. Or was it simply that she was thrilled with the intimacy suggested by his use of it? Instantly she told herself not to be silly. She was his employee, so he had every right to address her thus.

"And I am lucky that you chose to stay after the less-than-cordial welcome I offered you upon your arrival," he continued.

"That is understandable. You were surprised to learn that your son's tutor was a woman."

"Yes, I was surprised to learn that my son's tutor was a *beautiful* woman." The backs of his fingertips brushed a strand of hair beneath her bonnet. When she quivered at his brazen caress, he smiled.

Her linked hands longed to break free to touch him as boldly. What would he do if she did? Would he lambaste her for being so forward, or would he pull her closer and become *her* tutor in the delights of a man's lips on hers?

He picked up another strand and slipped it beneath her bonnet, but this one he curved up and over her ear with a single finger. She could not halt herself from stepping nearer to him as that finger traced the line of her bonnet's ribbons along her jaw and beneath her chin.

His finger rose along her chin to brush her lips. In her dreams his caresses were a forbidden delight, a joy in the midst of her concerns about teaching his son. But nothing in her dreams had been this splendid. Heat swarmed through her at this simple contact, and she longed for his mouth instead of his finger against her lips.

When she started to step back, his arm curved around her to keep her from moving. She put up her hand to draw his finger away, for she was not sure how much longer she could—or wanted—to be torn between good sense and the incredible rapture of his touch. His arm tightened to keep her close. As she looked into his shadowed eyes, all desire to pull away evaporated. Even though she could not see what was within them, she sensed his thoughts in his eager touch.

His fingers curved along the side of her face, not imprisoning, but offering an invitation she should ignore. Slowly his arm contracted, drawing her closer. As she was reminding herself that she should not become so involved with her employer, her hands slid along the firm length of his arms. His broad shoulders urged her to explore them. Her fingers tangled in the tawny silk of his hair as he tilted her mouth toward his.

Abruptly he turned away, releasing her. He cleared his throat and then said quietly, "I came out here to check on Rudyard when I discovered he was not in his room. Now that I have seen how well he is doing, I should . . ."

Elzanne blinked as his voice trailed off. She was still caught within the luscious enticement. Breaking its intriguing bonds, she walked a few paces along the path. Just putting space between them might prevent her from acknowledging these longings which must not be acted upon.

"Good evening, Elzanne," he said to her back.

"Yes . . . Thank you, my lord." She swallowed roughly as she fought to keep her voice from trembling. "Good evening."

As she heard his steps disappear into the darkness, she knew it was not *good evening* she longed for him to say to her, but as he held her close, *good night.*

Six

"You must stay for the quarter day, Elzanne," Lady Trowbridge said as she lowered her spoon with a soft clatter that added to the birdsong outside the open windows of the light blue breakfast parlor. "It is one of the most important events of the year here."

Rudyard exclaimed, "We cannot leave before the quarter day! I have not been here for it in so long."

"Master Rudyard's holidays may be over before then," Elzanne replied, realizing she had lost track of the time since she had left Lindenmere School. She was pleased to discover how many more days she would be at Trowbridge House. Smiling, she looked across the table at Rudyard and his grandmother. "We shall still be here by then, although we will be leaving the following day."

"The celebrations actually last for two days, so you must stay for both." Lady Trowbridge's eyes were as bright as Rudyard's. "There are all sorts of events." She put her hand on the boy's shoulder. "I have just the jolly, my boy. You must enter the kite flying contest."

"A kite?"

"You need to make it yourself and ready it to fly." She gave him an indulgent smile. "I believe, by now, the materials should have been delivered to your schoolroom."

He jumped to his feet, nearly knocking over his chair. As he steadied it, he said, "I will—"

"You will wait for Miss Corbett to help you with the project," Lady Trowbridge said quietly. Patting his arm, she went on as he began to frown, "However, you are welcome to go and look at what is there and imagine the kite you wish to build."

As he raced out of the room, Elzanne pushed back her chair.

"Where are you off to?" asked Lady Trowbridge. "My dear Elzanne, your breakfast is barely touched."

"I should go and supervise Master Rudyard."

"Nonsense. You should eat your breakfast." She picked up her cup and smiled over it. "Besides, I have two footmen guarding the materials so that my grandson does not do something out of hand like cut up the draperies at the same time he is designing his kite."

Elzanne smiled and sat back down. "You handle him so well, my lady."

"Practice. His father had much the same high spirits."

"He did?"

Hearing a laugh from behind her, Elzanne knew her cheeks were bright red, for they were as hot as the summer sun. She recognized the laugh even as Lady Trowbridge was urging her son to come in and join them for breakfast.

Lord Trowbridge walked around the table to give his mother a filial kiss on the cheek. Elzanne almost choked as she silenced her gasp when she saw what he was wearing. Every other time she had seen him, Lord Trowbridge had been dressed in prime twig, looking as if he were ready to take a stroll down a London street. This morning, he wore a casual dark green waistcoat that was unbuttoned over his buckskin breeches. No cravat closed his shirt, which was undone at his throat. Water droplets clung to his freshly shaven face. His hair was tousled, and her fingers longed to comb it back into place.

"Bradley," Lady Trowbridge scolded in the exact same tone she had taken with her grandson, "you know better than to come to the table directly from the stables."

"I am not coming to the table, for I wanted to let you know that I have already eaten."

"In the kitchen, no doubt."

"No doubt."

"Cook still spoils you, Son."

"That is true." He smiled.

Elzanne gripped her napkin as he turned that scintillating warmth toward her. How could she ever have considered this man cold? He needed only to look at her, and she melted like a sweet left too long in the sun.

"Good *morning*, Elzanne."

The slight emphasis he put on the word brought forth the memories of how his strong arms had enfolded her last night in the formal garden. She had spent the rest of the night trying to bury those thoughts and sensations, telling herself that she must consider this a lone lapse in judgment. A lapse in judgment that could not be repeated. Yet, as she gazed up into his silver-gray eyes, she wondered how long before she found herself drawn into making another foolish mistake. Foolish, only because he was her employer, for everything else about being close to him was wondrous and perfect.

"Good morning, my lord," she replied, taking care that every syllable was steady.

Lady Trowbridge's smile broadened. "Did you give us a look-in only to offer us a good morning, Bradley?"

"No."

He looked back at his mother, and Elzanne began to breathe. Had she been holding her breath in anticipation of him drawing her into his arms again? With his mother as a witness? Letting her thoughts lead her astray was guaranteed to take her right into the midst of trouble.

"I wanted you to know," Lord Trowbridge continued, "that I am going into the village to check on the arrangements for the quarter day."

"A capital idea." Lady Trowbridge set herself on her feet. "It will be a lovely day for a drive."

"I had planned going on horseback."

"Where would you put Elzanne? You can't expect her to ride pillion with you."

Elzanne had stood at the same time as Lady Trowbridge. Glancing at Lord Trowbridge's startled expression, she said, "My lady, I am not—"

"Exactly!" Lady Trowbridge said. "You are *not* riding pillion. You and Bradley can take the phaeton. It is time to shake some dust off it, for it has not been out of the carriage house in longer than I can recall."

"But, my lady, I was not intending to go anywhere but to help Master Rudyard with building his kite." *Dash her cheeks, which must be as red as her hair!* She wished Lord Trowbridge would say something to put an end to this uncomfortable conversation.

"I believe that is an excellent task for his grandmother to take on." She patted her son's arm. "Do you want me to have Rouse call for the phaeton?"

Lord Trowbridge chuckled. "It would seem that you have the whole of it planned."

"Elzanne has been spending too much time cooped up in that schoolroom trying to persuade Rudyard to finish his work. She could use some fresh air before she wilts away like a flower left too long out of the sunshine." She smiled. "A ride to the village will give her that fresh air and bring back her healthy color."

He glanced at Elzanne, and she could have sworn that he winked at her. She must be mistaken, for she could not imagine him doing such a thing.

Or mayhap she could, for he chuckled as he replied, "It appears she has no dearth of color in her cheeks at the moment."

"Because you are embarrassing her with your most ungallant failure to ask her to join you in an outing to the village," Lady Trowbridge said.

Bradley turned to Elzanne, who was listening to the exchange with wide eyes. Her eyes were the same color as a shadowed forest, and any man should think twice before exploring them.

"Am I embarrassing you?" he asked.

She shook her head, but her gaze remained locked with his. He could sense her bewilderment. Not that he blamed her. Just hours ago, she had been in his arms, when he was eager for her lips against his. Did she understand his hesitation to be alone with her? He could not explain how he was struggling to retain control of his errant emotions that would threaten the barriers she seemed determined to keep between them.

"*She* is being polite," Lady Trowbridge said with a smile. "Now ask her nicely to go with you into the village while I go and check on what your offspring is doing."

Bradley chuckled under his breath as his mother walked out of the breakfast parlor. Shaking his head, he said, "I would like to offer you an invitation to join me in a visit to the village."

"You don't need to do that," Elzanne replied.

"I know, but I find myself in the bothersome position of owing you an apology again."

Her brows dipped. "For what?"

"I believe it would be better if we did not speak of that when so many ears are sure to be listening eagerly." He glanced at the kitchen door and saw it abruptly close. "Mayhap a drive to the village would be the best venue for such an apology."

"I must get my bonnet and find Lurline. Shall we meet you at the stables?"

"That would be fine," he said, although he wanted to tell her to leave her abigail here. "Elzanne?"

She had started to turn, but paused and looked back at him, offering him an enticing profile that urged his fingers to explore what his eyes could. "Yes?"

"I want you to know that I appreciate what you have done for Rudyard."

"Thank you, my lord." She could not conceal her astonishment that he was repeating what he had said last night.

"And for the rest of this household."

"I haven't—"

"But you have. My mother and my son are closer than they ever have been."

She laughed, her face easing from its strained appearance. "That has nothing to do with me. Master Rudyard enjoys Lady Trowbridge's company."

"He has not in the past." He grinned when she nodded. "But apparently that does not surprise you."

"No, it doesn't. As I told you last night, my lord, being twelve is an awkward time for a lad. I recall Orson at that age arguing often with our parents." She abruptly smiled. "And your mother's comments hint you were much the same."

"So you are suggesting I should pity her for having to deal with such a recalcitrant lad twice?"

"I am suggesting that you should be very grateful for her patience."

Bradley gripped the back of a chair as Elzanne left the breakfast parlor. They had spoken of everything but what was truly on his mind. And hers? Her eyes had been heavy with a lack of sleep.

Too.

Had she been unable to sleep last night because she

was beleaguered by the same thoughts that had hounded him? If so, Elzanne was proving to be wiser than he was, for she was letting the canons of society keep her from putting them both in a situation that might lead to . . .

He cursed under his breath. Since he had come out of mourning for Nola, other women had candidly offered to take her place in his bed. He had gallantly turned down each of them. Now it seemed as if he had been walking in a deep mist through those evenings and those gatherings. That fog had cut him off from everyone else and had been simpler than putting himself at risk for pain and loss again.

Simpler, yes, but no longer enough.

Seven

Bradley slowed the carriage. He was not driving his fast phaeton, as his mother had suggested, but a slower carriage that would allow for Elzanne's abigail to join them. He paused in front of the stone and timbered building that served as the store and the meeting place for the village's leaders. Mr. Eustis owned the store, and he had served as mayor for as long as Bradley could remember.

"Look, Miss Corbett!" said Lurline from the back seat. "There are some roses that have already bloomed."

He smiled as he looked past the stone wall that surrounded Mrs. Keller's garden. Every child, dog, and possibly rabbit within a score of miles knew better than to wander, uninvited, into Mrs. Keller's rose garden. When he repeated that thought to Elzanne's abigail, Lurline tittered a laugh.

Beside him, Elzanne was silent. She had answered the questions he had asked in the hopes of sparking a conversation. *Blast!* If he had known that touching her cheek last night would mute her like this, he might have resisted. He wanted to let loose a wry laugh. She must know how difficult it had been for him to walk away from her, but he was not one of the peer who believed that *droit du seigneur* should never have gone out of practice.

Blast again! He was her employer, and she would be here only a short time longer. He should let her do the work she had come here to do, for already she had wrought changes in young Rudyard.

Even as he thought that, Bradley was handing her out of the carriage. Her slender fingers on his palm offered a temptation to succumb to the craving to sample her kisses. What was it about this woman? She was a delight for the eyes, but he had seen other beautiful women in the past year and not one of them had earned more than a passing glance from him. Mayhap it was her intelligence. She could challenge anyone in any conversation, proving that it was a true shame that her gender kept her from sharing that information in a classroom. It was both of those things, but he was also drawn to her by her gentle heart and her determination to help his son.

Mayhap he should have told her upon her arrival that she was only the most recent in a long line of tutors. Each one had given up as he tired of Rudyard's inattention to his lessons. Somehow, and Bradley had no idea how, Elzanne was reaching the boy as no one else had. Rudyard still was impatient and irritable when he did not get his way, but his son seemed to be finding some enjoyment in the work she gave him. That was such an amazing step in the right direction that Bradley was in awe of her skill as a tutor.

"Lord Trowbridge?" Elzanne's soft voice caressed his ears.

"Yes?"

"I am safely on the ground." She drew her hand out of his.

"So I see."

She glanced at him, then away as she moved to look at the village, which was only a collection of small houses and shops on either side of the road. "This is charming. These cottages remind me of the one I share with my brother at Lindenmere School, except that they have more roses growing around them."

"If you would like to look about while I talk to the mayor about the quarter day, it will save you from having to listen to all his reasons why we should not change anything about the day."

"He likes traditions?"

"He thrives on them." Bradley chuckled when she smiled. "The very idea that one iota of the quarter day might change is enough to give him apoplexy. I doubt if that would be a pretty sight."

"Thank you for sparing me." Elzanne turned to her abigail. "Shall we walk about the village?"

Bradley watched them amble toward the closest garden. He wished he had an excuse to be the one beside Elzanne as she delighted in the flowers that were bursting forth in each cottage garden. Mayhap, after they returned to Trowbridge House, she would accept his offer to stroll through the rose garden.

He was smiling as he entered Mr. Eustis's store. Before he had left Trowbridge Hall, he had changed into clothes befitting this call. What would the very proper Mr. Eustis think if Bradley arrived wearing his riding breeches? Most likely, the mayor would be deeply offended.

Following the twisting path through the collections of boxes that never seemed to move from the same spot year after year, Bradley reached the back of the store, where the mayor and his three council members sat in an arc. They came to their feet and offered greetings. He was not assured by their kind welcome, for Mr. Eustis was wearing a stubborn frown.

"You appear in uncommonly good spirits, my lord."

Mr. Eustis had been sitting in a chair that gave him a commanding view of the door.

"It is a lovely day." Bradley chose a hard chair at one end of the arc. He was not about to reveal that his smile had more to do with Elzanne Corbett than the sunny weather. As he listened to the rumors that had spread through the village about how Trowbridge House wished a multitude of changes in the quarter day, he let them go on until they had vented their distress. Only then did he say, "I do not know how such prattle gets its start. The only change I had intended to suggest was that the village allow me to provide fireworks for the first evening of the quarter day celebration."

"Fireworks?" Mr. Eustis's frown deepened beneath his balding pate. Glancing at his comrades, he leaned toward Bradley and said, "Those noisy things will frighten the livestock for a league. Who knows what damage that might cause?"

"If you don't want them . . ."

"No, no!" Mr. Kenyon, the village's doctor, jumped to his feet in his excitement. "Lord Trowbridge, this is a generous gesture."

"And something that would delight everyone in attendance," he said, fighting not to smile. During every other discussion he had with these men, they had never spoken against the mayor's edicts. Mayhap there was more changing around him than the differences Elzanne had brought to Trowbridge House.

He sat back and let the quartet argue it among themselves. It quickly became evident that for once the mayor's opinion would not sway his cohorts. The mayor relented enough to agree that the fireworks could be fired on the first night of the quarter day, but only if nearby residents were warned about what was happening.

"They might believe that the French are sending their cannon fire toward us," Mr. Eustis ended with a frown.

Bradley stood. "If you will do that, I shall arrange for fireworks to be delivered and someone to fire them off properly."

The other men stood and shook his hand again in the exact way they always did. As he walked out of the store, he could hear their raised voices as they launched into another brangle about what food should be served at the communal meal on the second day of the celebration.

He nodded to a woman who was herding her children up the street like a flock of chickens. Shouts came from beyond the houses on the opposite side of the road, friendly shouts of people working together and enjoying it. The breeze brought the scents of freshly turned earth and greenery.

He had brought his family here often in the past. How long had it been since he had noticed these simple pleasures? He knew the answer, for he had ignored them since Nola's death. He had come to Trowbridge House only to fulfill his obligations. Until now, he had not guessed how much he had missed this serenity, which was so different from the hullabaloo of London.

Hearing a laugh that soared through him like a bird taking flight, Bradley turned to see Elzanne and her abigail ambling back toward the carriage. The sunlight glistened on Elzanne's simple straw bonnet. Its single jaunty flower was the same color as the pink ribbons beneath her chin. Both were the perfect shade to match her cheeks and the lace on her gown which accented those curves that had been against him for such a brief moment last night.

He whistled a carefree melody that he was surprised he remembered as he went to meet them by the carriage. While Lurline chattered about the pretty blossoms they had seen and how wondrous it was going to be to return here for the quarter day celebrations, he helped the abigail into the rear seat of the carriage.

Not a single word she spoke entered his brain as he reached for Elzanne's fingers. She gazed up at him, and every other sound vanished but the urgent beat of his heart. He lifted her hand, and his gaze held hers while he kissed her fragrant skin. Her green eyes urged him to sink in their depths to drown in their hinted delights.

She tried to draw her hand out of his. His smile broadened as he held her fingers captive. Her lips parted in a gentle gasp when he turned her hand over to place another kiss against her soft palm. Her fingers quivered in his.

"My lord," she whispered, "we are standing in an open byway."

"That is true."

"We must remember ourselves."

"All I can remember is holding you last evening."

That pretty pink tint rose up in her face anew, but the color must come from her own memories because she replied, "Another subject that should not be discussed in such a public place."

"Shall we discuss it more privately?"

"Do you think that is a good idea?"

"I think it is the very best idea I have had in a very long time."

From the carriage, Lurline cleared her throat, and Bradley knew she was reminding him that Elzanne was well chaperoned. Not just by her abigail, he realized, but by the villagers, who were peeking out of their cottages. As soon as the carriage was out of view from the village, there would be a renewed buzz of gossip. *Blast!* He should have considered that and acted accordingly. Although he had long ago accustomed himself to the curiosity and wagging tongues of this village, he doubted if Elzanne would be immune to the questions that were sure to be fired at her when they returned for the quarter day.

"What is wrong?" Elzanne asked.

"Just my own thoughts." He would not be dishonest

with her, but neither would he fill her with apprehension over something that might not happen. A laugh bubbled in his throat. He could not be dishonest with himself either. Of course, those questions would be flying about like vexing insects. "I would rather not burden you with them at this moment."

Bafflement dimmed her eyes. "If I have done something wrong . . ."

"Rest assured, Elzanne, that *you* have done nothing wrong." He said no more as he helped her into the carriage and stepped in, sitting beside her. As he picked up the reins, he added, "If you enjoyed admiring the roses here, you must let me show you the ones in the red rose garden at Trowbridge House."

"Red rose garden?" Elzanne asked. "There is more than one rose garden?"

"Three to be exact. One for red roses, one for white, and the final one is a combination of the two. My gardener has a deep affinity for roses."

She turned to look back at her abigail. "You may wish to speak with him, Lurline, about how to get rid of the spots on our roses."

"An excellent idea, Miss Corbett," Lurline replied.

"It seems good ideas are all around us," Bradley said as he drove the carriage along the road, which was edged by a stone wall on one side and a hedgerow on the other. "Have you inspired all of us, Elzanne?"

"I doubt that."

"I don't."

She shifted to look at him. The light had returned to her emerald eyes, and he knew his words had pleased her. And her pleasure at them enchanted him. He could not recall ever looking forward to something as much as he was this walk among the roses.

Eight

Elzanne wondered why no one else was in the solarium. If she lived in Trowbridge House, she would spend every morning here. She longed to stretch out like a cat in the sunshine. She laughed at the very idea. What would Lord Trowbridge think if he came into the room and saw her draped across the wicker settee?

Her laugh softened into a sigh. She should not be thinking about Lord Trowbridge's opinions or how every emotion danced in his eyes. Fast when he smiled, and in a slow swirl when he was disturbed, but always with an intensity that threatened to set her heart beating at a frantic pace.

Frantic.

That described her each time she spoke to the viscount. She was unsure if he would be the stern, unsmiling man who had greeted her so reluctantly when she arrived or if he would be the disarming man whose smile melted every bone within her and threatened the last shreds of her resistance to the suggestion offered by that smile. When she had gone with him into the village, he had switched from a smile to a forceful frown and back so swiftly that she had not been sure what he had been thinking.

Hearing footfalls behind her, Elzanne turned, hopeful

that her thoughts had taken form. Her smile tempered when she saw Rudyard walking in, a wooden bucket in his hand.

"Oh, *you* are here," he said, pausing.

"Yes, I am. Were you looking for someone?"

"My grandmother."

"She mentioned something about spending the morning going over the accounts with the cook."

His nose wrinkled. "That sounds boring."

She smiled and sat on a bench next to the widest window. "What do you have in your bucket?"

"Worms."

"For fishing?" She laughed. "That is a silly question. They aren't for *you* to eat."

He grinned and sat next to her. "I have come up with names for fifty stars."

"So you can catch five fish. Fifty names are a lot."

Putting down the bucket, he began to count on his fingers as he named classmates and many of the servants in the house. She halted him before he could finish the whole list.

"I trust you that you have enough names even if you are lucky enough to hook six fish," Elzanne said, draping her arm over his shoulders.

He stiffened for a moment, then grinned up at her. "I may need some help with that."

"If you do, we can pull out your history textbook and find all sorts of peculiar old Anglo-Saxon names."

"Like Ethelbert and Edgar?"

"Yes. It sounds as if you like history far better than arithmetic."

He nodded with enthusiasm. "I like reading about the battles and how the English have won them all."

"Most of them."

"I don't read about the ones they lost."

Elzanne laughed. For the first time, she realized how

large a dose of his father's charm Rudyard had inherited, along with his mercurial moods. Before she could reply, she heard more footsteps.

Rouse paused in the doorway, looking about. The butler's eyes widened when he saw her sitting with Rudyard, but his expression did not otherwise change. She wondered if it ever did, for his face, as he walked toward her, was grim.

He held out a folded page. "This was just delivered for you, Miss Corbett."

"Thank you, Rouse," she said, lifting her arm away from Rudyard's thin shoulders to take it.

When the butler smiled back, she hoped her astonishment did not show on her face. The man had been, before this, as solemn as . . . as the Lord Trowbridge she had first met. She hoped *that* thought would be hidden.

Rouse walked out of the room as stiffly as a soldier on parade.

"What is it, Miss Corbett?" asked Rudyard, leaning in front of her to see.

She turned it over and pointed to the handwriting. "A letter from my brother."

"Mr. Corbett?"

She nodded. "He is in Leeds visiting a friend from *his* school days."

"What does it say?"

"You should know that a letter's contents are private."

He twisted his face into a scowl. "I want to know what it says!"

"So do I."

"Read it to me."

"Excuse me?" she asked, wondering how any child could be so self-centered. She had thought he might be setting aside his tantrums to be more reasonable. "I believe I just explained that this letter is for my eyes alone."

"But I want to know—"

"The fish are waiting." She smiled, although she wanted to ask him why he was so sweet one moment and so annoying the next. "The sun is out, so you should go before the light comes around to the pond and puts the fish to sleep down deep in the mud."

"It's already too late. Fish get caught best at dawn."

"But berries are best at this hour." She did not want him peering over her shoulder while she read what Orson had written. Orson was sure to have mentioned the boy, and she doubted it was in a flattering tone. Something must be vitally important for him to write her a letter when they would be seeing each other soon.

A twinge cut through her. When she next saw her brother, she would have already bid Lord Trowbridge *adieu*. The twinge became a wave of sorrow.

"Berries?" asked Rudyard, drawing her attention back to him.

"Strawberries should be ready to be picked now."

"Strawberries?" His eyes brightened.

"If you can pick enough, we can have strawberries for dessert tonight."

He jumped to his feet and grinned. "I can pick enough for all of us." He scurried through the door at one end of the room.

She watched when he ran past the window. He waved to her, and she raised her hand to wave back. When she saw a footman following close on the boy's heels, she lowered her hand.

Frowning, she realized that she never had seen Rudyard alone outside the house. Each time he had been in the gardens, either she or a footman had been with him. He was too old for such a close watch. She must remember to speak to his father or grandmother about this.

For now . . . She reached to break the wax seal on the letter. No, she would not read it here.

She went up to her bedroom, glad that she did not meet anyone and even gladder to see that Lurline was busy elsewhere. Closing the door to the dressing room and the one to the schoolroom, she sat on the bench by the dressing table.

The blue wax broke into pieces, scattering on the carpet. She would pick them up after she read what Orson had written. She unfolded the page to see his precise handwriting. Tilting it toward the window to catch the light, she read:

Dear Elzanne,

By the time you are in receipt of this letter, I shall be enjoying Lawrence's company at his home in Leeds. Our conversation on grammar and common spelling would be enhanced by your insights, I have no doubt. However, you must have realized by now that I was correct to send you to Trowbridge House with young Rudyard Trowbridge. The boy needs guidance in so many matters, not the least in how to think of someone other than himself.

I cannot wait to tell you any longer that I have asked Agatha to become my wife. She has agreed. You will always have a home with us, and we look forward to having you here to be a part of our wedding and our family.

Elzanne smiled broadly as she lowered the letter to her lap. "It is about time you asked her, Orson." She wondered why he had not mentioned his plans to do this before she left. Did he think that she had been unaware of the attraction between him and their housekeeper? Or, and she barely could complete this thought, did he think she would disapprove of the match?

Her smile returned when she realized the truth probably had nothing to do with either reason. Orson most likely had forgotten during the work to finish the term that he had failed to mention it to her. He became so focused on his students and helping them succeed that everything else—even something as important as a marriage proposal—fell right out of his head.

She lifted the letter again to finish reading what else her brother had written.

> *I trust your visit to Trowbridge House has not been intolerable. I know you will be doing your best. However, I do not expect you to have much success with the Honorable Mr. Rudyard Trowbridge. I do hope you have enjoyed living in a fine country house. You have been nowhere but Lindenmere School for too long.*
>
> *Belatedly I must write what I forgot to tell you at the time I arranged for you to go with young Trowbridge and act as his tutor. I know you were intrigued with his essay about his father. You probably have already discovered that the assignment for which young Trowbridge wrote those ill-penned paragraphs was an exercise I gave the class in expressing themselves through the use of irony.*

"Irony?" whispered Elzanne as she raised her gaze from the page to stare at the wall between the window and the painting of the elevation of Trowbridge House. "An exercise in irony?"

Rising, she knelt by the bed and drew out the bag which still held the essay that Rudyard had written. She pulled the ribbon from beneath her bodice holding the key. She unlocked the bag, opened it, and sifted through the pages there. Lifting out the one she wanted, she sat back on her heels as she read it again.

Tears filled her eyes as she read the words of excessive praise. Rudyard had lauded his father for what a boy would hope his father might be. Yet, instead of considering him the *best* father in England, Rudyard clearly believed Lord Trowbridge was the worst.

She lowered the page to her lap. A practice in writing irony? She was sad that such a chasm existed between the viscount and his son. In an effort to let his son have his way in everything to atone for his mother's death, Lord Trowbridge had created an appalling division between them.

She looked again at the last poorly written paragraph.

My father has introduced me to many important peoples, and he is teaching me all I need to learn to oversee his estates when I follow him as viscount. My father never tires of my company. During the last holidays, my father spent all of one afternoon fishing with me in the pond and then postponed a meeting with the local mayor so we could eat what we had caught. My father has taken me for a sail on a ship from London to Penzance and let me steer the ship. My father is teaching me to drive his coach-and-four and does not care if I drive it as fast as the wind. My father refuses to be away from home at night, so he can tuck me into bed and always read me a story. My father is the best father in England.

Coming to her feet, Elzanne walked out of the bedchamber. It did not take her long to find the butler. When she explained that she needed to speak with Lord Trowbridge straightaway, Rouse led her to a wing of the house that she had never visited.

She waited in the corridor while Rouse went into the viscount's office. She resisted the temptation to ease closer to the door, so she might hear the conversation within. The butler would return soon enough.

"He will see you now, Miss Corbett," the butler said as he emerged past the thick door.

"Thank you."

Elzanne went in and looked around, astounded. Orson's desk always overflowed with pages and books and half the time with an upset ink bottle that added to the stains. What did not fit on the desk was stacked on the floor. Although the room appeared to have suffered an explosion of paper, he always found what he sought quickly. She doubted if her brother would have been comfortable working in this sterile room.

"Elzanne, what is amiss?" asked Lord Trowbridge as he came to his feet from behind his desk. "You look as gray as death."

"You should see this." She held out a single page.

He took it and looked down at it. "This was written by Rudyard. I recognize his scrawling hand that I have seen when he writes the obligatory two letters home each term." He picked up a page from his desk. "Rudyard brought this yesterday to show off to me. Each letter on this new page is cleanly made, and it is as neat as anything my estate manager would have delivered to me. I can see you have made an inroad in teaching him to write something readable."

"I didn't give you that page to show how much better Rudyard's work appears. You should *read* what he has written."

"The Best Father in England?" Puzzlement filled his eyes, which widened as he continued reading the page. "But, Elzanne, I have not done any of these things with the boy."

"The task was, I did not realize until I received a letter from my brother today, to write something ironic." She took the page and looked away, not wanting to see his sorrow. "I'm sorry, my lord, but I thought you should know."

"So it is only in irony that he labels me a good and devoted father?"

"He seems to have tempered the anger aimed at you during these holidays." She turned her head to discover Lord Trowbridge's lips only a few inches from hers. His arm around her waist kept her from backing away. "My lord, I cannot concentrate on how to help Master Rudyard when you . . ."

"When I help myself to you?" He leaned his cheek against her hair. "Mayhap it is because I don't want to concentrate on anything but you, Elzanne. However, I must think of a way to make this better with the boy." He stepped away.

"It is not too late to do some of these things with him." She smiled. "He has been busy gathering worms to go fishing, and he is on his way to pick strawberries by the pond right now."

"By himself?"

She was astonished at the sudden anxiety in his voice. "No, with a footman. Why would Rudyard's being alone be a problem?"

"There was . . ." He stopped himself as if he did not want to add more, then said, "Of course, it is not a problem."

Although she wanted to ask him to be honest with her, she replied, "Mayhap if you join him, he might not be so quick to write something like this again."

"So you believe a single time of taking the boy fishing will ease this indignation he has toward me?"

"It cannot do anything but help."

He smiled as he curved his hand along her face. "Now you are being *my* teacher again, Elzanne. You are right. It is time I showed him that I am a good father in truth."

Nine

Lord Trowbridge was as good as his word. In the days leading up to the quarter day celebration, Elzanne had to smile when so many of Rudyard's sentences began with "My father and I." Her smile had grown wider when she watched Rudyard and the viscount put the kite they had made together into the back of the carriage. Rudyard had carried it carefully all the way into the village.

That was why, when it came time for the kite flying contest to begin as a fresh breeze came in off the sea, Elzanne was delighted to see Rudyard standing next to his father, the bright red kite in his hands. She went to where Rudyard was prattling. He halted when she put her hand on his shoulder.

"Good luck to both of you," she said. "If there is a prize for the most brilliantly colored kite, I believe you will win it."

"We are going to win for flying this kite the highest!" Rudyard crowed.

"Do you have it ready, Son?" Lord Trowbridge asked.

"Yes, I attached the strings while you were talking with Mr. Eustis."

Lord Trowbridge smiled at Elzanne. "The mayor is

most interested in making sure the fireworks are kept safely out of everyone's way until tonight."

Before she could reply, there was a call to ready the kites. A bell was rung, and the kites soared skyward . . . save for the red one. Rudyard was running about, but the kite bounced on the ground behind him like a broken-winged bird.

Lord Trowbridge halted him and looked at the kite. "You have it strung all wrong," he said. He took the kite from Rudyard and unhooked the string from the crosspieces. "It should be tie   n the other side so the wind can capture it and lift i

"I can do it!" Rudyard cried.

"Let me show you, and then—"

"Let me do it!"

Lord Trowbridge started to hand the kite to his son, then paused as he glanced toward Elzanne. "I will show you, Rudyard, then you will know how to do it next time."

"I want to do it!" Rudyard grabbed for the kite. When his hand burst through the paper, he cried, "Look what you did."

"Me?" Lord Trowbridge set the kite on the ground. "You were the one who was so careless, Rudyard."

"Because you wouldn't let me do it! You wrecked my kite!"

Elzanne stepped forward, but Lord Trowbridge waved her back away, saying, *"This* is my son. *This* is my problem. Rudyard—"

"I hate you!" the boy cried and tore the rest of the paper from the kite.

"Master Rudyard," Elzanne began, wanting to reach through his frustration as she had before, "your father just wanted to show—"

Rudyard snarled an oath at her, then raced away.

Lord Trowbridge started to follow, but she grasped his

arm and said, "You may as well wait until he cools his head a bit. He will not listen to anyone now."

He picked up the shredded kite. "I fear I have ruined the child."

"Nonsense," she said as she walked with him away from the competition and the many eyes that had watched Rudyard's tantrum.

He laughed tersely. "Must you sound like my mother when she chides me as if I were still a child myself?"

"Mayhap I must, because what you said was nonsense. Master Rudyard is not ruined. He simply needs to learn that he cannot always have things as he wishes. It is not an easy lesson for any child to comprehend."

"You are being generous." He turned, and the tension along his shoulders eased.

Elzanne followed his gaze and saw Lady Trowbridge talking with Rudyard. "I believe he is due credit for being much changed in recent days. You cannot expect the progress to be smooth, I am afraid."

He tossed the kite and the ball of string onto a table. "Afraid? You? I can easily imagine you jousting with some great multiheaded monster if you thought you could tame the beast."

"Is that how you view Rudyard? As a multiheaded monster?"

"Do not read meaning into my words that I have not intended, Elzanne," he answered sharply.

"I cannot help your son if you take that tone, my lord."

"What I intended to say," he said, as they continued past the edge of the field and into the almost deserted village, "is that I want to keep him from making the same mistakes his mother made, including the headstrong decision that ended her life."

Elzanne's steps faltered as she realized he had brought

her away from the others because he did not want them to hear what he had to say. "How did she die?"

"It was an accident, a riding accident. Like her son, Nola never would heed the advice of others. She knew about the ha-ha at the edge of the field where we were hunting, but she was sure her horse could jump the gap. She had been angry because I had insisted that she ride with the women instead of the men."

"Was she a good horsewoman?"

"No." He smiled sadly as he stopped by the small well at one side of the road. "That was why I told her that she must ride with the women. Even though she was told by her companions that she could not, she refused to listen and tried to make the jump."

"And did not make it?"

He shook his head.

"Oh, I am so sorry."

"That is why I have been tough with the boy. I want him to consider the consequences of his actions before he takes them."

Elzanne sighed. "You can tell him that, my lord, but I fear we all have to learn that lesson by difficult experiences. Mayhap if you took him to the place this happened and explained—"

"It happened at Trowbridge Hall."

"Which explains why Rudyard did not want to come here."

The sounds of the celebration beyond the church were muted by the stone houses along the single, twisting street, but his voice was even more hushed as he asked, "How do you know that he did not want to come here?"

"He flew into quite the pelter when we came through the gate of Trowbridge House. At the time I believed he was being outrageous as he had proven to be on other occasions during the journey here. I have changed my mind since I have come to know him better."

"Because you are now more familiar with his commonplace tempers?"

"I am afraid that is true." She leaned against the well's stones. "He was truly upset. He begged for us to turn the carriage around and take him to London. I had no sympathy for him because I thought he was just being as impossible as before. The poor child."

"Do not fault yourself. Rudyard gave you every reason to assume that he was simply being petulant. Like the boy who called wolf, he wasted your benevolence before he needed it."

"That is a heartless comment."

"I did not mean it to sound heartless, and I would never speak so to his face. However, you must own that he did nothing to earn your compassion."

"He was thinking only of his own pain and wanted nobody else to be happy when he was so unhappy." Tears gushed into her eyes.

"You are very understanding when he has given you so much trouble."

She ran her fingers along the uneven stones. A pebble came loose and fell into the well, splashing. "I am trying to be."

"And you are succeeding."

"Most of the time, my lord."

He rested one hand beside hers and gave her an easy smile. "Today is a quarter day, Elzanne, when it is every Lord Trowbridge's duty to be treated with as great a lack of courtesy as possible. As half the village elders are addressing me by my given name, I see no reason why you should not as well."

"It would be inappropriate for me to do so. The elders of the village are not employed by you, my lord."

"I could make it an order, but it would be much better if we leave it as a request to honor an old tradition."

Her eyes widened, and she wondered if he had been

visiting the kegs of ale at one side of the field. "You would order me to do something like this?"

"Do I need to?"

She laughed. "No, but do not expect it to be easy for me to address you so."

"Ah, the ever-proper Miss Corbett. It is not so difficult to say 'Bradley.' "

"Not the word itself."

He put his fingers on either side of her mouth and squeezed gently as he said, "Bradley. Say it after me."

"Bradley," she mumbled. Reaching up, she drew his hand away from her mouth. "It would be much easier to say if you did not try to help, my—Bradley."

"Much better."

Elzanne laughed. "Do you always expect to get your way?"

"I always hope to." He wove his fingers through hers, shocking her. As he drew her hand up to press it over the buttons on his brightly embroidered vest, he chuckled. "My son and I are much alike in that."

"And in other ways."

"Ouch," he replied. "I believe I have persuaded you to show as little respect to me as possible today."

She smiled, despite the ambiguity within her. Bradley's teasing soothed her. As she watched a smile spread across his lips, the uncertainty dissolved. She put her hand on his and delighted in his fingers engulfing hers. She longed to be in his arms. With her face against his strong shoulder, she could close her eyes and shut out the world. The only danger would be succumbing to desire.

It was a risk she needed to avoid. She was his son's tutor. She was supposed to be thinking of ways to help Rudyard learn. All thoughts of the lessons she would like to experience in Bradley's arms must be banished from her head . . . and her heart.

* * *

Elzanne was astonished to find Rudyard nowhere in sight when the food was spread out across the tables. Although he had been avoiding his father, she had seen him running about with some of the village boys, but those lads were here, ready to eat.

"I don't know," she replied when Lady Trowbridge asked where Rudyard might be. "Is he with Lord Trowbridge?"

"No, for here comes Bradley now." She waved to her son and called, "Where is the boy?"

"I thought he would be here with you." The viscount frowned, his expression out of place among the many smiles at this *fête champêtre*.

Elzanne smiled. "I am sure he is busy with one of his friends. If we each go in a different direction around the field, we are certain to see him."

When Bradley and his mother exchanged worried glances, Elzanne could not understand why they were so distressed. Did they fear that Rudyard would do something out of hand like his mother had? She started to reassure them that this village should provide no danger to a lad.

Lady Trowbridge cut her off in mid-word, proving how distressed Rudyard's grandmother was. Taking Bradley's arm, she turned him toward the village. She called back over her shoulder, "Elzanne, look around here."

Elzanne wanted to shout that they were overreacting, but saw the nervous glances among the villagers. Did they believe that Rudyard was as headstrong and doomed as his mother had been? Recalling how the boy was never alone outside the house, she guessed that was the case. Poor Rudyard! No wonder he rebelled against such restrictions.

She began to walk in the opposite direction from

where Bradley and his mother had gone. When she saw an area under some trees that had been cordoned off with a thick rope, she realized this must be so no one would wander near the fireworks. Bradley had arranged for it. She started to walk past. She paused as her eyes were caught by a motion within the shadows. A motion and a spark.

With a cry, she bent beneath the rope. She ran to where Rudyard and a boy she had not seen before were crouched in front of an open wooden crate. The hiss of a fuse added speed to her feet. She grabbed both boys by the arm and jerked them to their feet. As they shouted, she propelled them toward the rope. She ran after them as fast as she could, shoving them forward again when they faltered.

The crate exploded behind them. She dove to the earth, pulling the boys down with her. Sparks peppered the ground, and she winced when one struck her arm. One of the boys moaned, but she could not guess which one, because her head rang with the concussion of the explosions that had ripped into the trees behind them.

People ran from everywhere, shouting and calling for water to put out the small fires in the grass. Men tugged the crates away before they could explode, too. As Elzanne rolled to sit, hands under her arms lifted her to her feet as if she were no older than Rudyard.

"Are you hurt, Elzanne?" asked Bradley, his eyes like thunderheads.

"I am all right." She winced as she touched the red spot on her arm. "It's nothing."

He reached past her and brought Rudyard and the other boy to their feet with a single tug. The village boy looked horrified, but Rudyard's defiance burst from every inch of him.

"How could you be so foolish?" demanded Bradley. "You could have killed Elzanne and yourselves."

"I am sorry," mumbled the village boy, his head hanging as his mother rushed up to him.

As the lad's mother seconded his apology, Bradley waved her to silence. "Your son is no more culpable than mine."

She smiled at him and led her chagrined son away, scolding him as they went.

"We are deeply grateful to you, Elzanne." Lady Trowbridge squeezed her hand, then frowned at her grandson. "I believe Rudyard has learned a lesson that he will not soon forget." The boy scowled back at her, but she appeared not to notice.

Elzanne knew she was overstepping her place, but she said, "All of us have. Rudyard needs some room to be a boy, but he needs to learn the obligations that go with freedom."

No one spoke for a long moment, then Lady Trowbridge patted her son on the arm. "Asking Elzanne to stay here to teach Rudyard may have been one of the smartest things you have ever done, Bradley."

" 'Twas upon your insistence, as I recall," he answered with a taut chuckle, but fury burned in his eyes. A fury that was now aimed at Elzanne as well as his son.

"I am sure that Elzanne would remind you that it is a wise man who heeds the counsel of others around him."

"And what is your advice now?" he asked in the same sharp tone.

"You should remember that what happened in the past won't necessarily happen again." Lady Trowbridge's voice trembled with emotion. "As well you should recall the day that you set the stables on fire."

"He did that?" Rudyard gasped.

"You and I are going to talk about your misdeeds, my boy, while your father considers his own." Lady Trowbridge took Rudyard by the arm and steered him to where several men were checking the crates to make sure they would not explode. Her scold drifted back to where Elzanne still stood beside Bradley.

"Excuse me," he said. "I have a few words to say to my son as well." He started to brush past her, but she gripped his sleeve, startling herself as much as him.

"Wait!"

He lifted her hand away. "I have heard what you have to say about this. Now *he* needs to hear what *I* have to say. He must learn to think of what will happen when he makes his choices." His voice cracked as he added, "As his mother never did."

"But he is *your* son, too, Bradley! Why are you assuming that his wild spirits come from your late wife? Your mother has hinted often that you were as mischievous at your son's age as he is now."

"But I learned."

"So will he, if you give him a chance. You have coddled him for so long in fear that he will endanger himself that you have not let him learn the lessons he must. Let your mother handle this now. It is important that you not damage the trust Master Rudyard is beginning to feel toward you."

"So you expect me to act as if nothing happened?"

"Of course not. Talk to him while you are eating or watching the fireworks tonight. That will give you both a chance to clear your heads before you speak your minds." She glanced toward Lady Trowbridge, who was wagging a finger right in Rudyard's face. "I do believe one scold at a time is enough. I cannot believe he meant to harm anyone. He was just curious about the fireworks."

"And did not stop to consider the consequences."

"Bradley, he is just a child. He is going to make mistakes. You cannot judge him as you would an adult. He is changing slowly, but he is changing. He is growing up. You have to give him time to do so."

"Is that so, Elzanne?"

Before she could answer, Rudyard ran up to them. He scowled at his father, but turned to Elzanne. "I am so sorry, Miss Corbett, that you got hurt trying to save me from my own foolishness."

"Did your grandmother tell you to say that to me?" she asked.

He nodded, then shook his head. "She did tell me to apologize, but I really am sorry, Miss Corbett. I wouldn't hurt you for anything." He threw his arms around her in a quick embrace, then raced away.

"Mayhap I have been a fool not to heed your counsel," Bradley said quietly as his gaze followed his son.

"I am not certain I would use the word 'fool.' " She wished she could find the words to ease the rigid lines in his face.

"I would. Now, I shall do something intelligent. I'm going to take you to Mr. Kenyon. I want him to look at that burn." He offered his arm, astonishing her anew.

She put her hand tentatively on his. When his hand covered hers, a pain even more fierce than the burn on her other arm surged through her. Like Rudyard, she must recall her lessons and remember that, in two days, she and the boy would be returning to Lindenmere School.

Ten

Rudyard tumbled out of the carriage as soon as it stopped at Trowbridge House. His grandmother followed more slowly. When Bradley offered his hand to Elzanne to assist her down, she fought to keep from yawning.

"Am I boring you?" he teased.

"Of course not. It is very late for those of us who have never enjoyed the hours the *ton* keeps." She could not halt the yawn as she stepped down out of the carriage.

"Do you think you can stay awake a few more minutes?"

"Barely." When he drew her hand within his arm and turned her away from the door, she asked, "Aren't we going inside and to bed?"

His voice became low and husky. "You do ask the most provocative questions."

She hoped the starlight hid her blush. "You know that was not what I intended."

"So much more the shame." He laughed and led her toward the red rose garden. "As you can see, we are in clear view of the house, so you need not worry about me doing something untoward."

"I was not worried about that."

"You should be."

Elzanne drew her hand off his arm. "I think it would be best if I said good night, Bradley."

"Why?"

She looked everywhere but at him, because she was unsure if she could resist the enticement that might be on his face. Just his fingers gently rubbing her arm warned her of the extraordinary danger of remaining here. Slowly she forced out words. "I don't think we are thinking very clearly just now."

"Good."

She looked up to discover his starlit smile was as alluring as she had feared. It was almost impossible to fight the temptation it suggested, but she said, "I bid you good evening."

"I'm sorry you feel that you should leave now, Elzanne. You can't guess how wrong you are."

"You *do* need to think more clearly."

She started to walk past him, but he took her uninjured arm and whipped her back against him. His eyes blistered with silver fire. In a low growl, he said, "I have thought about this very clearly. I want you right here, Elzanne." He turned her into his embrace. Holding her face between his hands, he captured her lips.

She raised her hands to push him away before someone took notice of them in the shadows, but his silent, fiery persuasion urged her to wrap her arms around his shoulders. The luscious flavor of his kiss was so succulently flavored with the ale he had downed with the villagers. Delight seared her as brilliantly as the fireworks had burnished the sky.

He raised his head and smiled. "I don't want you to think clearly, Elzanne. I want you to stay here with me."

"I should go inside."

"I am not talking of just tonight. I am talking of tomorrow."

"Tomorrow, Rudyard and I must make the final preparations for our journey back to Lindenmere School."

"Do you want to go back?"

"It is my home."

"You could stay here. Now that I am holding you, I do not intend to let you leave me."

"And if I wish to go?"

"Do you?"

Her answer vanished into a gasp as he pressed his lips to the curve of her neck. His fingers sweeping upward sent her hair cascading along her back.

With a soft moan, she pulled out of his arms again. "What I want is irrelevant. What I must do is."

"And you must leave?"

"What would be said if I stayed here after your son returned to school? People would think—"

"To perdition with what other people might think!" He tugged her closer again. "You know, Rudyard could be the one who understands how life should be lived. Mayhap it is time we learned a lesson from *him*. He is willing to take a chance."

"And he could have gotten himself killed today."

"Yes, but he also could have escaped without anyone's help." He brushed her hair back from her face. "You are right. I have been trying so hard to protect him, that I have not given him a chance to be the mischievous boy that I was."

"You should tell him that, too."

"I believe I shall." Bradley looked past her and crooked his finger. "Rudyard, you might as well come out. I know you are hiding behind that rosebush." As the bush rustled, he added, "Rudyard has refused to allow himself to be constrained by other people's expectations. Why should you and I be?"

She heard Rudyard's giggle as he bounced out onto

the path between the bushes, but did not take her gaze from his father's face.

"I only know what *I* believe I must do," she whispered.

"And that is to leave Trowbridge House?"

"Lindenmere School is my home." She smiled sadly at Rudyard. "As it will be your son's until he graduates."

Bradley turned to his son. "What would you say, Rudyard, if I told you that you need not go back to that school? That you could stay here, so you and I can learn to love each other again without the shadow of the past coming between us?"

"But I *do* love you, Papa." He hesitated, then flung his arms around his father as he had around Elzanne at the quarter day celebration.

"I want you to think I am the best father in England. Not in irony, but in actuality." He ruffled his son's hair.

Elzanne bit her lower lip to keep it from trembling. She could not have imagined this ending to her visit to Trowbridge House. As she turned to go into the house and let father and son have this moment alone, Bradley's hand settled on her arm.

"You don't need to leave," he said softly.

"You two have much to share, and I will be in the way."

"I wasn't talking about tonight. I was talking about *you* going back to Lindenmere School."

She glanced at Rudyard, who was listening avidly. "Bradley, I don't think the discussion of such matters is appropriate in front of your son."

"Why not? He will be in need of a teacher now that he will not be returning to Lindenmere School."

"I am sure my brother can suggest an excellent one to you."

"He already has." He drew her back into his arms.

"A teacher who can help me learn to be the best father in England to my son."

"You need only listen to your heart to know what to do."

"I have listened, and I know what to do." He dropped to one knee and ignored his son's giggle as he added, "Will you marry me, Elzanne?"

"You want to marry *me?*"

"I believe I just asked that." He winked at his son. "Without a touch of irony. What do you say, Elzanne?"

She looked from father to son. They had found their way into her heart, and she did not want to let either of them go. She held one hand out to Bradley and the other to his son as she whispered, "Yes, I will marry you."

Rudyard cheered and hugged her again.

His father plucked him away and said, "The groom-to-be should hug his betrothed first, Son." When he put his arms around her, she smiled up at him. He lowered his mouth toward hers and whispered, "And now you can teach me, Elzanne, to be the best *husband* in England."

"It might take a while, for you are as stubborn as Rudyard."

"I hope it will take a lifetime, my love." He kissed her as his son let out a cheer and embraced both.

A FATHER'S
LOVE

Valerie King

One

Lord Westbury stood at the windows of the school-room on the second floor of his country house, his heart tight with misgiving. His gaze was directed toward the rose garden below where he watched his betrothed, Lady Esther Adstock, toss several red blossoms onto the gravel at her feet, blow her nose heartily, and afterward sneeze quite violently for the hundredth time since her arrival a fortnight past. The windows rattled at the unexpected sound. He sighed heavily as she fled the garden.

He knew something was amiss with the lady he had chosen to make his wife, but for the life of him he did not know what. He had courted her over the course of the recent London Season and had thought he had found in her the necessary makings of the next Countess of Westbury. She possessed excellent breeding, agreeable manners, and a certain gentleness of spirit he had enjoyed exceedingly. She had appeared to welcome his advances and in the end had accepted his hand in marriage with a dignity becoming her rank as the daughter of the Duke of Adstock. If she seemed to be indifferent to his kisses, he felt confident that time and patience would improve any lack of affection between them.

Until her arrival at Ludgerwick Hall, therefore, he had

been confident in his choice. However, from nearly the moment she crossed the threshhold of his home, she seemed to have altered beyond recognition. She had adopted an autocratic manner of governing his house to the point that she had offended nearly every servant on his staff, all gentleness of manner had disappeared entirely, and she had not stopped sneezing! He had begun to feel he had made a dreadful mistake yet he could in no manner account for her wretched change of disposition or manner.

A flutter of movement caught his eye and he shifted his gaze to a point at the opposite end of the garden. Alison, that was, Miss Russell, was leading his four nieces into the garden. He knew their routine well. At this time of afternoon, they were speaking French, all five of them, one of three continental languages Miss Russell spoke fluently and which she was presently teaching her pupils. Miss Russell had been governess to his brother's daughters for the past seven years.

Poor Harry! A twelve-month past, he had fallen into a ditch that had become swollen after a heavy rainstorm, and had drowned. Water alone had not sealed his fate. Harry had been in his cups that night as he was most nights and had been for years. Lord Westbury had mourned his brother's death quite deeply but a blessing had followed quickly. Because he was guardian to Harry's children, Mary, Jane, Sarah, and Arabella had come to live with him along with their governess. His life had never been so complete nor so joyous as with the presence of his nieces in his home.

His gaze rested in this moment on the governess, on Miss Russell, on Alison, whom he had known for more than eight years. How beautiful she was, carrying her wide straw bonnet on her arm, her expression lively as she spoke her French nouns and verbs. He could hear her laughter and the answering merriment of his nieces.

Her delicate hands were sheathed in pretty white lace gloves. He knew what her fingers looked like beneath the gloves, for he had kissed each one numerous times. Her soft curves were cloaked by a gown of light blue silk. He knew the lines of her figure well, for he had embraced her on countless occasions. Her hair was caught up in a jaunty knot of curls atop her head. He knew what each strand felt like laced between his fingers. He had caressed her locks every day for weeks.

But that had been eight years past. Ever since, he had been allowed only to gaze upon her and to remember.

She chanced to glance up at the window and wave to him. Faith, but she was so very beautiful. His breath caught every time he but looked at her, just as it had from the first moment he saw her so many years ago. Her hair was the color of sunshine and her eyes as blue as the sky overhead. August suited her.

An old familiar sadness drifted through him. He had loved her for so long now. The passing of the years had not dimmed his passion, his affection, his love for her. He had been betrothed to her at one time. He had courted her for weeks during the summer the mad king, George III, had failed to return from an excursion into the fantasies of his mind. He had asked her boldly to marry him and she had agreed, only then had he told her the truth, that he was not Mr. Twyford, the son of a squire in Lincolnshire, but rather heir to the Earldom of Westbury. She had stared at him in such a way, as though he had just informed her he was the devil himself. There was nothing so futile, so abhorrent, so impossible as an unequal alliance in her opinion. She had easily forgiven him for the lies he had told her about being a mere Mr. Twyford, but she could not forgive him for being the future Lord Westbury.

He understood in part her reasons for ending the betrothal. He had witnessed for himself the manner in which her mother, Lady Katherine Russell, argued heatedly with her husband, a mere major of the Horse Guards, about matters of household economy, of social standing, and of fashion. There had been nothing discreet or pretty in their marital arguments. The result had been to deprive Lord Westbury of the wife of his choice—their eldest daughter, beautiful Alison, who refused to marry him because her parents had been at war ever since she could remember.

She had instead become a governess to his brother's children, four beautiful, lively girls, and he had never stopped loving her.

In the intervening years he had been able to see Alison frequently, for Harry Longley, though a wholly incompetent clergyman, had held the living at nearby Whitbourne. Her presence had always been a mild torture, for she had never once relented in her refusals, though he had approached her several times, hoping to rekindle what had been a very passionate courtship.

The youngest of the girls looked up at him and waved. Delightful Arabella. Bella. He smiled and waved at her in turn. Her sisters followed suit, Mary, Jane, and Sarah. He loved them all. He had the care of them as their legal guardian, but the relationship was nearer and dearer than a mere guardian or even an uncle to his nieces. He stood in their father's stead. To some degree, he always had, particularly since their mother had perished as well, so many years ago.

Alison looked up at him and waved as well. Oh God how his heart swelled. He smiled and waved in return. Dear, precious Alison, whose kisses were sweeter than a fine East Indian Madeira. How he hated the thought of losing her, but lose her he must. Lady Esther did not believe in housing beautiful governesses beneath her roof. He might have argued with her on that score, but because the lady was Alison Russell and because he could not look at her without remembering, regretting, wishing, he allowed his bride-to-be to have her way.

Later that afternoon, Alison sat on a settee in the library, her fingers clenched about the spindly handle of a fine teacup. She was situated across from Lady Esther, who occupied a noble wing chair and who had just given her the terrible news. Alison felt as though she were trapped in a nightmare from which she could not escape no matter how hard she tried.

She had been dismissed.

Lady Esther had just told her as much and though she had always known the day would come when she would be required to part from her pupils she had not been prepared in the least to be commanded to leave dear old Ludgers in but five days!

"In five days?" she queried, stunned. Why must she leave so soon?

Lady Esther lifted her chin, lifted a brow, and sneered faintly. "You heard correctly. Five days."

Alison continued to stare at Westbury's bride-to-be. She had thought she would have had the training of the young ladies until the youngest, Arabella, was introduced to society the year of her eighteenth birthday, which would have been five years from now.

Lady Esther softened slightly. "You must understand, Miss Russell, Lord Westbury simply no longer has need of your services. We are in agreement. If I am to be mistress of his home, then I must have the choosing of the servants. I am sure you are well enough in your way, but Mama is arranging for a superior governess to take over your duties."

Alison gave herself a shake. The lady before her was two-and-twenty, quite pretty with curly brown hair and large, expressive brown eyes. She might even have been accounted a beauty had she not had a tendency to pout or scowl in turns. She chanced to glance at her hands and saw that they were trembling.

From the time Alison had first made Lady Esther's acquaintance upon her arrival at Ludgers a fortnight past, she had been attempting to comprehend the lovely young woman. She had as yet been unsuccessful in part because Lady Esther had made herself accessible to no one. Yet for all the lady's imperiousness of demeanor, there were times when Alison had found Lady Esther a warm generous creature, as though in coming to Ludgers she had adopted a role and not a life.

"A new governess?" Alison queried, still reeling from the shock of the dismissal. She lowered her teacup to the saucer at her elbow.

Lady Esther continued. "Surely you did not think you would be staying forever in the earl's employ, particularly since the entire staff tends to seek you out for advice. Why, I have been given to understand that you even have the approval of the menus! Cannot you see how inappropriate this is?"

Alison smiled faintly. "I thought it excellent for I always took the menus to Lord Westbury's nieces and we discussed each of them at length. Mary will be mistress of her own establishment undoubtedly within the next few years, Jane not long to follow. I felt the exercise to be highly beneficial to their training as well as to the training of the younger girls. If I was also of service to his lordship, so much the better."

Lady Esther smiled condescendingly. "Miss Russell, I am certain you were well intentioned, but the Longley ladies will be my particular charge once Westbury and I are wed and it simply will not do to have the girls clinging to you as they are wont to do."

"I beg your pardon, Lady Esther, but the Ladies Longley do not *cling* to me."

"Now, now, do not take a pet, Miss Russell."

Alison felt her temper spiral upward but she suppressed her anger in favor of a rational response. "I am not taking a pet," she stated. "I am taking strong exception to what you have just said to me. The Longley girls have known me for the past seven years as a mainstay in their lives from the time of the death of their dear mother, and the past year since their father perished. I know an affection for them as someone who has served their interests devotedly these many years and more and I believe they are fond of me. However, I have also had the training of them and to refer in any manner to their conduct as *clinging* I tell you I quite resent."

Lady Esther's spine grew rigid. "How dare you speak to me in that insolent manner! You are an employee in this house and I beg you will remember your station. Westbury did not want you to leave, he even asked me not to dismiss you, but I knew what you were. Undoubtedly, you have had your eye on him from the moment you crossed the threshhold of his brother's house. Governesses always seek to marry their betters."

The coldness, the bitterness, emanating from Lady Esther stunned Alison. From whence did such inexplicable hostility arise? "You are sadly mistaken, my lady," Alison returned in a quiet voice. "I do not have my eye on Westbury. As it happens, I rejected a proposal of marriage from him some eight years past for the very reason you have intimated as being abhorrent."

The color in Lady Esther's cheeks receded ominously and she quickly retrieved her vinaigrette. "And now you have taken to telling the worst of Banbury tales! Who, of your lowly place, would break off such an engagement? I . . . I do not believe you for even a moment!" She sniffed the pungent sponge held within the small box, coughed, and sneezed. "Westbury would never have offered for a mere governess!"

Alison watched Lady Esther carefully. Her fingers trembled anew as she lifted the little box to her nose and sniffed yet again. She would not meet Alison's gaze. She should have been infuriated by her words but she sensed there was something more beneath her accusations. "You may not credit it, my lady, but there was a time when your betrothed fancied himself in love with me. But that was many, many years past. Of course, his present affection for you must eclipse even the smallest residue of his prior sentiments."

Lady Esther glanced at her sharply.

A maid suddenly walked into the chamber, bearing a large vase of roses. Lady Esther turned to her. "How dare you enter without making your presence known!" she cried, gaining her feet.

"I . . . I . . . I . . . oh, m'lady, I do beg yer pardon. I thought ye and Miss Russell was in the drawing room. I were told as much."

"And what are you doing bringing roses into the library! I have forbidden them from the principal rooms."

"I . . . I . . . were also told that m'lady did not care fer the library, that ye had no use for books. Oh, dear. I mean, that the books ye desired would be fetched fer ye by Miss Longley, or Miss Jane or Miss Sarah or Miss Arabella."

Lady Esther sneezed, not the polite expulsion of a Lady of Quality, but that of an elephant. "Aaaaaachoooo!"

Alison braced her footing as the windows rattled. "Do take them away immediately, Bonnie," she said gently.

"Yes, Miss Russell." Bonnie dipped a quick curtsy and scurried from the room.

Lady Esther retrieved her kerchief and blew her nose. "You . . . are . . . aaaaaachoo! . . . dismissed, Miss Russell. I expect you . . . to . . . aaaaaachoo! . . . be gone from Ludgerwick Hall by Monday."

"As you have said," Alison murmured.

When Alison quit the library and turned down the hall, she saw the last bit of at least two muslin gowns racing up the side stairway to the second floor. She would have laughed at the sight of what she knew to be her charges spying on her had she not been so angry and so stunned by her recent confrontation with Lady Esther. The faint sound of another sneeze reached her as she, too, mounted the stairs to the schoolroom.

Her thoughts turned to Lady Esther's odd sufferings, for she had been sneezing for one cause or another since her arrival at Ludgers. Thus far her ladyship had blamed her troublesome nose on the quality of the candles and of the soap, on all the flowers in the garden except bouquets of lavender which she said were her favorite, on Arabella's black-and-white cat, named Mr. Wellington after the famous duke, and lastly upon the dust in what she said over and over was an extremely unkempt house, thereby offending the housekeeper, who was an elderly lady of Flemish descent and extremely particular in her standards.

In a private moment, she had asked Westbury quietly if Lady Esther had suffered in a similar manner in London, to which he had answered a decided negative. His expression had grown furrowed with worry. "I do not believe she is happy here," he had confided.

Alison could not have agreed more. Nor was the household content to have Lady Esther at Ludgers. She had succeeded in the space of a fortnight, since her arrival, in offending each of the retainers to the last man, even advising Cook on getting rid of her poultry, for her own mother kept a far superior breed at Chanfield.

Good God, *Chanfield Hall.*

Alison knew there was not a single inmate of Ludgers who did not dread hearing the word "Chanfield" spill from her ladyship's lips.

Entering the schoolroom, she found the young ladies

sulking. "And who was it that sent Bonnie to the library with roses?" Alison queried, closing the door softly behind her.

"We all did," Sarah stated firmly. "We could not help it for we knew what Lady Come-the-Crab meant to do. The servants have been gossiping about it these three days past."

Ordinarily, Alison would have reproved the most heedless of the Longley girls but of the moment her spirits were far too distressed to do anything more than shake her head and cluck her tongue. "I suppose you were listening at the door," she said, sitting down beside young Arabella, who was holding Mr. Wellington on her lap.

Mary, turning a silver tatting shuttle between her fingers, shrugged. "Of course."

Bella's lips quivered. "How can she turn you off, without so much as a by-your-leave?"

"She has every right to do so since she will very soon be mistress of Ludgers. Besides, she discussed the matter with your uncle before speaking with me."

All four girls turned to stare at her, each expression wounded. Jane gasped. "Uncle James has permitted this?"

"Of course he has," Alison stated strongly. "And he was right to do so because his bride-to-be wished for it. She is to be his wife and it is his duty to abide by what she believes to be best for his home and for you."

Shoulders drooped, expressions fell.

Sarah's mouth grew pinched. "She does not mean to stop with merely dismissing you. She will not be content until she has sent all of us to Miss Amesbury's Young Lady of Quality's Seminary for the Insane!"

Her sisters first gasped then laughed heartily at her witticism. Alison, however, felt it necessary to reprove Sarah. "You will not say such things about one of England's finest schools."

"I can and I will," Sarah countered. "After all, who will be here to prevent me." Alison might have said more, but Sarah's eyes filled suddenly with tears.

Jane moved to stand next to Alison, laying a hand on her shoulder. "Lady Esther should not have spoken to you as she did. We were all appalled."

Alison covered her hand with her own. "In that, I must agree. As mistress of her home, or at least her future home, she should have shown me a greater respect, and I tell you this for I have every confidence that one day each of you will be happily settled as mistresses of your own establishments. Any servant or employee of a house should be treated with great dignity—" Here she stopped, suddenly unable to restrain her own tears. "Why am I attempting to instruct you even now?"

She rose hastily, not desiring for the young ladies to witness her sadness. "I must go. I shall return later; in the meantime, please continue with your French. Mary? Be so good as to instruct your younger sisters on the verb *avoir.*"

"Of course Miss Russell," she murmured, her expression pale.

Alison had nearly reached the door of her bedchamber, which was fixed very near to both the schoolroom and the young ladies' bedrooms, when she was hailed from some distance down the hall. "Miss Russell!"

Alison recognized the deep voice at once, for it was as familiar to her as her own. She hastily swiped at her tears and turned to face Lord Westbury. She wished he had not found her in this moment when her heart was choked with so much agony. She clasped her hands in front of her, striving to regain her composure, and waited.

Watching him walk toward her, however, she could not help but smile a little. Had there ever been a more handsome gentleman born than James Westbury? His hair was a thick, wavy black, his features strong and angled sharply, his eyes dark and penetrating. This morning he wore buckskin breeches, a blue coat that he favored, and glossy top boots. He was an athletic man, his frame powerful yet lean, which gave an impression of wild untamed lands like the Colonies or India. She smiled a little more. He was the stuff of novels, as Bella was wont to say.

Perhaps it was because she knew she would be leaving in but a scant five days or perhaps because she was merely overset, but in this moment she was transported back to a time eight years past when she had first met him. She had been sitting on the banks of a river, angling rod in hand, her bare feet dangling into the cold water. The summer day had been hot, her parents were at the cottage house, wrangling over her mother's reckless purchase of a phaeton her father could in no way support, and the fish had beckoned to her.

She had heard a horse come galloping down the lane, heading toward the bridge, which she could see from her perch on a large flat rock. Her bonnet was somewhere behind her and she was already nicely sun-bronzed from her scandalous summer sport.

She thought her dear friend, Freddy, was coming to join her, and so she had not bothered to do anything in preparation for his arrival, except to lower her skirts a trifle so that at least her knees were not exposed.

Instead of Freddy, however, a wonderfully handsome man had ridden across that ancient stone bridge, caught sight of her, and after inclining his hat, made his way down to her. He dismounted his horse, tying up the reins on a nearby thorn shrub, and joined her on the rock.

She had shared her angling rod that day, but neither of them had caught any fish. They had been too boisterous in their conversation. He had been a mere Mr. Twyford that afternoon and when he had taken his leave, she had stood with him professing her need to return to her home as well. He had then done the unthinkable, he had taken her boldly in his arms and she had let him. She doubted she would ever forget what that kiss had been like, from a man who was a veritable stranger besides being the perfect embodiment of every foolish schoolgirl's dream. She had fallen in love with Mr. Twyford that day and for always.

Now he was before her; eight years had passed, and she was leaving Ludgers on Monday.

"Miss Russell," he said, drawing near.

"Yes, Mr. Twyford—I mean Lord Westbury?" She felt her cheeks flame at the slip of her tongue.

His smile was crooked nor did she mistake the sad look in his eye. "Do you think of that day often as well?" he queried softly.

She shook her head. "I will be leaving," she stated, refusing to discuss the past with him.

"I know. I came to speak with you."

She began to weep. She had not meant to, but the tears began to fall. He opened her door and escorted her inside, then, to her surprise closed the door behind her. They were . . . alone.

She removed a kerchief from the pocket of her gown and once more wiped at her cheeks. "I did not mean to become a watering pot. I beg you will forgive me. Only, how shall I bear being parted from your nieces?"

Alison met his gaze and saw reflected in his eyes the dreams she had held of her future so many years ago. She recalled again that first kiss with the summer sun bathing her hair in warmth, his strong arms locked about her.

"Alison," he murmured softly, like a breeze soughing gently through the tops of trees. Before she could protest, he enfolded her in his arms once more, holding her very close. "You should have married me, Alison. We could have spent our days angling and our nights . . ."

"Do not speak it," she whispered against his ear.

"How very much I am going to miss you."

"And I, you."

He settled his lips gently on hers. She felt the tenderness of the kiss for what it was, an expression of affection, of regret, of comfort. The soft kiss became a search and then a yearning. A powerful sensation of longing and desire rushed through Alison. She flung her arms about his neck and kissed him passionately in turn, a forbidden, wicked kiss for the man holding her so tightly was betrothed!

"Alison," he whispered hoarsely.

He tried to kiss her anew but she forbade it, struggling from his arms. "Forgive me, Westbury! I should not have . . . you are to be married!"

She stared at him, feeling panic-stricken. How could she have done anything so ignoble as to have surrendered to his embrace, except that she was feeling desperate and painfully sad.

She could see that he was restraining himself with no small degree of effort. He grimaced and drew in a deep breath. Finally, he said, "Why the devil did you not marry me? No, do not speak! I do not wish to hear your arguments again. I will say only this, you were, you are mistaken, Alison Russell, in your belief that our disparity in station would have been the undoing of our love. This alone has undone our love—your stubbornness!" With that, he quit her bedchamber, the door slamming shut upon her.

She stared at the fine-grained oak for the longest moment, struck dumb by his harsh words as well as by the suffering so evident in his every feature. Was she merely being stubborn?

She did not know. Regardless, the tears flowed freely that afternoon until there were simply no more to be shed.

Two

Alison had thought, given the general air of sadness in the house, that Lady Esther would be grateful that the Longley ladies had expressed a desire to partake of their dinner that evening in the schoolroom. She could not have been more mistaken.

Her ladyship, having dismissed the governess, meant to take charge of the ladies and demanded not only their presence in the dining hall but Alison's as well. She would brook no refusal, no pretense to illness, no excuse whatsoever. The Ladies Longley were to learn by her own hand proper comportment in the house of a peer.

Alison, knowing the girls to have been overset by her ladyship's commands, took great pains to compose herself. After having assured herself in the looking-glass that her afternoon tears had not left her scarred with a swollen nose and hideously reddened eyes, she quit the safety of her bedchamber. Beginning in Mary's room, she assisted each of her charges in adjusting to Lady Esther's demands and insensitive comments. She combed tresses, chose gowns, spoke of patience and long-suffering as virtues, and then made as many jokes as possible in order to enliven the saddened brood. For her own sake, as well as theirs, she wanted them on their best behavior.

When she reached the drawing room, with the ladies

in tow, she could have laughed for all her concern at her own tear-drenched features, for Lady Esther's nose was bright pink from all her nose-blowing. Her ladyship nodded imperiously to her future nieces, squinting at each one from swollen eyes. The girls made their best curtsies, after which Lady Esther honored them by sneezing. The windows rattled anew.

"Lady Esther," Jane said in her soft, sympathetic voice, "you seem to be suffering greatly. You cannot be well. Perhaps you should retire to your bed."

Lady Esther attempted a grin, which reminded Alison that though the bride-to-be marched about Ludgers as a hostile dowager might, she was still very young. "You cannot trick me, Miss Jane," she said jovially. "I know you mean to get rid of me, if you can! But you cannot! I am here to stay! A—a—aaaaaachoo!"

Lord Westbury, who had a glass of sherry at his elbow, quickly snatched it in hand.

Lady Esther once more set to blowing her nose.

Alison glanced at her charges and was particularly alarmed by the sudden conscious expression on Bella's young features. Mary, seated beside her, elbowed her gently.

"What?" Bella murmured.

Mary glowered down at her.

"I did not say anything!" Bella whispered urgently.

"What was that, Miss Jane?" Lady Esther called out.

Bella seemed startled. "I am not Miss Jane, I am Arabella."

"Of course you are. Only tell me, what were saying to your sister? It must be of some import since you interrupted me."

"But I did not interrupt you," Bella responded innocently, "for you were not speaking at all but blowing your nose."

Lady Esther's eyes fairly bulged from her head. "I beg

your pardon! Do you now mean to contradict me? Where are your manners, Miss Arabella?"

"I beg your pardon, ma'am, that is, my lady."

"Better," Lady Esther responded with a quick nod of her head. She struggled to allay another sneeze, wrinkling her nose and grimacing. Having succeeded, she said, "Now, tell me just what you were saying to your sister?"

Bella chewed on her lower lip, her eyes darting about nervously. "I . . . I was merely saying that we were enjoying very fine weather and . . . and that a full moon is rising even though the sky is as light as a winter's day."

"Ah," Lady Esther murmured, her brows lifted in surprise. Clearly she was taken aback by this long speech. She slid her gaze to the windows. "A full moon is it?" Her voice was barely more than a whisper and an oddly sad expression took possession of her face.

Alison watched her, wondering what such a momentarily woeful expression could mean.

"I noted the moon earlier myself," Lord Westbury said, rising from his chair to cross to Lady Esther. "Come. I daresay you will be able to view it from the windows to the east." He extended his arm to her.

"Th—thank you," Lady Esther murmured, her cheeks flooding with color. She seemed rather startled by his approach as she rose to her feet and overlaid his arm with her own.

Alison was struck again with her youth and wondered if it was possible Lady Esther had not entered into the match willingly.

She watched Westbury gently coax her arm about his own and smile tenderly down at her. Alison's heart began to ache quite furiously and for the most profound moment she found herself wishing above all things that she was Lady Esther, that Westbury was holding her arm as sweetly, that he was looking at her with such love in his eyes. She gave herself a shake, lowering her gaze to her lap, where she began to smooth out the creases of her gown. This would not do, this sudden longing, and wishing, and being overtaken by sentiments she had buried so long ago! She drew in a deep, steadying breath. Only then did she realize the girls were whispering to one another.

"You should not have put three in the pitcher I tell you," Sarah said, addressing Bella. "They will stand on one another and leap out."

"What will leap out?" Alison asked.

The ladies turned to her, each pretty face smiling and innocent in expression. "Nothing to signify," Mary said lightly. "Bella was in one of the succession houses earlier today and found three, er, young doves. She had put them in, what was it, Bella, a pitcher?"

"Yes," Bella responded, her eyes wide.

Jane's brow was puckered as she addressed her older sister. "I believe you are right, Mary," she said firmly. "They will leap out even if they cannot fly."

"Whatever are we to do?" Bella asked, startled by her sisters' concerns about the doves.

"You may tend to them tomorrow," Alison said, smiling, her heart gentled by the innocent conversation. "If they are yet fledglings, I doubt they will be able to climb one another's backs either."

"I suppose you are right." Bella nodded.

At that moment, Brill arrived, announcing that dinner was served.

Save for Lady Esther's numerous eruptions and fierce nose blowings, dinner was a quiet affair. When she had succeeded in extinguishing three of the candles nearest her with the ferocity of her sneezes, Lord Westbury called to her from the end of the formal table. "My dear, are you certain I should not send for Dr. Winslow? I am beginning to be terribly concerned for your health."

She shook her head. "I am frequently in such a state when I am dist—that is, I am certain once we are wed, I shall be perfectly well. However, I begin to think these candles are having an—an—effect. Aaaaachoo!" Two more flames disappeared and her end of the table fell to darkness.

"The candles must go tomorrow," she said, nasally. "I am become persuaded there is something in the wax. Westbury, do summon the housekeeper at once."

Westbury seemed astonished. "You wish to speak with Mrs. Pitchcott? Now?"

"Yes, I believe it best."

Westbury glanced at his butler, Brill, and with a slight shrug nodded his acquiescence. A silence fell over the table punctuated by the sound of the clock on the mantel.

At last, Mrs. Pitchcott arrived, somewhat out of breath. Lady Esther had her say.

Mrs. Pitchcott listened to her in some bemusement. "But the wax is of the finest quality, I assure you, my lady."

Lady Esther lifted an indignant brow. "A good servant never questions her mistress."

Mrs. Pitchcott lowered her gaze deferentially and dropped an apologetic curtsy. "I do beg your pardon, my lady. Do you wish me to replace all the candles?"

"Yes, I have said so. You may write to my mother's housekeeper at Chanfield. She will know where you might procure a superior quality of wax. Of course, if you had attended to your duties a little more carefully, I daresay this conversation would have been wholly unnecessary." This last comment, so derisive in nature, was accompanied by a smile apparently meant to soften her strictures.

Alison did not know where to look, whether to stare

in some horror at Lady Esther, or at Mrs. Pitchcott, whose complexion had become heightened, or at Westbury. She chose the latter, but his gaze was fixed upon his bride-to-be. There was a question in his eyes to which the answer he was seeking could not be a happy one. Lady Esther may have reprimanded Mrs. Pitchcott for a breach of staff etiquette, but her own conduct was in Alison's opinion so wretched as to border on the uncivil. Where, she wondered, had Lady Esther learned that it was in any manner appropriate to address matters of the house at the dining table in view of not just the family but of a butler and three footmen as well?

After a very long moment, Mrs. Pitchcott spoke in a tight voice. "Very good, my lady. If that is all?"

Lady Esther nodded imperiously.

The long-suffering housekeeper turned on her heel and with her back stiff, strode from the room.

Lady Esther took a sip of claret and sneezed anew.

Sometime later, after the tea tray had been presented to Lady Esther in the grand salon and she had begun dispensing in her precise manner cups of tea, Alison excused herself. Throughout dinner, particularly after the young bride-to-be had treated Mrs. Pitchcott so wretchedly, the Longley girls had taken to exchanging pointed glances and smiles.

Alison was now convinced that some mischief was abroad, which no doubt had something to do with Lady Esther. She had pondered the previous conversation she had overheard about three doves climbing out of a pitcher. She had never heard of doves in the succession houses, for the estate dovecote was on the other end of the property near the home farm. There were, however, other creatures that made their way into the houses—insects of every kind, an occasional squirrel, even frogs from time to time.

Alison moved swiftly to the east wing, knowing that

a prolonged absence from the drawing room would be thought an insult by Lady Esther, even if she had already been given her notice. She lifted her amethyst silk skirts and climbed the stairs in light quick steps to the first floor. She did not hesitate to go directly to her ladyship's bedchamber.

The moment she opened the door, she heard a loud croaking—no, two . . . no, three separate vocalizations—which confirmed her darkest suspicions. Doves, indeed! She moved swiftly to the large pitcher and basin settled on a table by the window and peered within.

"Oh dear," she murmured. The poor frogs were in a desperate state, climbing over one another in an attempt to escape their porcelain prison. "Come with me," she whispered.

She turned around swiftly, but nearly dropped the pitcher in her sudden fright.

Westbury stood in the doorway, his expression somber as he regarded her. "What are you doing, Miss Russell?" he asked.

Lord Westbury had sensed something was amiss the moment his nieces sat down to dinner. There was an air of excitement, even anticipation, among their quiet, polite exchanges. When Alison had excused herself, he had not been long in also expressing a need to withdraw. He saw her reach the landing and turn in the direction of the east wing. He was in no doubt now what his niece's governess was about and took the stairs stealthfully two at a time as he followed in her wake.

The real question, however, which plagued his mind presently, was why he had deemed it necessary to pursue the matter at all. If what he suspected was true, that his darling nieces had played a prank on Lady Esther, he knew quite well that Alison was perfectly capable of managing the situation. He trusted her implicitly. Yet he had been unable to resist the impulse to hurry after her.

"What do we have here?" he queried, watching her closely.

"Nothing of the least interest to you," she responded, lifting her brow to him and turning the pitcher aside so that he could not see within. "I . . . I merely felt that your bride-to-be ought to have fresh water. I am, er, taking the pitcher to the kitchens myself to make certain the task is accomplished properly."

He could see that she was telling whiskers. "How very kind of you, only I should like to offer my assistance. We can go together, if you like." He was amused by her Banbury tale and could only smile. "Allow me." He extended his hands, but she turned the pitcher farther away from him.

"On no account!" she cried. She tried to sidle past him all the while keeping the contents of the pitcher hidden from view.

"No, I insist!" he exclaimed, tickling her at her waist as she passed by.

"Do stop, Westbury! Let me *fetch the water.* Oh, what a beast you are! I beg you will cease tickling me—at once!"

He was charmed at this moment. With all her squirming and complaining, he could still see that a smile hovered at the corners of her lips and that twice she had withheld a burst of laughter.

Since one of the frogs chose to croak loudly at that moment, he began to laugh but then stopped almost as quickly. "Someone is coming up the stairs," he whispered.

"Oh, dear," she murmured, "if Lady Esther should find me in her bedchamber . . ."

He glanced up and down the hall. There was only one thing to be done. He must hide Alison if he could from the censure of his bride-to-be. "Come!" he commanded, gesturing for her to follow him.

She was quickly on his heels, the heavy pitcher in hand. He opened the door to the bedchamber opposite and she swished in after him. He closed the door swiftly but silently, then turned immediately to listen, his ear pressed to the wood.

"Where did she go?" Lady Esther's voice could be heard down the long hall. "And where is Westbury?"

One of the frogs croaked. He turned and watched as Alison rather squeamishly shoved her hand into the pitcher in an attempt to keep the little beasts silent. Perhaps in their fright at having their prison thus invaded they would be unable to croak again. The trick seemed to suffice.

She carried the pitcher to the far wall near one of the windows and settled it on a table.

"Someone has been in my room!" Lady Esther cried. "Mrs. Pitchcott, has one of the maids been here? I do not see my water pitcher. I can only suppose that one of the under maids has been remiss, only why is the door open?"

Mrs. Pitchcott murmured something indistinguishable.

Westbury watched as the door handle moved. He extended his hand to the door, prepared to hold it firmly against any pressure his beloved might exert on it.

He heard a faint choking sound from behind him and knew that Alison's sense of the absurd was suddenly getting the better of her. She was right, of course. Was there anything more ridiculous than a gentleman of four-and-thirty years hiding from his *beloved* and all because of a frog or two?

He cast his hand at her several times in an attempt to quiet her growing mirth. The choking sounds were replaced with barely audible murmurs from her throat. He knew her so very well. He could imagine to perfection how she would at this moment be biting her lip, holding her sides, tilting her head just so, all in an attempt to keep from laughing aloud.

Dear, dear, Alison.

The door handle turned farther still.

Mrs. Pitchcott was then heard to call to her. "My lady, that bedchamber has not been used in some time. I daresay *the dust* will be heavy on the furniture."

He knew then that his housekeeper had seen one or both of them enter the room. Despite Lady Esther's criticisms of Mrs. Pitchcott's worth, he felt at this moment he would be forced to increase her wage as a reward for intervening as she just had. Her words had a happy effect on Lady Esther.

"Indeed?" the young woman cried. The door handle flipped to its resting position. Westbury finally took a breath.

"Why do you not return to your tea," Mrs. Pitchcott added, "and I shall set the staff to hunting for both Miss Russell and Lord Westbury?"

"Oh, very well," Lady Esther grumbled. "Only I think it very odd in them both and I still do not understand why the door to my bedchamber is standing open."

"I will speak with the upper maids at once."

"Just as you should. I hope you will have the room opposite dusted as well!"

"Of course, my lady."

Their voices disappeared down the hall. When all was silent beyond the door, the earl crossed the chamber to Alison. She began to giggle and could not stop.

"What a dreadful girl you are!" he cried, still whispering. "I could hear you only barely restraining your laughter. What do you think would have happened had she walked into this room and discovered us here?"

"Perhaps she would have thought we . . . were dusting?" she suggested, still holding her sides.

"Vile woman," he responded, narrowing his eyes at her.

"Do you not think it absurd that you and I have been hiding from your future bride?"

"Absurd in the extreme," he responded.

He watched her grow quite serious. "Your nieces are overset that I have been dismissed."

"I know," he murmured. "No less so than the household staff, my head groom, who is inordinately fond of you, all the stableboys, the vicar, the villagers, half the neighborhood, and even surly old Gibbons, my bailiff."

She chuckled. "How can any of them, save your staff perhaps, know of my dismissal?"

"They will, before another day has past I daresay, and then they will be saddened, to the last man."

A deep silence followed. He searched her eyes, asking the same unspoken question over and over, the answer to which had been given so many years ago but which had been a thorn in his side. "Somehow I had supposed you would be here always," he said.

"I know," she responded softly.

His gaze slid over her face, memorizing every detail. "You should be married with children of your own."

She smiled, if sadly. He wondered what her thoughts were and was enlightened a trifle when she lifted a hand to his cheek and let her fingers drift down his face. She should not be standing before him with three frogs now croaking softly behind her and with only a dusky sky and a full moon by which to see and to be seen. His gaze dropped to her lips. Everything was in shadow and weighted with the past as well as with the future.

"Darling Alison," he whispered. He watched her lips part expectantly. He caught her quite suddenly about the waist and dragged her against him. No protests this time! He would kiss her, by God he would kiss her.

He slanted his lips over hers, kissing her roughly. He demanded entrance and as if by magic her lips parted. He drove into her mouth, taking possession of the tender warmth just as he had done so many years ago, in passion, longing, and love. How he loved her. How he would always love her. This was the reason he had not argued with Esther about dismissing Alison Russell. He loved her far too much to have her underfoot while he danced attendance upon a young woman who cringed at his every touch.

A gentle wave of murmurs sounded from her throat. He had forgotten the sweetness of that particular sound, the delight he experienced when she warbled so. He slid his hand into her hair dragging her head backward that he might slide his lips down her throat. She did not protest. Her breath came in small gasps of pleasure until he heard a painful catch followed by a barely suppressed sob.

She then tore from his arms. "You are to be married in a fortnight!" she cried. A moment more and she ran from the chamber, the pitcher in hand.

Three

On the following day, Alison sat in the schoolroom, working on her most recent French project, a translation of Rousseau's *The Social Contract*. Her four students were gathered about her, each employed on a particular project of their own. One and all were trying to forget that but four days remained before Alison would be leaving Ludgerwick Hall.

Repressing a sigh, Alison settled her pen on a tray and glanced about the long, rectangular chamber where she had spent the past year of her life. The schoolroom had been an eccentric creation of a doting countess a century past who had desired for her children not just a view of the northerly front drive, but of the westerly home wood and the southerly rose garden as well.

The chamber was quite large, which allowed for a diversity of occupations throughout the seasons. In the summer, great portions of the room were devoted to the collecting of every manner of herb, weed, leaf, and seed that were presently displayed and identified in nearly every unused space of the room. In the winter, the floors were heavily polished and the young ladies skated over the glossy wood in heavy stockings they had learned to knit. An entire wall held dozens of efforts with watercolors. A succession of windows formed the opposite wall which overlooked a beautiful, hilly skyline topped with oak, ash, and elm and through which Alison had taken the Longley girls on numerous walks.

Much of the activity of guests at Ludgers, therefore, could be seen from the schoolroom, whether just arriving, or taking a walk in the direction of the woods, or traipsing through the flower gardens that banked the back of the house.

The rumbling of carriage wheels on the drive caused Bella to leap from her seat and race to the windows that overlooked the front avenue.

"Miss Russell!" she cried. "A very fine carriage is coming up the drive drawn by *six* horses. A second coach and a wagon follows!"

"Undoubtedly, Her Grace, the Duchess of Adstock, is arrived," Alison said. She glanced at Bella, who was craning her neck in the direction of the front door of the expansive Elizabethan mansion.

"A lady with very red hair has just emerged," she reported.

"Very red hair?" Alison queried. She could only smile as she closed her book. "That would be the duchess, I believe."

The Duchess of Adstock, mother to Lady Esther, had been an acknowledged beauty in her day. Even with the advance of years, her hair had remained a startling hue nearly the shade of carrots.

The three remaining Longley ladies took up positions at the two windows as well. Sarah stood beside Bella while Jane and Mary sat side by side on an adjacent window seat.

Sarah, who was bent at the waist, also craned her neck. "She is not traveling alone. There are two young gentlemen with her. One is very handsome and the other has a decided brooding look, as though his stomach ails him."

"He is very handsome, though," Jane added. "Oh."

"What is it?" Alison queried, crossing to the windows in their wake.

"I do not think very much of his manners. He just scowled at one of the footmen."

"He must have had a reason."

"The young gentleman bumped his head and I believe he felt it to be the footman's fault."

"And what do we think of such young men?"

"Brutish," Mary responded.

Jane murmured, "A veritable crosspatch. I wonder why he is so out of temper?"

Alison thought it might have been because he had been traveling with Lady Adstock, but refrained from venturing an opinion which would hardly serve to endear the girls to their future aunt's mother.

"I think him uncivil," Sarah stated emphatically.

Bella sighed. "Such men, however, are frequently found between the covers of novels."

Alison turned to stare at her as did her sisters. "And when have you been reading novels?"

"I was referring to *Pride and Prejudice,* of course, which you read to us last month. Mr. Darcy was rude in just that fashion."

"I do not think he was rude."

"Elizabeth Bennet would surely disagree with you."

Alison laughed. "I suppose she would."

Once the party disappeared within the house, the ladies left their post by the window and returned to the round table situated in the center of the chamber. "Do you think Lady Adstock will be as obnoxious as her daughter?" Mary asked.

"You must not speak so of the new mistress of Ludgers," Alison reproved firmly, taking up her seat before Rousseau's text. "And I think it time we discuss the matter of . . . *the frogs.* No, no. Do not turn away, do not grimace, do not shake your heads. No guest, and particularly not the future Lady Westbury, deserves to be treated so shabbily as having frogs put in her water pitcher!"

The girls sat down, one after the other. Her tempering words, however, had an opposite effect.

"You are right," Jane cried. "She deserves far worse! She ought to be boiled in oil after having pinched at Mrs. Pitchcott as she did last night and that in front of you and Uncle. It was most improper. I hate her!"

"Jane," Alison reproved, stunned by her outburst. "This is not like you to speak so harshly and I hope you will hate no one."

Bella, seated next to her, crossed her arms over her chest and scowled heavily. "I will not hate her, if that is what you wish, but I cannot like her. She smells very peculiar."

Alison gasped. Bella's older siblings burst out into peals of laughter. "It is the pastilles you smell. She does not sleep well so she burns them at night."

"It is a horrid odor," Bella complained further.

Alison felt weary of a sudden. Perhaps had she been given longer than a scant five days—now only four—she might have had sufficient time to reconcile the Longley girls to the future mistress of Ludgers. As it was, their growing dislike of Lady Come-the-Crab, as Sarah was wont to refer to her, had become complicated by her own dismissal.

"Regardless of your present opinions of Lady Esther I ask that you not repeat last night's prank."

Mary eyed her in mock innocence. "You may be assured we will not put frogs in her water pitcher again, if that is what you fear."

Alison rose from her chair and rounded the table to slip her arm about Mary's shoulders, embracing her warmly. "You know very well that was not what I

meant," she chided gently. "You are all far too creative
to actually *repeat* the same absurd antic."

When the young ladies merely exchanged knowing but
stubborn glances, she released Mary's shoulder and settled her hands on the table, glaring at each of them in
turn. "I beg you will desist, if not for my sake, then for
your uncle's. How do you think he will feel knowing
that his bride-to-be has become the target of your childish capers?"

Every expression fell.

"Why does he have to wed her at all?" Mary asked.
"Why not you?"

Four pairs of eyes turned to her expectantly.

For reasons she could not explain she wanted the girls
to know the truth. "We were betrothed once," she confessed as she began a slow circuit about the table. She
could not have shocked them more and was not surprised
when they demanded to be told as many details as they
could provoke from her.

"Why did you not marry?" Jane asked, her blue eyes
wide.

Sarah blinked several times quite rapidly. "Did you
fall out of love with our uncle?"

"Why did you never tell us before?" Mary gasped.

"Did you reject him like Elizabeth Bennet because
you thought him proud and disagreeable?" Bella inquired.

Alison smiled anew. There was something so charming in the countenances that watched her so expectantly.
From the first time she had met the Ladies Longley she
had loved them. They were beautiful, each bearing so
similar a shade of blond ringlets that from certain van-
tages they were entirely indistinguishable. Each was
blessed with sparkling blue eyes, and more than once,
particularly when she had first taken up her post as governess to the girls, she had been told by those not know-

ing her true relationship to them that she had a fine brood of daughters.

She could not look at them now without a measure of pride and affection tearing at her aching heart. She glanced at Arabella, suspecting that in her thirteen-year-old world she was becoming utterly bedazzled by the notion of romance as young girls were wont to do. Dear Mary, as the eldest and nearly seventeen was tottering between two worlds as she joined less and less in the girlish occupations of her sisters.

Jane—sweetest Jane!—would hold her sisters together no matter what happened, while Sarah, so full of spirit, would charge into the world eagerly and joyously. She loved them all.

As Alison roved each expectant face, she wondered just how much she should say about her former relationship with Westbury. They were of an age, however, which caused her to open her budget a little. "I did not marry your uncle because he told me a whisker about who he was. When he came into Berkshire where I lived, nearly eight years past, he told everyone he was a mere Mr. Twyford, the son of a squire from Lincolnshire, and since I was the daughter of a soldier, I felt safe in giving my heart to him. Had I known he was—goodness!—the future Earl of Westbury, I should never have exchanged two words with him because—"

All four young ladies finished her thought, *"You do not believe in unequal alliances."*

Alison was a little startled to find she had so completely made her opinion known to the girls. She felt uncomfortable by it, as though she had erred in some manner that she did not quite understand. Westbury's words of last night came back to her suddenly, *This alone has undone our love—your stubbornness!*

"Never mind that!" Sarah cried, clearly intrigued. "Why did Uncle James pretend to be a squire's son?"

"Why, indeed!" Bella exclaimed, her eyes shining. "I think it terribly romantic. Did he already know you would not have approved?"

Alison shook her head. "I do not know. I think his purpose that day was very different. I believe he had grown fatigued of being heir to an earldom. He wanted to be ordinary for a time and to meet ordinary members of the gentry, my father for one, and many of the families of our neighborhood. We all adored him and by the end of the summer, he and I were betrothed. Only then did he tell me the truth, but as you have just expressed, I am adamantly opposed to marrying above one's station. Such alliances can only bring the greatest unhappiness. Your uncle's world is one of London, politics, the future of England, while a soldier's daughter's largest concern is whether another war will separate her from her father. Do you see?"

The girls were thoughtful but it was the eldest, Mary, who tried to solve the puzzling dilemma. "But you loved him. How could you forsake someone you truly loved?"

Alison chuckled, if ruefully. "By crying myself to sleep every night for a twelve-month."

"Oh," Jane murmured. "How tragic! And now Uncle means to marry the witch from hell!"

Alison was properly shocked, particularly since such horrific words fell from gentle Jane's lips. Her sisters, however, fell into renewed peals of laughter.

That evening, Alison brought the schoolroom misses to the withdrawing room to meet Lady Esther's guests.

Her mother, the Duchess of Adstock, was what she expected—cold and imperious, delivering a dozen dictums and commands at once. "Do close the window, Alfred," she called to her son and heir, Lord Thornton. "I feel a draft on my neck. Esther, sit up straight. You young ladies may be seated. Mr. Ackeley, I beg you will smile a little more. You put me forcibly in mind of Byron at the moment and I never could abide the man! Westbury, you have a charming home."

"Thank you, Your Grace. I have always—" He was not allowed to finish his sentence, the duchess preferring to trample his words quite thoroughly.

"Although, I believe you have too much silk in this chamber, but my daughter will mend that soon enough. In my day, the heavier brocades were the fashion and they endure so much better than these thin, shabby textiles. Better a sturdy damask than a silk."

"What about a silk damask?" Alison queried facetiously.

She heard Mr. Ackeley choke on his sherry.

"Ah, now a damask silk will do in a pinch," Lady Adstock remarked knowledgeably. "You shan't hear me complain of silk damask. Prinny is most fond of the fabric."

Alison was fascinated as much by the duchess's belief that she had a right to issue commands in another man's home as by the manner in which Lady Esther began to shrink into the sofa with each word her mother spoke. The only advantage the presence of her parent afforded the young woman was that to all appearances she had finally stopped sneezing. The windows had since stopped rattling and the tip of Lady Esther's nose was no longer quite the shade of a strawberry. Only, what precisely had brought about the transformation?

A half hour later, the young Misses Longley were dismissed. "You may go now," the duchess commanded.

The ladies rose with alacrity, which Alison comprehended perfectly. She was herself grateful to be allowed to escape Lady Adstock's overbearing presence in the drawing room.

As she escorted her charges from the chamber she

overheard Her Grace address her daughter in an audible whisper. "Have you dismissed her yet, Esther?"

"Yes, Mama."

"You must be very strict with your servants and discharge the prettiest of the staff. Only trouble will ensue when a beauty is allowed to remain beneath your roof."

"Yes, Mama."

"And you must be firm. Firm, I say, 'else your servants will believe they can rule the roost."

"Yes, Mama."

Alison only wished that the duchess had been discreet enough to save her remarks until the girls' hearing was out of range. She could see by their expressions they were disgruntled by Lady Adstock's remarks. However, unlike Her Grace, the Longley ladies reserved their disparaging comments until they were safely within the schoolroom once more. Two of the windows were open, allowing a refreshing breeze to cool the chamber, which tended to grow overly warm during the summer months since it was unprotected from the western sunlight.

The chamber, with the fine muslin drapes dancing in the light wind, was quite inviting, even more so when Mrs. Pitchcott entered bearing a tray of fresh-baked macaroons, glasses of milk, and a warm, affectionate smile on her lips.

All the young ladies gathered round her, thanking her prodigiously and guiding her to the round table, where she settled the tray.

"You are kindness itself," Alison cried.

Mrs. Pitchcott smiled and nodded. "Thank you, Miss Russell. I was sorry to hear that you will be leaving us, and that so very soon, but there are some what think you may have the advantage of us all. However, more on that subject I shall not say." Her sentiments concerning the future mistress of Ludgers were subsequently expressed in a loud sniff.

When the girls were happily employed savoring the macaroons, Mrs. Pitchcott drew Alison into the hall for a word in private.

"I debated mentioning this to you, Miss Russell, and it goes against my inclination of the moment to intervene, but I thought I should warn you that earlier, when you were taking your daily walk by the brook, the Misses Longley were in the rose garden."

Alison chuckled. "I believe I can understand why."

"I fear they were not just there to enjoy a little relief from *certain personages*. They were instead cutting flowers—a great many of them. *A very great many.*"

Alison blinked at Mrs. Pitchcott. Understanding dawned on her in one fell swoop. "Oh dear." The nature of the Longley girls' latest attempt to unseat Lady Esther became perfectly clear.

"I will attend you, if you like, in remedying the situation."

"On no account, for I have little doubt that if it was learned you were anywhere near Lady Esther's bedchamber, the blame would fall solely at your feet."

When Mrs. Pitchcott breathed an obvious sigh of relief, Alison knew the good housekeeper shared a similar opinion.

Alison thanked her for revealing the nature of the girls' latest prank. She did not hesitate, but set her feet quickly in the direction of the east wing of the house, where Lady Esther's chambers were situated. When she arrived, she found Lord Westbury just leaving his betrothed's room, carrying not one but two vases of roses.

He was not amused.

Indeed, he seemed to be in the boughs, glaring at her as he approached her. She planted herself against the wall, allowing him to pass by without the smallest hindrance. He carried the vases down the hall to the landing and set to shouting.

"Brill! Ah, there you are! See to it that at least three footmen are brought to Lady Esther's chamber. At once!"

Why ever would he need three, Alison wondered.

A sense of dread flooded her as she eased to the threshhold of the chamber. She winced as she gazed upon the extravagant display of flowers now present in Lady Esther's bedchamber. She rather thought that had the Longley girls not been intent on frustrating her ladyship, the results of their foraging in the rose garden would have been a lovely gesture, indeed.

Westbury was behind her. "My bride-to-be nearly went off in a fit of apoplexy! I escorted her but five minutes ago only to find this!" He waved his arm over the chamber.

Alison found herself curious about one point. "I suppose she began sneezing almost immediately."

"As it happens, she did not!" he cried irritably. "But what the deuce does that have to do with anything?"

Alison thought it curious in the extreme. Yesterday, when Lady Esther had been in the process of dismissing her, one of the maids had arrived with a vase of roses and before Bonnie had taken three steps into the room, Lady Esther had begun sneezing. For her to have refrained upon arriving at the portal of this veritable garden of flowers seemed quite odd.

"Nothing to signify," she responded quietly. Her gaze drifted over the numerous vases. "Well, regardless, I think it lovely beyond words." There remained within the chamber no fewer than eight large vases of roses, the blossoms in a multitude of colors and placed rather artistically, probably with Jane's eye, around the room. Even the counterpane, which was a cornflower blue in color, was covered with deep red and white rose petals. The effect was astonishing, even charming, and the fragrance quite exquisite.

A sudden fear bubbled within her. Lady Esther had not hesitated to dismiss the girls' governess for no reason at all, but if she believed that the Longley ladies were purposely trying to aggravate her, what would she do? There was only one answer—the girls would be shipped off to school, to the Seminary for the Insane, as Sarah had called it.

"I only wish Lady Esther was able to appreciate how beautiful it all is. I . . . I meant no harm, truly I did not."

"What do you mean, *you* meant no harm?"

"Well, that I made this entire arrangement for your bride-to-be," she said, turning to gaze wide-eyed and innocent upon his outraged face.

"The devil you did!" he cried, frowning more heavily still.

"Of course I did! Who else would have done so?"

He narrowed his eyes at her. "Yet you knew my betrothed despised these flowers. How then do you explain your conduct?"

Alison lifted her chin. "I thought, given the proper amount of exposure, she might grow to love the simple, elegant rose."

"I think you did this in order to punish her for having dismissed you."

She did not at all like the baiting, suspicious light in his eye.

"I suppose if you are to press me, then yes, you have the right of it. And also for speaking to Mrs. Pitchcott as though she was not the superior creature we all know her to be, and for continually speaking of Chanfield as the model for all homes and . . . and for ignoring your nieces."

Westbury clasped his hands behind his back, the furrows lining his face relaxing. "I have since addressed these matters with her," he countered softly. "She means to do better. She has confessed to a belief that she must be like her mother. I recommended she follow her own conscience in future."

She stared up at him surprised. "You spoke with her? And she truly intends to improve her conduct?"

"Why do you seem so amazed? No, do not answer that. I only wish you had seen her in London. There was a sparkle to her eye and a lightness of movement and speech that truly delighted me. I never thought . . . well, I never expected her to dismiss you, for one thing."

Alison felt there were a hundred things she wished to say of the moment, yet could not bring even one to her lips. She was passing through the difficult circumstance of being part of the household yet certain to leave in but a few days.

The three requested footmen arrived in that moment and he commanded that every vase, flower, and petal be removed from the chamber.

"Where do we take them?" the eldest of the three asked.

Westbury seemed bemused. "I do not know."

"Might I make a suggestion?" Alison queried.

"Yes, of course."

"Since Lady Esther suffers so in whatever chamber they might be placed, perhaps some of the maidservants would enjoy them."

"I believe they would," Westbury responded. He waved a hand in the direction of the flowers. "Pray take them to Mrs. Pitchcott and have them distributed to the servants at her will."

"Very good, m'lord."

Westbury led her from the chamber so that the footmen might perform their duties. "Where are the girls?"

"In the schoolroom enjoying some macaroons."

"I have missed them," he confessed. "Would you come with me while I bid them good night?"

She smiled faintly. "I should like that."

A few minutes later, the young ladies, in what no doubt neither Lady Esther nor Lady Adstock would have thought was an appropriate manner, cast themselves upon his person. He embraced each of them in turn and when they pushed the tables and chairs back, he swung them in wide circles, as he had been doing since they were toddlers. Only Mary declined the treat, which was perhaps appropriate since she was nearly come-out.

Alison moved to stand beside her and watched as Westbury twirled the three younger ladies around in circles until they were dizzy and giggling with glee.

"Do you think she will send us away?" Mary asked in a small voice.

"I cannot say, my darling. Whatever your concerns, though, I beg you will tell your uncle about them. He loves you as a father. He wants only your happiness, you know that."

Mary nodded, but tears brimmed in her eyes. "He will be thinking of her now, and not us. Perhaps it would be best if we did go away. Is there a chance we might accompany you wherever it is you mean to go?"

At that, Alison smiled. "I only wish you could and were I circumstanced differently, you would, one and all, be extended just such an invitation. However, I intend to visit my sister in Bath for but a fortnight or so, just long enough to secure a new position."

Mary embraced her quite suddenly, holding her fast. A moment later, she raced from the schoolroom. Alison was left to watch Westbury for a time as he read to Jane, Sarah, and Bella. She once more took up her French translation, but some of the joy of the task had been lost in the harsh truth that she must be thinking of just how to transport her furniture and other belongings to her sister's house in Bath in but three days.

Four

The next day, Alison entered the morning room for breakfast, where family and guests were partaking of a generous meal served from an ample sideboard. She prepared her plate, aware that the table was rather quiet this morning, then seated herself between Sarah and Arabella. Lady Esther sat rigidly opposite the girls, Lord Thornton and his friend Mr. Sylvester Ackeley flanking her on either side. Westbury sat at the head of the table and the Duchess of Adstock imperiously at the foot. Alison felt as though she had intruded on a conversation that had ceased the very moment of her appearance, yet there had not been the smallest sound of chatter upon her approach to the high-ceilinged chamber.

At first glance, Alison thought perhaps Lady Esther was punishing everyone present for the rose prank of the night before, but after a moment she came to believe that some other unnamed, perhaps even hidden, force was present.

Westbury caught her eye and grimaced slightly. She knew that particular expression and immediately took up his hint.

"Mr. Ackeley," she said with a smile, addressing the dark gentleman, "I understand you to have traveled a great deal."

"You are correct," he responded, turning his attention toward her, his gaze having been fixed previously on a brown ringlet draped over Lady Esther's shoulder. "I have recently returned from the East Indies. This past spring, as it happens."

"Were you gone very long?"

"Five years."

"That is an extraordinary amount of time. I have always longed to travel to distant lands and explore the novelty of cultures so disparate from our own."

"I did not explore so much as I would have liked. I was much occupied with business." He glanced at Lady Esther, who was consuming her eggs in a meticulous fashion, her eyes downcast. "Alfred joined me for a time."

"Did you?" Alison queried, glancing at Lord Thornton. "In which country?"

"India," the gentlemen chimed together.

"Calcutta," Mr. Ackeley added. "It is a fearsome city and India is an extraordinary land. A great many poor and the climate—not to be believed."

"So I have heard time and again. Did you find England very much changed when you returned?"

He shot a brief almost accusing glance at Lady Esther. "A few things, incredibly so, but generally everything was as I remembered."

Alison glanced at Lady Esther and found that a faint blush was climbing her cheeks. How curious.

"Were you in London for the Season, then?" she asked.

"Yes."

"Oh, my yes!" Lady Adstock cried, intruding abruptly into the conversation. "He was so very sun-bronzed upon his arrival that you would not have credited the stir he made. He fairly set every feminine heart to beating wildly. I daresay there were no less than two score of young ladies who set their caps at him."

Alison, quite taken aback by this speech, glanced at Mr. Ackeley, who was fairly seething with indignation.

"It is a wonderful thing to be greatly admired," she interjected quietly.

Mr. Ackeley lifted his gaze to her. "When one cares for only the attention of a certain lady, the rest is but the worst sort of nuisance."

Alison could not mistake his meaning, particularly given the flame now burning on Lady Esther's cheeks. Even the four Longley ladies gasped at his pointed comment. Westbury had paused in taking a sip of coffee but otherwise appeared unmoved. She could not help but turn her attention to Lady Adstock to see what effect his words might have had upon her, but that grand lady seemed entirely disinterested save in just how fine a strip she might cut from her kipper.

Lord Thornton took that moment to laugh heartily, which in turn set the Ladies Longley to giggling.

Lady Esther, however, would have none of that and finally lifted her gaze, but strictly for the purpose of glaring at the girls. Alison thought this completely unfair. She in turn fixed her gaze upon Westbury, hoping this time he would take up her hint and redirect the conversation himself. He was however frowning at his bride-to-be, who apparently would not meet his gaze but instead reverted to staring at her scrambled eggs.

Oh dear, she thought distractedly. She ought to say something, to once more take charge of the conversation, but she found she simply could not think, nor frame in her mind even the smallest scrap of harmless information to present to the table at large for discussion.

Mary, however, took up the slack and inquired of Lord Thornton how he had enjoyed his sojourn in Calcutta. Lord Thornton, having finally laughed himself out, relieved everyone of the present tension at the table and spoke at length of his adventures, in particular an intriguing hunt for a tiger which he considered the pinnacle of his adventure in the hot, exotic land.

Later that day, Alison, who was leaning over Jane and directing her in the use of watercolors, turned toward the westerly windows. "Who is doing all that shouting?" she inquired.

Bella ran to the nearest window. "It is Mr. Ackeley," she cried. "He is arguing with Lady Esther."

Alison stood upright, greatly stunned, and moved to the windows, as did the rest of the young ladies. It was one thing to have hinted so broadly at his feelings for Lady Esther at the breakfast table but quite another to be arguing with her in plain view of anyone in the western wing of the mansion.

She found Bella to have been quite accurate as her gaze landed on the pair in question. Lady Esther began hurrying away from the house in the direction of the home wood and Mr. Ackeley did not hesitate to follow after her. A repeated flinging of Lady Esther's hand seemed to indicate she wished he would leave her in peace. Instead, he remained close behind her, the sound of his voice just reaching the schoolroom windows, if not the actual words themselves.

"What do you suppose it means?" Mary asked.

"I do not know," Alison returned, shaking her head.

"I think they must be in love!" Bella cried.

"How can she marry our uncle if she loves another?" Jane queried.

A scratching at the door brought Westbury into the chamber. The girls each in turn whirled around to greet him, although more brightly than usual. For herself, Alison thought it the oddest circumstance that he had arrived but a few seconds after his bride-to-be and Mr. Ackeley had disappeared into the woods.

"What is it?" he asked, glancing from one visage to the next.

"N—nothing!" Sarah cried.

"We just did not expect to see you so early in the day, Uncle," Mary remarked.

"Indeed," Bella added, swallowing visibly.

"Should I go?" he inquired. "For it seems I have disturbed you."

Jane moved forward instantly and linked arms with him. "On no account. You must stay. We have a great deal to show you for even though Miss Russell is leaving so very soon, she will not permit us, even for a moment, to forsake our studies."

Alison received Westbury's warm smile, her heart dancing at the appreciative gleam in his eye.

"She has done precisely what I would have wished her to do," he said.

Alison smiled in return. Moving away from the windows, she suggested he take up a chair. He agreed readily and for the next hour sat happily with his nieces, asking to see the progress of each of their employments, Mary with her needlework, Jane's watercolors, Sarah's struggles with the Italian language, and Bella's latest Mozart sonata, part of which she performed on the pianoforte kept in the schoolroom for the purpose of practice and an occasional performance for their uncle.

Alison watched him with infinite pleasure, particularly given the knowledge that in so short a time she would be departing Ludgers forever. She smiled and laughed at each ridiculous antic the girls would use to attract his attention. At the same time, a terrible sadness descended on her.

She had thoughts. *Desperate thoughts.* Perhaps she should inform him that Lady Esther was having a tryst in the woods with Mr. Ackeley. Perhaps she should throw herself at his feet and beg him to marry her in Lady Esther's stead. Perhaps she should . . .

"Miss Russell?" a quiet voice intruded.

Alison turned to find that Mary was at her elbow. "Yes?"

"I addressed you three times," she whispered. "Is anything amiss?"

"No," she responded, chuckling. "I was lost in reverie but I am now returned. What is it?"

Mary glanced at her younger sisters, who were even now gathered round Westbury, listening enrapt to a continued reading of *Robinson Crusoe*. She drew her aside. "I should not be telling you this and were my sisters to discover my disloyalty they would surely have my head, but there is a plan afoot, at midnight, to travel the length of the secret passageway that leads directly behind Lady Esther's bedchamber."

"Oh dear," she murmured, walking with her to the opposite end of the chamber which overlooked the rose garden. "Tonight? But to what purpose?"

Mary smiled. "To make ghostly sounds and frighten her ladyship away from dear old Ludgers."

"Why are you telling me, Mary?"

"I do not know, precisely. I think because however much I dislike my new aunt-to-be, she does not deserve to be frightened out of her wits. I know if I thought a ghost was in my bedchamber, I should jump from my skin!"

"As would I," Alison responded. "Thank you for telling me, Mary. I shall speak with the girls as soon as your uncle leaves the room."

"No!" she cried, laying a hand on her sleeve. "It would not serve in the least, for they would refuse to abide by your strictures and attempt the fright anyway."

"That determined, eh?"

Mary was silent apace, but a very sad expression overcame her lovely features. "You cannot know how despondent we all are. It is not just you we are losing, but Uncle James as well. Lady Esther is a demanding sort of woman and she will not like the attention he showers upon us. Surely you know that to be true."

What a muddle!

"I have every confidence that in time she will discover for herself how wonderful you are, each of you."

"How can she discover anything when she does only what her mama wishes her to do?"

Alison was stunned. "I begin to think you are far too perceptive for your age."

She drew in a deep breath, a frown pinching her brow. "I will tell you what I truly think. I am convinced that Lady Esther no more loves my uncle than she loves any of us."

"Is this truly your opinion? How . . . why have you come to believe as you have?"

"Because I know what love is." Here she smiled. "For I have seen the way you look at my uncle every day and not less so than by how his expression softens the moment you but enter a room."

"Oh, Mary, you mustn't believe, that he, that I, any longer—"

"I know what I see," she reiterated, appearing far wiser than her sixteen years. "And never once have I seen any such gentle, warm, or passionate expression on Lady Esther's face."

Alison felt a blush climb her cheeks. "I have been indiscreet," she murmured.

"You still love him," she stated quietly. "I believe you always shall and pray do not insult me by telling me a pack of whiskers I shan't ever believe." With that, she walked away and joined her sisters.

* * *

At teatime, Alison stood outside the grand salon, her heart twisted into a knot. Lady Adstock's voice had reached her the moment she drew near the doors, but the subject had forced her to remain without. An argument was underway.

"You must send them all away to school!"

"But, Mama, I have already dismissed their governess, how can I—"

"Esther, you were always far too tenderhearted a creature to be of the smallest use! I had hoped by now you would be exhibiting more sense, more understanding of the nature of the world in general. I have seen Westbury with his nieces. Unless you act speedily, you will find them underfoot the rest of your life. That may seem of little significance now, but wait until you have children of your own. Trust me, you will want these orphans gone in an instant!"

Alison felt despondent beyond words. Mary was right. Lady Esther had no choice but to bend her will to her mother's. Lady Adstock was one of those powerful creatures who could only be overborn by drastic measures. She wondered if she should warn Westbury about his wife's predicament, but her common sense prevailed. After all, if Westbury did not comprehend the lady he was marrying, then all her protests and warnings would avail nothing. He must discover for himself the truth about his bride-to-be.

"Eavesdropping?"

Alison flinched and turned to find Mr. Ackeley smiling somewhat benevolently upon her. "I did not know what to do," she confessed quietly. "Lady Adstock's voice will carry."

"To the ends of the earth," he returned ruefully. He offered his arm. "Come. I shall take you in. And do not worry. If she sees we are linked she will be less likely to fire upon one or the other of us. Our unity will be our strength."

Alison could only laugh for even though he was being ridiculous he was also likely to be correct.

"Now," he murmured conspiratorially, "do trill your laughter as a measure of warning to *Her Highness* that we are on the approach."

She could only chuckle. "I fear that I cannot *trill* on command."

"Then we will just have to be brave."

With that, she allowed him to escort her into the grand salon, where it soon appeared to Alison that Lady Adstock was setting up court by arranging her skirts just so in a winged chair by the fireplace and directing her daughter as to the precise position of the footstool.

"There, child! What are you about! More to the left! No, no! The left! The left! How do you do, Miss Russell? I did not expect to see you this afternoon, at least not alone. Esther, you are the clumsiest child! Where are the Misses Longley?"

"I imagine they must still be in the schoolroom with Lord Westbury. I thought they would be here by now. Undoubtedly they will be down shortly."

"What did I tell you, Esther! You must be firm!"

"Yes, Mama."

Lord Thornton appeared at an open window at the end of the chamber, beyond which was an expansive garden. "Ackeley!" he called out. "Come have a ride with me. The day is yet very fine and there is a cooling breeze."

Alison watched as a quick glance was exchanged between Lady Esther and Mr. Ackelely. There could be no doubt now that some prior and quite significant relationship existed between the two.

"Will that suffice, Mama?" she asked, reverting her attention to the footstool.

"Yes, I suppose it will have to do. You have fiddled enough and you are crushing the skirts of your gown. Ackeley! Do help my daughter to rise!"

"It is not necessary," Lady Esther murmured. She began to squirm and gather her skirts from under her knees and feet but Mr. Ackeley hurried to her side.

"I should be happy to assist my good friend's sister." He gently took her arm.

"Ackeley!" Thornton cried. "There's a good fellow. Come have a ride."

"Tomorrow, perhaps," Ackeley returned.

Alison, who took up a chair as far from Lady Adstock as would not seem rude, watched the intriguing pair carefully. Mr. Ackeley was solicitous in the extreme, holding her arm gently, his fingers lingering as he lifted her to her feet. She glanced at the duchess, wondering again if she was in the least aware of her daughter's obvious connection with Mr. Ackeley.

Lady Adstock, however, had apparently found a loose thread on the sleeve of her gown and was nibbling it off. Alison could only laugh, for she thought the duchess was the strangest combination of the vulgar and the sophisticated. She wondered just who the lady was.

At that moment, the distant sounds of the Longley ladies' laughing and joking with Lord Westbury drifted down from the landing above.

"Do you hear that?" Lady Adstock whispered angrily. "Be firm, Esther. Ackeley, my daughter is perfectly situated now. You may go. Have your ride with Alfred." She waved at him dismissively.

"I prefer to remain here," he stated strongly. After seeing Lady Esther settled on the sofa, he took up a seat beside her.

Lady Adstock was first startled, then astounded. "You should ride," she commanded. "I tell you, go with Alfred—at once!"

"Never mind, Mama," her son called from the window. "Ackeley was never a great rider. Besides, the wind is picking up and I see that a dark bank of clouds is moving in from the west. I daresay it shall rain before night descends."

"No, Alfred, you wish to ride and Ackeley should accompany you. It is all settled. Besides, a little summer shower will harm neither of you."

"But I prefer to remain here and converse with you, Your Grace. How do you find Ludgerwick Hall? I think it a lovely country house. Not so grand as Chanfield but then what house is?"

His expression was so sardonic, and his attitude so indifferent to her ladyship's belief in her own importance, that Alison found herself astonished and not a little amused that Lady Adstock took him seriously. She began to boast anew of her husband's magnificent home. Lord Thornton, resigned to Ackeley's indifference to riding out, entered the room by climbing through the long window. He had no interest in his mother's pontifications and took up a place by a chessboard, studying the present positions of the pieces.

"Ludgers is well enough in its way," the duchess pronounced, "but not really a great house in the tradition of so many of our fine, ancient homes. Chanfield, as I am certain you have observed, is equal in stature to Chatsworth."

Lord Westbury entered the chamber with Bella on one arm and Sarah on the other. Mary and Jane followed behind. "I would have to agree," he said, congenially.

Alison glanced at Esther, who seemed intensely relieved by his affability. At the same time, she rubbed her temple and attempted a faltering smile.

"Are you well, Lady Esther?" Alison asked sympathetically. "You seem rather pale."

Her mother answered for her. "My daughter is never ill. She is blessed with my excellent constitution."

"Strong as an ox, eh?" Mr. Ackeley queried.

Lady Adstock grew flustered. "I . . . I . . . I suppose so though I must say, Mr. Ackeley, I do not like the comparison a great deal."

"Forgive me," he stated coldly.

Lord Westbury intervened. "Mary, will you honor us with your most recent piece on the pianoforte?"

"I should be happy to, Uncle."

Mr. Ackeley turned to Alison, caught her gaze, and winked at her.

Alison turned away, lest Lady Adstock see her smile. She was beginning to think Mr. Ackeley a genius.

For the next half hour, as tea was brought before Lady Esther and complained over by Lady Adstock, the Longley ladies each performed their favorite pieces on the Broadwood grand.

While Jane was playing Beethoven, Westbury's voice drew the attention of everyone present as he addressed his bride-to-be. "I cannot allow it," he stated heatedly. "I can respect your desire to hire a new governess but my daughters, that is, my *nieces,* will remain here at Ludgers!"

Alison glanced at him, startled that he had raised his voice to Lady Esther, particularly in the presence of her mother. Even Jane ceased playing. "Is something amiss, Uncle?" she inquired gently.

Westbury rose to his feet. "No, of course not, Jane, pray continue. I . . . I have just remembered something I must discuss with the bailiff immediately."

Lady Adstock nodded to her daughter, encouraging her to follow after him. When Lady Esther rose to her feet and trailed in Westbury's wake, her mama cried out, "For God's sake do not be hen-hearted! Remember, you will be mistress of this house. Be firm!"

Alison thought if she heard that particular command one more time she would go mad. Glancing at Mr. Ackeley, she watched him cross his arms over his chest and smile hugely at Lady Esther's retreating back.

Five

Alison readied herself for bed, braiding her long blond locks and slipping into a nightdress. She glanced at the clock on the mantel. She had little more than an hour before she would need to intercept the young ladies in their mischief.

Betwixt times she climbed between the sheets and began to read. The candle burned steadily; she scooted down in her bed. The candle burned a little more; she scooted down farther, rereading one or two paragraphs of *Emma,* which for some reason had not made the least bit of sense to her sleep-laden eyes. She scooted a little more and turned on her side. Mr. Knightley was very much like Westbury, an excellent gentleman, strong and handsome, and tomorrow . . .

She awoke with a start, sitting up abruptly.

"Lady Esther's chains!" she cried to the walls of her bedchamber, then laughed. She had been so deeply asleep that her dreams had become entangled with visions of Lord Westbury walking down the aisle of a church with Lady Esther beside him but bound in chains.

She glanced at the clock and found to her dismay that the hour was well past midnight. She would not be surprised if the entire east wing was in an uproar by now and once found out, the young ladies would be shipped off to the Seminary for the Insane!

She leaped from her bed, grabbed her plaid wool shawl from the nearby chair, took hold of the candlestick, and began as quick a progress as she could without the flame blowing out across the exceedingly long Elizabethan mansion.

At the grand staircase, she climbed speedily to the second floor. There were numerous secret passageways connecting both the ground and the first floors as well as the first and second floors.

The original owner of the mansion, some centuries past, had been born in the era of political turmoil in which Charles I had been executed. His house had been designed with hiding places and a series of no less than twenty secret passageways linking both room to room and floor to floor. Mary, upon first arriving at Ludgers, had heard her uncle speak of the veritable rabbit warren of routes in and out of a variety of chambers and had led her sisters on a hunt for them all. Alison had been told of their adventures in some detail and had permitted the girls to guide her once through one particular maze of entrances and exits. She hoped she could remember enough to make her way to the secret passage that ran adjacent to Lady Esther's room and with dispatch bring the errant ladies back to their bedchambers.

She found the access from the second floor, which she believed descended nearest to Lady Esther's chamber. She stood in an alcove in which was situated a chair and a rarely used fireplace. She pressed the appropriate panel beside the brick mantel and a narrow, low door swished inward. She quickly slipped into the small space and gently pushed the door shut behind her.

Holding her candle aloft, she stared down into the precariously narrow stairwell. At the same time, she fairly jumped, for she heard a distinct rattling of chains, then silence. Descending with great care, she spiraled down to the first floor. She listened at the secret door and heard sounds from within the chamber.

Someone was approaching.

She backed into the corner and awaited events. Undoubtedly the young ladies were returning. Perhaps her timing was more propitious than she had thought.

A moment more, and Westbury slid into the opening, carrying a candlestick in one hand and a loop of chains in another.

"Alison?" he queried, stunned. "Have you been the author of this mischief tonight?"

As startled as she was to see him, she did not hesitate to prevaricate. "Y—yes," she whispered.

He entered the small space and settled his candlestick on a shelf near the staircase. "I see. I must say I am grievously disappointed in you. I had supposed you far past the age of engaging in such pranks, whatever the reason. What are you—thirty now, one-and-thirty, five-and-thirty?"

She gasped. "I am just seven-and-twenty."

"I had no notion you had become such an ape-leader."

Alison stared at him. "What a dreadful thing to say to me!" she whispered hotly.

"And how much more dreadful that you would stand here telling me whiskers! I know very well you would do nothing of the sort. Why were these chains in the next passageway? What are they doing here?" He turned and settled the length of chain into the far corner.

"I am so very sorry. Mary warned me earlier, and I had meant to intercept the younger girls before they accomplished their mission, but I fell asleep. They had intended to steal into the passageway nearest Lady Esther's bedchamber and frighten her from Ludgers."

He chuckled and shook his head. "They have quite

missed their mark, just as you did. *I* was awakened, not Lady Esther."

"Is this your bedchamber?" she queried, gesturing at the door.

"No, but the one beyond it is. Lady Esther's is two rooms in the opposite direction. I was hunting for our mischief-makers when I found you here, but it would seem they have disappeared."

"Oh, I see. And Lady Esther is still in her slumbers?"

"I believe so."

"Then I am greatly relieved."

His gaze fell to her nightdress, shawl, and her bare feet. He was dressed in only his nightshirt, which was open at the throat. On his feet were the pair of slippers she had embroidered for him last Christmas.

"You are wearing my slippers," she said, smiling.

"I always do."

She lifted her gaze to his face. Her thoughts began darting into places they should not. He was so very handsome and she loved him quite desperately.

"I suppose I should let you go," he murmured.

"I should return to my bed."

He drew in a deep breath but made no move to step out of her way that she might ascend the narrow stairs. He lifted a hand and pushed back an errant curl from off her forehead. "Yes, to your bed."

She suddenly felt very faint, particularly since a certain hungry light had entered his eye. She knew she should leave but she could not seem to command her feet to move.

Suddenly, it was too late. He closed the very small distance between them, slipped his arm quite violently about her waist and planted his lips firmly on hers. The kiss which ensued sent her hurtling into a place of bliss so wondrous she could hardly breathe. He had always known just how to kiss her, his lips warm and soft yet demanding.

"Alison," he murmured against her lips. "Alison."

"My darling," she returned.

Again, he kissed her fiercely, dragging her against him. Through the thin fabric she felt the entire length of him. Desire, pure and primal, raced through her, thrust forward by the sure knowledge that in but three days she would see him no more.

His tongue requested entrance and she obliged him readily, the sensation weakening her knees and every proper resolve. She loved him, she would always love him, but he was not hers to have.

"Westbury, no," she whispered, drawing back from him slightly.

"You are leaving me and I shall never see you again. My heart is breaking."

"James," she returned, sliding her arm about his neck, "do not say such a terrible thing to me. How shall I bear it?"

"My heart is breaking," he reiterated strongly, "and I was a fool to have thought I could bring any woman into this home and not compare her to you." He kissed her again, the passion he was feeling for her working in her strongly.

She loved him so very much.

She loved him and wished she were wedding him instead of Lady Esther, who did not love him.

"I thought I was doing the right thing," he whispered. "I was following your advice. I went to London to find a wife, a woman from my rank, a mother for my dear nieces and hopefully for children we would one day have. I never suspected the lady I chose would be so indifferent to me, that her heart would be so cold. Oh God, what am I doing? I will vex myself no longer with what I cannot have." He released her suddenly. "Come. You should not be in such a damp passage at this hour. You will contract an inflammation of the lungs and perish before my eyes."

She laughed, though disheartened. "I am not so fragile," she said.

"No, you are not."

She passed into an elegant if infrequently used bedchamber. He brought the candlesticks with him and blowing one out, led her to the door. "Go first, Alison. I shall remain here until you are safely away. If anyone should ask, say that you thought Bella had come to my chambers with a nightmare and you had followed after to fetch her."

"Very well."

She moved to the door and opened it quietly. A bedchamber door was open thirty feet away and light poured into the hallway.

She gestured for Westbury to draw close. "I cannot leave just yet," she murmured. "Someone is about."

"Let me see," he whispered. She drew back and allowed him to peer into the hall.

A loud crashing sound followed from the direction of the open door.

"Good God!" Westbury cried. "What was that? And who the devil is in Lady Esther's bedchamber?"

A certain suspicion pierced Alison's mind.

Westbury immediately left the chamber, making a quick progress in the direction of his betrothed's room. She followed after him, her heart beginning to beat erratically in her breast.

"Sylvester, you must not!" Lady Esther's voice swept into the hallway.

Alison now understood perfectly what was going forward, but trembled at the sight of Westbury charging toward the door of Lady Esther's bedchamber.

Lady Adstock appeared in the doorway across from

her daughter's. Her nightcap was askew and she was blinking and squinting against the dim lights. "Why is there so much shouting?" she cried. "What broke? Miss Russell! What are you doing here? Why are you barefoot and wearing only your nightdress?"

Alison ignored her, following swiftly behind Westbury. He stopped at the open door of his bride-to-be, his expression as one stunned. "Good God," he murmured.

Alison joined him and was astonished yet somehow not surprised to find Mr. Ackeley in but a shirt, breeches and his stockinged feet, kissing Lady Esther quite passionately. Behind her was a shattered vase. The young woman wore but a thin, muslin shift. The entire portrait was scandalous in the extreme.

Alison turned away, leaning her back against the wall. She covered her mouth with her hand but could not keep from laughing.

Lady Adstock reached Westbury's side and also peered within. "Esther!" she exclaimed. "Whatever are you doing with . . . with . . . with . . . ooooh!" She fainted in a hard thump on the carpeted hallway not far from Alison.

"Mama!" Esther cried, releasing Mr. Ackeley summarily. "Oh, hallo, Westbury. I am so sorry, but I cannot marry you and I—I truly did not intend to be so vile to your staff and your nieces. Miss Russell, do you have a vinaigrette per chance?"

Alison, who stared at Lady Esther in some amazement, shook her head. She appeared younger still with her brown hair draped to her waist and with all the false imperiousness of her demeanor cast aside. "I fear I do not."

Lady Esther dropped to her knees and began patting her mother's face quite vigorously. "Mama! Mama! Do wake up! All will be well, I promise you."

"Is she all right?" Mr. Ackeley inquired, standing over her.

Alison glanced at him and saw that Westbury was watching him as well, but with a cloud of angry possessiveness mounting over his head. She intervened. "I would remind you, *James,* just what it was you were doing and regretting not five minutes past before you do anything hasty—like challenge someone to a duel."

At that, Westbury turned toward her. Enlightenment dawned and he burst out laughing. "Of course you are right. Of course." He addressed Ackeley. "You are, I believe, in love with my betrothed?"

"She is not your betrothed!" he cried. "Damme, she's mine. We were engaged to be married before I quit England five years ago. She was able to withstand her mother's pressure until this past Season when you appeared ready to win her heart. You failed to tell her, however, that your heart had already been won."

He glanced meaningfully at Alison.

Any fight which had arisen in Westbury disintegrated in that moment. He opened his mouth to speak, but Lady Esther, who was still trying to awaken her mother, was before him.

"I am sorry," she said, looking up at him. "I am fond of you, Westbury, but I cannot, I will not marry you."

"You may consider the matter settled, Esther," he returned with a faint smile. "I wish you every imaginable happiness."

"Thank you. You are being most gracious in this moment."

Alison glanced at the figure lying prone on the floor, then turned to address Mr. Ackeley. "Have you a sufficient fortune to marry Lady Esther and provide a home for her?"

He smiled. "You have heard of the Golden Nabob?"

She drew in a sharp breath. "You?" she cried.

"The very one."

"No wonder you had not the smallest compunction in contradicting Lady Adstock!"

The lady in question moaned.

Lady Esther drew back as one bitten by a viper. "Oh, dear," she murmured, still holding her mother's arm in hand. "She is coming round." She lifted her frightened gaze to Mr. Ackeley.

"She will never understand," Alison murmured.

"She will never accept my love for Sylvester."

Mr. Ackeley shook his head. "I suppose it was too much to hope the old goat would remain prostrate for the remainder of the night."

Alison repressed her smiles but only with the greatest difficulty. "Might I suggest . . . an elopement?"

Lady Esther, who had been holding her mother's arm in the air and patting it gently dropped it altogether. It landed with a thump on the carpet. "Oh, yes, indeed, Sylvester—Miss Russell is right. We must elope! Now! Mama will never permit me to marry you otherwise. She is a complete toady, I fear, without the smallest understanding of love. Nor will she ever forgive me."

"Oh, I think she will," Westbury said conspiratorially, "for there is something my father once told me about her that is not commonly known and which I have every confidence you may use to your advantage to bring her down a peg or two. For the present, however, I would agree with Miss Russell—you must away to Gretna Green on the instant!"

The following morning, Alison watched in some amusement as Lady Adstock marched into the morning room, her arms flailing. The entire family was present, save for Mr. Ackeley and Lady Esther, but she focused her wrath exclusively upon Lord Westbury. "Where is my daughter, you . . . you . . . rascal! What have you done with her! Last night when Miss Russell helped me to my bed, you told me Esther was asleep and . . . and that I had suffered the ill-effects of a terrible nightmare, but I know now it was all a hum! Where is she? Where is Mr. Ackeley? Where is my daughter?"

"On her way to Gretna," Westbury said, a forkful of potatoes suspended in midair. "She has decided to keep her promise to Mr. Ackeley to become his wife, a solemn vow she had made to him some five years past. His was the superior claim. I felt I had to let him take her. Besides, she seemed most willing to go. Indeed, she told me she could not marry me because she loved him." He slid the potatoes into his mouth.

"And you listened to her? What a complete gudgeon you are! She is but a child and does not have the sense of a flea! She cannot wed Ackeley, he is but the son of a clergyman, even if he is as wealthy as Golden Ball Hughes! I will not allow it! To disgrace the family in such a manner! It is not to be born! The Duke will set things to rights when he arrives today!"

Lord Thornton rolled his eyes. "But she loves him, Mama. She always has, since they were children. And he loves her. Why the deuce do you think he risked his life in India as he did—to earn his fortune that he might have the right to marry her."

"I do not give a fig for that! Golden Nabob or not!" she exclaimed. "Adstock will set things to rights; see if he won't. I intend—"

"Do stubble it, Mama. Westbury let her go quite willingly since he is in love with Miss Russell and besides, he knows all about Drury Lane."

. Alison watched as Lady Adstock once more opened her mouth, as she had last night, in an attempt to catch her breath. There was only one thing she could do, however. Her eyes rolled back in her head and she dropped yet again into a dead faint. It would seem Her Grace's breeding was not of an exalted nature. When quite young she had been an opera dancer whom the present Duke of Adstock had taken a fancy to. He had sent her to be reared by a vicar in Shropshire until she was of such an age that he could present her to society as the daughter of a clergyman and wed her.

Later that day, a much chastened Lady Adstock and her son quit Ludgers in the company of the duke. The latter sensible gentleman had arrived just past nuncheon and once having learned of the circumstances, laughed heartily, much to the chagrin of his incensed wife.

"It could have been worse, my dear," the duke said dryly. "She might have become attached to a truly reprehensible creature, like one of those low-born actors at the Royal Theatre or, God help us, Drury Lane!"

Later, just before nuncheon, instead of descending to the drawing room where the family usually gathered, Alison remained sitting on the edge of her bed, a familiar anxiety wrenching her heart. She knew what was expected of her now that love had been confessed and so many kisses had been exchanged. How could she tell Westbury, though, that her doubts had never truly been eradicated and that she was still haunted by the terrible strife which had existed in her parents' home?

Finally, summoning the courage to leave her bedchamber, she found Westbury awaiting her at the bottom of the stairs. His expression was solemn, as though he already understood what it was she meant to tell him.

"I cannot marry you," she whispered.

"I know," he said. "I did not suppose all your fears would have ceased merely because my engagement was put off."

She marveled at him. "I . . . I thought you would be angry."

He shook his head. "Disappointed . . . again, but not angry."

"What do you intend to do?" she asked.

At that he smiled. "Why, to see to the raising of my brother's daughters, of course."

She stared up at him as he led her in the direction of the drawing room, where she could hear Jane playing Beethoven again. She could not credit that he was so calm, almost disinterested, as though when he had kissed her so passionately in the passageway on the previous night, he had been a different person entirely.

"Do you wish me to continue as governess to your nieces?" she asked, feeling strangely numb.

"Yes, for a time, if you wish for it."

Oddly, Alison felt quite hurt by his passive acceptance of her refusal yet again to marry him. Even more so when, upon entering the drawing room, he offered her a glass of sherry quite blandly, then asked if she had completed her translation of *The Citizen*.

Six

A sennight later, Alison was conducting her usual course of studies with the Longley ladies in the schoolroom when a coach was heard on the drive. Bella raced to the northern window.

"Someone is coming, in a yellow bounder," she cried, "one of those horrid coaches let from the Crown. They smell awful! Who do you suppose it is?" She was quickly joined by her sisters.

Alison was not long to follow. A charged air of expectancy always accompanied the arrival of an unexpected visitor.

"The door is opening," Sarah announced.

A maroon bonnet, exceedingly fashionable, appeared. The green silk pelisse which followed was of a mode which Jane had exclaimed over only yesterday at Ackermann's Repository.

"What an exquisite parasol," Mary observed, "with so many tassels dancing in the wind."

Jane sighed. "She is certainly of the first fashion. I only wonder who she might be?"

"Good God," Alison whispered, as the older woman turned her face upward and in the direction of the schoolroom. "That lady is my mother!"

With the Longley ladies in tow, Alison hurried from

the chamber, quickly descended two flights of stairs, and met Lady Katherine Russell as she crossed the threshhold.

"My dearest child," she whispered, catching her up in a warm embrace. "Do you know it has been three years since last we met?"

"I know, Mama, only, why have you come?"

Her mother glanced at Westbury, who had just emerged from the grand salon. "Must I have a reason to visit my daughter?"

"You?" Alison queried. "Yes, definitely. You hate being drawn away from, where was it this time?"

"Brighton with the Regent. I am a favorite of his, you know. He always sets aside a bedchamber for your father and me during the summer months."

"And how is Papa? Does his hip ail him very much?"

"Only a trifle. But you would not need to ask after him if you but once saw either the Regent's stables or his billiard room. He is quite content particularly since Prinny thinks of himself as a military man. Do you know he actually believes he saw battle during the French wars?"

"I have heard as much."

"Oh, but he is a delight, if a bit eccentric." Drawing off her gloves, she cast her gaze about the expansive entrance hall. "Ludgers is as beautiful as I remember it. My sincerest compliments to Mrs. Pitchcott. I vow there is not a finer housekeeper in all of England."

"She will be glad to hear you have said so," Westbury returned.

Lady Katherine then greeted each of the Longley ladies and as they were walking in the direction of the drawing room, Sarah addressed Lady Katherine. "Are you here to persuade Miss Russell to wed Lord Westbury?"

"Whatever do you mean, child? I thought your uncle was to be married to Lady Esther Adstock."

"The wedding is off!" Bella cried, scarcely containing her happiness.

"It is? I am greatly astonished to hear of it."

Only then, when Alison heard her mother profess to being astonished, did she know she was telling a whisker.

Later that evening, when Westbury and his nieces had retired to their bedchambers, Alison found herself alone with her mother.

"Why have you come, really, Mama?" she queried. She was seated in the library opposite her parent, who was sipping a glass of brandy and smoothing out the silk of her lavender gown.

"To apologize to you," she said.

Alison was surprised. "Whatever for?"

"For making you believe an untruth which I do not know how to make right at this point."

"What untruth? What are you talking about? You are being quite mysterious."

"Yes, I know," she responded solemnly, settling her glass on the table at her elbow. "As it happens, Westbury wrote to me. He said you were as stubborn as ever and that you were throwing away happiness with both hands. He felt there was nothing he could say to convince you to marry him."

Alison felt her complexion pale. "So Sarah was right. You have come to persuade me."

She shook her head. "I do not think I can. Even as a child, once you had made up your mind, you were incredibly hard to dissuade, whatever the subject." She let out a gruff sigh. A silence followed in which her mother seemed pained, greatly so, as she stared into the past. "My dear, there is something you must know, you must understand, but I do not know how to explain it to you after I have behaved so very badly all these years." She turned to look at Alison. "I *never* regretted marrying your father. Never. Do you hear me?"

"But, Mama—"

"Never. I was young and madly in love but I was also childish and immature. I stamped my foot and complained loudly all the time about what I had given up in wedding him. Wisdom does not come overnight, however, my precious one. I wish it had for I greatly fear that during the years when I was sorting out my decision to wed the dashing Major Russell, I passed to you this ridiculous notion that unequal marriages are disastrous."

Alison recalled the numerous quarrels she had overheard while growing up.

"Your father was wiser than myself, however. He stoicly let me shout and complain and rail against my terrible fate until like a once-powerful storm I was all worn out. In the aftermath, however, your sweet sensiblities took a beating and for that I am sorry particularly since I believe—though I may be wrong—that your refusal to marry Westbury is because of my professed unhappiness.

"In truth, I was never unhappy. Just spoiled. You know what an exemplary man your father is. Who, once knowing him, could not love him or admire him or esteem him?"

Alison nodded. "What you have said is true. He is exceptional in every way."

"He is and I love him to the point of madness; I always shall." She rose to her feet. "And now, I require my bed. I have been traveling too many days to be anything more than beyond fatigued. So I will say good night." She bent down and placed a kiss on Alison's cheek.

"Good night, Mama."

Alison sat before the empty grate upon which Mr.

Wellington reclined, fast asleep. She sighed deeply. She was stubborn, admittedly. Even Westbury had said so. What she did not understand, however, was what precisely her mama's words should mean to her.

Her mother, the daughter of a duke, had wed a mere major of the Horse Guards. Lady Adstock was at one time an opera dancer and had married a duke. Lady Esther, the daughter of a duke, was on her way to Gretna Green, eloping with a clergyman's son.

"Alison."

She turned to find Westbury in the doorway.

"May I come in?"

"Yes, of course, but I thought you had long since found your bed."

"I needed to speak with you, so I have been waiting. There is something I must say to you."

She felt nervous of a sudden for she had never seen him so solemn. He sat down beside her, so close that his knee touched her own. Without the smallest degree of ceremony, he took up her hand and pressed his lips to her fingers.

"I love you," he said, shaking his head almost sorrowfully. "I have from the moment I espied you on that flat rock, angling for fish in the noonday sun, your skirts quite scandalously revealing a pair of shapely legs."

A certain queasiness attacked her stomach. "James, I wish you would not—"

"I have a confession to make—I sent for your mother, hoping she might be able to persuade you to marry me."

"She told me as much."

He nodded. "But I have since realized that doing so was a ridiculous notion. Your mind was set long before I chanced upon you that day by the bridge and it was only the queerest impulse that caused me to pretend I was not the future Earl of Westbury, otherwise we should not even today be in this fix. But I have determined that I will not press you further on the subject of matrimony."

"Thank you," she said, wondering then just why he had come to the library. "I did not know if you could possibly understand."

He frowned at her searching her eyes. "I daresay it does not matter whether I understand or not. However, I must be long-sighted about the future which is why, after much deliberation, I must ask you to resign your post as governess to my nieces."

"What?" she cried, a certain panic seizing her heart. "But why? Why must I go? Why have you so suddenly changed your mind?"

He turned toward her, meeting her gaze fully, his hand still in strong possession of her own. "I have many duties beyond my love for you, beyond my desire that you set aside your fears and agree to marry me. I have a profound obligation to the Earldom of Westbury."

"You need an heir," Alison murmured, her spirits sinking.

"Yes, I do," he responded pointedly. "Which was what sent me to London in the first place. However, my choice of bride proved to be less than adequate for many reasons not least of which was because poor Lady Esther was still in love with Mr. Ackeley." He smiled ruefully but after a long pause and a furrowed brow he added, "I mean to do better next time, but I shall never achieve my object if you remain here to remind me every day of what I have lost. When I wished Lady Esther a mountain of joy as she entered that coach with Ackeley, I promised myself that the future Lady Westbury would have only my memories of you to contend with and not you, as you are, moving through my house as you do, lighting each chamber with your loving presence, delighting in my brother's children as if they were your own, guiding them with your infinitely patient hand in their accomplishments and education. No, you cannot remain here if I am to know a mote of happiness with my future wife."

Alison felt as though her heart would shatter at any moment. She saw the absolute conviction in his every feature as never before.

"Please do not send me away," she whispered, her voice catching.

He dropped her hand and rose to his feet. "I must. There is no other way. My love for you is too great to be more than the worst hindrance to my future. I must have an heir for Ludgers, I must take a wife, I must have a mother for Harry's girls. I had wanted that woman to be you, but you are, as your mother has already told me, firmly fixed on your course. Good night, Alison, and good-bye. I hope you will respect my wishes and leave Ludgers by noon tomorrow. You will have no need to speak with my nieces. I shall perform that office for myself, explaining this second, terrible dismissal as best I can."

He said nothing more. He did not even smile, if faintly. He merely turned on his heel and strode purposefully from the room.

Alison stared at his retreating back. She had never thought he could be so cruel.

She rose unsteadily to her feet and found that she was trembling. Why would he not even permit her to bid farewell to the girls, to Mary, Jane, Sarah, and Bella? How could he do this to her!

Late the following morning, having partaken of breakfast in her bedchamber, Alison arranged for her portmanteaus to be carried downstairs to a waiting coach. She had remained within the walls of her room, respecting Westbury's harsh orders and communicating with her mother only through brief notes carted between the west and east wings for the purpose of arranging the hour of their joint departure. She would go first to Brighton, her furniture to follow, and later to her sister's house in Bath. Afterward, a new post.

When she finally descended the stairs, a bandbox in hand, she found the house strangely quiet. Not even a single maid or footman awaited her at the bottom of the stairs to bid her farewell. Was this then to be the end of seven years of labor? The expulsion from Ludgers as though she had been a disgraced servant? Only, why was there such an extraordinarily heavy fragrance in the air of . . . roses?

The butler appeared at the closed entrance to the grand salon. "Miss Russell, Lord Westbury requests a word with you if you please." He gestured at the doors.

"Thank you."

He cleared his throat. "You will probably wish to give me your bandbox, your bonnet, and your pelisse. Yes, I know it must sound odd in me, but there is a guest, a rather prominent guest, who wishes to meet you before you depart."

"Odd, indeed," she murmured. She sniffed the air once more, wondering at the strong fragrance. Extending the bandbox to the butler, she smiled. "Are you perchance wearing perfume, Brill?"

The old servant rarely smiled but he did so now. "On no account, Miss Russell. You are perhaps smelling the fragrance of roses?"

"Yes, quite markedly," she responded, draping her pelisse over his outstretched arm. "Can you explain it?" She set about removing her bonnet.

"The Misses Longley could not resist picking a great many roses now that Lady Esther and her sufferings have quit the house."

"Ah, I see," she murmured, settling her bonnet in his waiting hands.

She moved to the closed doors as Brill arranged her belongings on a long, polished table near the grand salon. He then strode in a quite formal manner to stand beside her and with an uncharacteristic wink, threw the doors wide. He announced her in an equally formal manner, which caused her to wonder if the Prince Regent himself was awaiting her.

Alison took but one step into the chamber, drew to a sudden stop, and gasped. She had expected to see two or three large bouquets but much to her astonishment an even grander display greeted her eyes. A score of vases, each containing the abundance of not just the rose garden but of the cutting garden as well, were scattered everywhere. In addition, numerous exotic plants, ferns, and trees had been brought over from the succession houses. She felt as though she were entering a secret garden which had been growing in the grand salon all these years and was just now being unveiled.

She advanced into the chamber slowly. She had thought she would be leaving Ludgers without saying good-bye to anyone, but apparently that was not to be the case. The Longley ladies were present and dressed most curiously in their finest gowns. Her mother stood beside a winged chair, also gowned as elegantly and wreathed in smiles. She could see that someone—undoubtedly the prominent guest that Brill had mentioned—was seated in the chair but she could not see who it was. A pair of fine leather shoes proclaimed that a gentleman was present but a palm leaf hid his face from view.

Whoever he was, he must be of the royal family, for she could not otherwise explain either the state of the grand salon or the fancy dress of everyone present.

The vicar, a frequent guest at Ludgers, was also present. He nodded to her graciously. Next to him, Lord

Westbury stood resplendent in a fine coat of gray super-fine, an elegant, embroidered waist coat, charcoal gray knee breeches, black stockings, and black leather shoes. His costume as well was inordinately formal for the middle of the day. She felt decidedly nervous of a sudden and was grateful that whoever this most important person might be, at least her gown of cornflower blue silk was of classic lines and creaseless since she had not yet sat in a coach for hours on end.

The path through the vases, chairs, and tables, brought the winged chair into view. She prepared a welcoming smile, then uttered a spontaneous cry of delight.

"Papa!" she exclaimed, hurrying to him. "Is it really you? When did you arrive? How long have you been here? Why did no one tell me? Have you been waiting very long? Oh, how could you have traveled so many miles with your hip paining you as it does?"

He rose from the chair, cane in hand. She cast herself into his arms and he held her in a tight embrace. "My dearest Alison. It has been far too long since last I saw you."

"I have missed you dreadfully," she said, pulling back from him slightly. "You can have no notion. But how happy I am that you are here, only do not tell me that you have traveled such a long distance on my account."

"Can you give me a better reason any father should make a journey?"

"Oh," she murmured, her eyes flooding with tears, "I love you so very much, Papa. Only tell me, does your wound give you much pain?"

"Only when it rains." He chuckled.

"But, Papa, it rains two days out of every three."

"Then I have a third of the year in which I am in a state of complete contentment."

She glanced at everyone assembled. "Why are you all dressed in your finery at eleven o'clock in the morning and why is the room decorated like a . . . oh!" She glanced at Westbury, her heart picking up its cadence so quickly she thought she might faint.

"You must make a choice," her father said. "Remain here in a house full of love, or leave to your next post, which is one of the reasons I have come. A lady in Brighton has a large family of eight children—five daughters—and would be happy for you to become her next governess. At least then I shall be able to see my eldest daughter as often as I wish. Although I must warn you three of the girls are quite the most obnoxious creatures I have ever before met. Not that you will be unable to work your wonders, for you are quite skilled in managing children, but I for one hope you choose to remain here."

"But, Papa," she began quietly.

"I know," he responded. "I did not come to argue you into staying. I do comprehend fully why you feel as you do and in that matter both your mother and I are at fault." Here her mother slipped her arm through her father's. "However, you are old enough to know your mind. Whatever you choose, we will support you in that decision."

Alison turned to look at Westbury. She recalled sitting on the flat rock that day so many years ago, tumbling in love with him before he had even dismounted his fine black horse, kissing him so recently in the secret passageway and afterward feeling as though her heart would break because she would soon be separated from him.

"I have loved you forever," she said quietly.

"And I you." A faint, uncertain smile touched his lips. "Will you be my wife, my dear Alison?"

She waited, looking into his dark eyes, pondering, waiting a little more. Everyone was perfectly silent, even Bella, who would usually set to sighing on such an occasion as this. Should she stay? Should she go? Should she leave this house of love?

No. A voice came from deep within her soul. Again, *no.*

How could she leave when all that she loved was here?

"Oh, James," she cried, casting herself into his arms and weeping against his shoulder. "I have been so foolish, yet I meant well. I did. I did."

"Then will you wed me?"

"Yes, yes of course I will."

A sudden, rousing cheer rose up from her mother and father, and the Longley ladies. Even the vicar cried out a warm, "Huzza!"

Westbury gripped her shoulders and forced her away from him slightly in order to dry her tears. He smiled encouragingly at her. "Excellent," he murmured, dabbing at her cheeks with his handkerchief. "And here is our good vicar prepared to conduct the ceremony, for if you must know I have a special license already in hand."

She drew back from him. "You mean now? Today?"

He released her and nodded quite firmly. "I do not want to give you a moment more to ponder your decision. Why else do you think I had every maid in my household bring flowers and plants to the salon this morning?"

His smile and the light in his eye was a decided challenge.

She chuckled. "Very well but I hope you know that at last having agreed to marry you I would never break such a promise."

"I had rather be secured of the prize immediately. Even you must admit I have waited a very long time."

Alison smiled anew as more tears flooded her eyes. She inclined her head in acquiescence and before a scarce five minutes had passed she was speaking her vows and hearing his spoken in return.

* * *

The celebration of her nuptials lasted an entire fortnight as guests arrived from all parts of the kingdom, after having been informed of the unusual change of brides. Alison knew the gabblemongers could not resist coming merely to hear the extraordinary story of a mere governess oversetting the plans of the Duchess of Adstock. Although she rather thought the entire company was properly shocked and delighted when at the highlight of the wedding ball, Mr. Sylvester and Lady Esther Ackeley arrived to congratulate the bride and groom.

When Alison and her new husband had finally bid the last of the guests farewell, she asked Westbury to escort her outside, where the early August night had filled the sky with stars. He took her to the rose garden and drew her into his arms. The kiss which ensued had become as familiar to her as the sound of her own name, which he murmured provocatively against her cheek now and then. How infinitely dear was the feel of his lips on hers, the possession he inevitably took of her mouth, and of the manner in which he drew her so close that she could feel the entire length of him.

"I love you so very much, James," she whispered against his lips.

"And I, you. Happy?"

"Tremendously, you can have no notion."

"I think I do, a little." He kissed her again, warmly, deeply.

After a time, when she was cradled gently against his chest, she said, "I will always be indebted to my father. His encouragement opened my heart to the notion of becoming your wife. You were very wise to have brought him here." She looked up at him, smiling.

"Actually," he said, also smiling, "my nieces were the ones who suggested I do so."

"What?" she cried, surprised.

"Yes. Mary told me that a father's love was more important than anything in a young lady's life."

"I believe she was right. She thinks of you as her father, you know. They all do."

He nodded. "Their presence at Ludgers is one of the two great joys of my existence."

"And what is the second?" she asked, though certain of the answer.

"Only this . . ."

He once more took her in his arms, kissing her again and again until even the moon, at last growing weary of waiting for them to discreetly retire, slipped behind the wooded hills to the west.

A FATHER'S
DUTY

Jeanne Savery

Colonel Lord Cranston, Rath Moorhead to his friends, shifted from one foot to the other. Even the most casual observer would guess that the notion he was at ease was poppycock. The prospect of once again meeting his daughter and under circumstances that were not of the best was more nerve-wracking than facing hostile troops. Just in case anyone *was* watching, he cast what he fondly hoped was a casual glance around his mother's salon. The room, he concluded, looked just as it had for as long as he could recall. A bit more faded. A bit grayer, more grimy . . .

My mother is the worst sort of miser, Rath thought, his mouth set in a bitter line.

He fingered the letter he'd read so often it was torn along one fold and illegible along another . . . not that he needed the words. He knew the brief missive by heart. Now, that same heart beat a rapid tattoo. His daughter! It was more than four years since he'd last seen Constance. Five? In any case, before orders sent him to India, where the long-delayed missive finally reached him.

Had his wife succumbed to illness, as she predicted? Few survived the wasting disease. . . .

And his daughter? Had the poor child already been married off as his mother had married off his sisters? Was he too late? Had he failed *both* wife and daughter?

Once again Rath did the fateful calculations in his head and concluded it was all too likely. The chit had celebrated her eighteenth birthday some months previously and his mother was not one to allow a female child time to find her feet. Eighteen, to his mother's way of thinking, was already too long on the shelf.

Because, if she had time to gain poise, to feel secure, to attain a certain maturity—and wish to have some say in the matter—it might, the cynical thought crossed Rath's mind, *be more difficult to marry her off to Mother's notion of the best possible match.* Thinking of the blackguards to whom his sisters were wed, Rath felt pity for them. Well, perhaps Mary was only to be pitied for the fact *her* husband was the biggest bore in England!

Had that been his daughter's destiny?

Why, he thought bitterly, *can His Majesty's mail not be delivered more expeditiously?*

The letter from his wife informing him she feared she'd not live to see their daughter happily married was dated very nearly two years in the past. He opened it still again, tipped it so the faded ink caught the light, and smiled, as he'd done each time he read his wife's most acid comment.

"The dowager, Lady Morlande's only requirement in a husband for Constance," wrote his wife, "is that the marriage place our child as far as possible toward the head of a line going into dinner."

Rath's smile faded. His wife had forgotten that a well-filled purse might set the bride back a place or two. What a terribly difficult choice for his mother, having to balance status against wealth when choosing the best suitor, *from her point of view,* for her granddaughter.

Rath refolded the page and regretted that it had taken him the better part of six months to reach England. *Perhaps I should not have stayed that last month, not seen to handing over my duties in proper form,* he thought uneasily.

How long after writing the letter had his wife lived? How long had his mother waited before presenting the girl? He was too late. He knew it. Rath's overly well developed conscience beat at him, as it did for any perceived failure where his duty was concerned.

His *daughter.* The notion she was old enough to wed was a facer all in itself. It was true that, when last seen, Constance was leaving childhood behind and occasionally presented a frighteningly adult facade. But not the day he'd arrived for that last visit! His favorite memory of the girl filled his mind. She'd known he was coming, had been waiting for him. When she saw the carriage turn into the drive she'd run toward it, long plaits flying out behind. Despite her protests her skirts had not yet been let down and, that particular day, revealed highly polished little black shoes twinkling when the sun caught them.

Rath smiled as he recalled she had lost a button from one shoe, the leather puckering slightly at the side . . . such a lively child. Happy and, as he recalled, exhibiting the curiosity of the intelligent young and a willingness to question new notions and—Rath's smile widened a trifle—a flattering attention to his stories.

The smile faded.

That was his last visit home. The last time he'd seen his wife. Another pang of guilt slipped under his guard and slipped away. It was not her fault their marriage had failed, but neither was it his. He'd his duty to his king and she had known that when they wed, had accepted it—but refused to follow him around the world as some wives did, living somewhere not too far from where his regiment was based.

But there had been no acrimony between them as might have been the case and gradually they had become friends through their letters. Rath regretted, for the both of them, the possibilities they had missed, the love they each might have known if wed to another. Sometimes he thought the only good thing to come of their marriage was Constance.

Consciously, Rath brought forward the mental picture he treasured of that young girl. The long braids. The child who laughed and sang and was never still.

He looked up as the door opened.

Standing there was an attractive and self-possessed young woman. Very slightly taller than average. Long hair neatly braided and wound around her head, clearly revealing classic features. Even though she was dressed in deepest mourning he enjoyed the vision of femininity—until he realized it was his daughter!

Constance.

Shock passed through him. A fleeting sadness followed. The child was gone and this young woman, this *stranger,* had taken her place. With his usual self-control Rath put aside regret. Eyeing her black skirts, he said, "I am too late."

His daughter nodded solemnly. "Mother died just over a year ago. She told me I was not to mourn her, but I could not help it. Grandmother Morlande is losing patience with me, that I refuse to put off deep mourning."

Then the mischievous smile he recalled in the child lightened her features—and he was glad the younger Constance had not entirely disappeared.

"Deep mourning was," she continued softly, "the only ploy we could contrive to keep Grandmother from immediately beginning the marriage market maneuvers necessary to bring her quarry up to scratch!"

Rath smiled slightly at his daughter's vocabulary. She sounded as if she were quoting. But whom? Had his wife spoken to Constance about her grandmother in such terms as these? And then her wording caught his attention.

"We?" he asked—and turned toward the door as another woman entered. She was ten to fifteen years older than Constance. No more than thirty-five at the outside, he decided.

The stranger looked from Rath to Constance. "Constance?"

The heavy black skirts swirled around Constance's ankles as she turned. "Ah! Annabelle. Father, you remember Miss Adams, do you not? My governess and now my companion?"

Rath nodded, happy to realize he need not lie. He did remember her, vague recollections from the visits he'd made after Constance was old enough for a governess. A quiet well-behaved woman always in the background, effacing herself, but keeping an eye on her charge, ready to remove her when his wife indicated Constance should return to her schoolroom.

"Miss Adams." Rath bowed. "You, then, are the 'we' who has managed to keep my daughter free of my mother's scheming?"

Annabelle chuckled. It was a warm brown sound that ran up Rath's spine like the bristles of a bath brush. He took another, more searching, look at his daughter's companion and liked what he saw. Liked it a lot. Not a beauty. Very likely never a beauty, but her features had a great deal of character and her eyes were made brilliant by the intelligence and humor lurking there. He felt very slightly guilty when he saw a blush warm her throat at his impertinent stare—but he could not bring himself to look away.

Annabelle cleared her throat. "We did the only thing we could think of and, by the grace of God, we succeeded."

"Succeeded?"

"You, sir, have arrived in time to see to your daughter's presentation and organize her Season."

Rath's brows arched. "Why so I have!" A modicum of relief filled him. "I have *not* failed my daughter! Constance"—he turned, his head following, his eyes leaving Miss Adams's face at the very last—"you and Miss Adams must tell me exactly how to go on. I have been away from tonnish things far too many years to have a notion of what must be done, but I promise you, rough old soldier that I am, I will do my best."

His gaze returned to Annabelle and, despite the guilt, he felt satisfaction when, once again, a rosy color crept up her throat. He didn't bother to analyze why he was pleased, but allowed himself to relax as he rarely did and simply enjoy the sight of a good and intelligent woman. Such had been all too rare in his life as a soldier.

The trio seated themselves and again Annabelle cleared her throat in preparation for speech. She then proceeded to outline the steps that must be taken to make ready for her charge's presentation and Season.

Constance listened to the verbal exchange between the two but more interesting by half was the silent communication of flicking glances, long looks, and the lowered eyes whenever one or the other became conscious that he or she was staring. Constance remembered her mother's rambling monologues concerning her husband. The sick woman had lain on her bed and, with Constance holding her thin hand, spoke of her regrets that she had not been a better wife, that, most importantly, she'd not given him a son. She told her daughter now, that he'd be free to do so, she hoped he would find love and remarry. She warned Constance his remarriage was likely and she prayed Constance would help her father's bride feel welcome and not, as some children did, make life difficult for them.

Constance had promised she'd do all she could to help her father. And then, curious, she'd asked how she would know if he was falling in love. Lady Cranston had chuckled weakly and then smiled mistily at her daughter. "You will know by how he looks at the woman. There will be a stunned look about his eyes. He will stare rudely and be unaware he does so. And he will find it difficult to look away. Oh, yes, you will know when he has met a woman he may wed—once he thinks of it!"

"Wed?" whispered Constance too softly to break into the others' conversation. "My Annabelle?"

Her gaze went from her father to her companion and back again. A barely repressed giggle rose up inside her at the thought of her grandmother's reaction to such a connection. *But why not? I'd not lose my beloved Annabelle if they were to marry,* she thought. She watched them, careful not to disturb the discussion between the other two.

Either discussion.

Or both. Neither that which concerned Constance's coming Season nor that other, silent, communion that passed from eye to eye, a man-woman communication so blatant that even Constance could not mistake it.

"Grandmother would be so angry," she whispered gleefully.

Lady Morlande did not like Constance's companion, who had the temerity to object to her plans. Disliking Annabelle, her ladyship would be appalled at the notion the penniless young woman might raise her eyes to the exulted heights of a Moorhead son.

Whatever her grandmother's sensibilities, the knowledge of the social distance between her father and her companion didn't persuade Constance one whit that the notion was not a good one! She immediately put her mind to thinking up ways of promoting a match between the two most important people in her life.

"In the salon? My son? Nonsense. No note was sent round that I was to expect him."

The harsh voice carried clearly through the closed door but roused neither of the speakers. Constance, wanting to protect them, moved to stand before them. She waved her hand between the two and, quite rudely, broke into their conversation, saying in a clear young voice, "It is so good to have you home, Father. You cannot know how I have longed to see you again."

Rath had not risen to the rank of colonel by being stupid. He flicked a glance toward the door and back to his daughter, who nodded. "Yes, well, I came as quickly as I could. I only regret that I was not in time to see your mother one last time."

Annabelle, who had been in the middle of listing the purchases necessary merely for a girl's presentation, looked bewildered—but for no more than a moment. She, too, flicked a glance toward the door and then, pushing herself back in her chair, crossed her feet at the ankles and clasped her hands in her lap. Instantly, she turned herself into a properly reticent hired companion— and then spoiled it by blushing when Rath winked at her even as he continued speaking to his daughter.

"I have already set a few things in motion, my dear," he said. "My solicitor opened up the town house where you and your mother lived each Season. He informed me your grandmother *suggested* he see it rented, but that he refused to do so until he communicated with me. His letter to me with respect to this and other things, is, very likely, even as we speak, on its way back from India. And I have visited . . ."

"It *should* be rented," interrupted Lady Morlande. She stood just within the door to the hall. "You will go to Colemore Hills, of course, to see to your property. Constance will stay here. I have plans in place for her presentation. . . ."

Rath, in turn, ruthlessly interrupted his mother, the only way one could ever get a word into the flow of her monologues. "How pleasant to see you again, Mother dear," he purred in a dangerous tone. "Thank you for your joyous welcome."

Lady Morlande scowled. "You know I hold such conventional chitchat in abhorrence, Rathbourne. You must, of course, stay here tonight since it is too late to begin a journey. Adams, see to it."

Annabelle rose to her feet, but Rath held out his hand, stopping her. "No *Miss* Adams, it is unnecessary. I will stay in my own home, of course."

Her ladyship ignored her son's hint that Miss Adams was more than a servant and should not be addressed as one. "At Cranston House? But I have said it must be rented!"

"It is, perhaps, your house for you to order as you please?" he asked politely.

Lady Morlande bit her lips. "Why have you returned to England?"

Rath pretended shock. "My wife has died and left our daughter alone and unprotected and you ask why I have returned? It is my duty to see to her. You know I am not one to shirk my duty."

Lady Morlande compressed her lips. "You cannot mean you think to see to her presentation and Season!"

"And why should I not?"

"You . . ."

"I," he interrupted before she could say something that would force him to be still ruder, "am her father. Constance," he added, turning to her, "I must go now, but you and Miss Adams are to be ready to leave this house tomorrow morning. Early. I am certain you have no wish to impose upon your grandmother a moment longer than necessary, and will expedite a move to Cranston House as expeditiously as possible!"

He bowed to Miss Adams, placed a quick peck of a kiss on Constance's cheek, and moved toward his mother, who barred the way to the door. He could, he thought—for him it was an unusual whimsicality—see steam coming from her ears. Would she, like an overheated steam engine, explode?

Lady Morlande exploded, yes, but not until after she'd sent Miss Adams upstairs to begin the packing. "You are a fool, Constance," she began, "to continue to retain that idiotic woman. She does not know her place! Sitting here in the salon with my son as if they were equals! And she is forever giving me looks no servant should think of giving her betters! If only your skitter-witted mother had not written it into her will that the creature was to remain with you until you were wed! Of what possible use is she? She is only in the way—" At which point, fearing she had said too much, her ladyship turned her thoughts toward her son. "—and you should have nothing to do with your father. How can you trust him when he is very likely to receive orders and be off somewhere just when you need him most? Why, he wasn't even here for your birth, although he'd *promised* your mother he would be. My son has never understood what is important. *Never . . .*"

Her ladyship ranted on, but Constance, although appearing to listen attentively, dreamed her own dreams of the future. Or, rather, of her father's future. With Annabelle.

". . . so you agree that you will remain here." Lady Morlande smiled a cold hard smile. "Be a good girl now and run upstairs and tell that Adams creature she is to unpack." Lady Morlande settled back, a complacent expression softening her features.

Constance, when she realized the voice had stopped,

straightened. "Grandmother? I fear"—she knew she blushed—"I missed something."

Lady Morlande sighed hugely. "It is all of a piece. And *just* like your father! Now pay attention. You have agreed that it is impossible to trust him to see to your Season and that it is best you stay here."

"No thank you," said Constance politely but firmly. She rose to her feet. "I'd best join Annabelle and help with the packing."

Constance, afraid of the anger she'd obviously roused in her grandmother's breast, sped from the room, her skirts flying around her. Seeing the shocked expression the newest footman wore—Lady Morelande's servants, those below the upper servants, left her service and were replaced with great regularity—she rolled her eyes, jerked her thumb back over her shoulder as she passed him, and took the stairs at an equally unladylike pace. She didn't slow down until she entered her bedroom, closed the door, and leaned back against it.

"Annabelle," she said when she could speak without panting, "be so good as to remind me that I am never again to drift off into a daydream when Grandmother is in the middle of a tirade!"

Annabelle straightened, one hand still on the half-folded gown laid across Constance's bed. "Almost agreed to wed the marquise did you?"

It was a jest between the two that Lady Morlande would try to wed Constance to the ancient widower who appeared in Lady Morlande's salon with some regularity, and reference to him brought a smile to the girl's face. "Not quite so bad as that. She appeared to think I had agreed that my father is not to be trusted and that I should stay here with her. I am chagrinned to admit that I may have nodded at the wrong place and led her to believe she had the right of it."

"So?"

"So let us get these trunks packed. I fear she will throw anything we forget into the street, washing her hands of the both of us!"

Constance went to the door and looked down the hall toward the room the maids used for linens and caring for the women's clothes. The door was ajar. She went to see who might be in there. It was her favorite among the maids.

"Daisy, come help. We've a great deal to do and no time in which to do it."

"I'd be happy to help, miss, but I've been ordered to sort the clean linen and put it away and I daren't do otherwise."

Constance frowned. "Daisy, do you *like* working for Lady Morlande?"

Daisy swallowed and her eyes widened. Almost fearfully, she whispered, "Do you want the truth, miss?"

"Of course."

"Then, no. She's . . . she's . . ."

"An ogre to work for." Constance nodded. "Would you come be under maid to Annabelle and myself? Work for me? I suppose I'll have to have a fully trained abigail, but you can help care for our clothes and, when she needs assistance, do for Annabelle . . . ?"

"But . . . ?"

"Ah. You do not know. My father has reached London and we remove to Cranston House tomorrow morning. Do come," coaxed Constance.

Daisy tossed the linen towels she'd held to her bosom onto a table and moved toward the door. "You don't have to ask twice, miss. I'll be happy as a Whitstable oyster at low tide to be a-coming with you."

About nine, Constance sent Daisy down to the kitchen for a tray of bread, cold meats, and fruit, which she and Annabelle shared with the maid—to Daisy's obvious embarrassment—and then the three continued their work long into the night. Finally they finished and looked around the bare rooms with satisfaction. Only then did Constance think about Daisy's possessions. "Oh dear. Can you pack before morning? You may sleep all day tomorrow if you need to."

"Won't take long to bundle up my things, miss," said Daisy. "No time at all. Shall I return with morning tea?"

"Yes." Constance bit her lip. "I suppose it is necessary that we tell Bloom that you will be leaving her service."

It was half a question and the three eyed each other. None of them looked forward to that particular task. Lady Morlande's butler was a strong-minded individual who had Notions. He disliked above anything to change them. It would be very difficult to convince him that Daisy actually preferred to work elsewhere.

"I know," said Constance, her expression lightening, "I will write him a letter."

All three relaxed. Then Constance's jaw cracked, she yawned so widely. The others yawned simultaneously and the three grinned at each other. "Did we pack all my night rails?" Constance asked, fighting another yawn.

"Every one." Annabelle went to the second trunk and lifted the lid.

"Never mind. I will sleep in my shift. Off with you. The both of you." Constance could barely wait to find herself stretched out on the bed. She knew her nights, once the Season was under way, would end still later, but, right now, she was unused to such hours and her eyes would barely remain open long enough for her to brush out and braid her hair.

An army man, Rath arrived at his mother's door at an unconscionable hour. Or so her butler told him. He also told the colonel to go away.

"It would appear that dictatorial behavior is catching,"

retorted Rath, eyeing the man much as he'd have done one of his subalterns who got above himself. "Bloom, is it? Step aside and allow me entrance. Then send a maid up to rouse my daughter, assuming she has not yet awakened."

Bloom stuck his nose in the air. "The maids are about their work."

"And you?"

The butler's eyes bulged from his head at the implication. *"Me,* sir?"

"You. If you do not care to climb the stairs, then you may take on the work of one of the maids, since it cannot be stopped for even a moment. Then send her to do as I've ordered."

The butler goggled. Rath's request, if it could be called that, did not suit his Notions at all, but it had occurred to him that this was Lady Morlande's son—merely a second son, of course, but the first did not look to be getting on with the business of providing an heir, so the heir presumptive was more important than he might otherwise be. Perhaps it behooved one to Do Something.

Cogitations complete, Bloom put his nose in the air and announced, "I will, my lord, see that Miss Moorhead is informed of your arrival."

"That will be unnecessary, Bloom, since you see I too have arrived. Have you come for us, Father?" She continued down the stairs in that light airy fashion Rath found so disturbingly adult. She came up to him and, putting her hands on his chest, rose on tiptoe to place a kiss on his chin. She grinned up at him when she saw his ears turn red. "Good morning, Father."

"Harrumph. Good morning to you too, child." He turned slightly, saw that Miss Adams had followed in that quiet calm way she had. "To you too, Miss Adams." He bowed.

Annabelle, when she'd finally reached her bed the

night before, had found her mind filled with disturbing thoughts of the distinguished military man who was her charge's father. She had been so certain she'd totally rid herself of the unsuitable dreams that always followed his rare visits. Such dreams would not do and she had scolded herself roundly. Now she stood quietly, her hands clasped loosely before her, and nodded gravely. "We are ready, my lord. Have you arranged for a cart to transport our trunks?"

"It comes shortly. And who is this?" he asked when, racing in a manner entirely unsuited to a gentleman's residence, Daisy arrived in the hall.

Daisy saw that Bloom was looking down his long nose in a decidedly disapproving manner and she stuck out her tongue at him. "You old slumguzzler!" said the maid in a tone she mistakenly thought suitably hushed and for his ears alone. "Don't you go a-looking down your nose at *me*. You got nothin' to say about me. Not any more you don't!"

Constance hid a grin. "You are correct, Daisy, that he is no longer responsible for your behavior, but I am. Please recall where you are and who else is here."

Daisy blushed to the roots of her carrot-colored hair. She curtsied to the colonel. "Sorry, I'm sure," she said in more genteel and far more subdued tones. And then she grinned at Constance. "Got my bundle," she whispered in the manner in which she'd spoken to Bloom, one certain to be heard by far more people than if she'd used more normal tones.

Bloom, realizing he was losing a maid, appeared to swell. The fact he'd been considering letting the impertinent chit go without a character was irrelevant. Letting her go and having her leave were two entirely different things!

"Never mind, Bloom," said Rath, reading the man's

mind with pretty fair accuracy. "You'll find another soon enough. Constance? Miss Adams? Shall we go?"

Daisy, hugging her bundle to her considerable bosom, cocked a snoot at the butler as she went by him. "Cabbage-head," she said under her breath, insulting him to his face rather than behind his back, as she'd been doing ever since first coming to Lady Morlande's.

When they reached Cranston House, Constance introduced Daisy to the housekeeper, who took the girl into the back part of the house. Rath, who had appointments with his solicitor and his tailor, bowed to the two, told them to do what they must to settle in, that he would return home in time for dinner, and then left them standing in the hall.

Constance looked at Annabelle, who looked back. "I believe we have our orders, Annabelle!"

"I believe we do, but our trunks have yet to arrive. How should we begin?"

"I don't know about you, but I will be unladylike and admit to hunger," said Constance, "so perhaps we might indulge in a nibble of something? Since we did not eat before leaving my grandmother's house?" She raised a querying eyebrow at the footman, who stood by the salon door. He bowed slightly and moved to throw open the door. "Miss Moorhead," he announced, ignoring Annabelle.

"And Miss Adams," said Constance quietly but firmly, wondering to whom they were being announced.

"And Miss Adams," he repeated, his ears red.

Constance looked around the room and suddenly it was as if the sun came out in her face. "Auntie Jo! Aunt Freddy! Oh, how wonderful to see you!"

She raced across the salon and hugged first the one and then the other and then looked at the third lady, a bright-eyed perky little lady whom Constance very much feared she recognized. She sank into a curtsy. "My lady?" she said a trifle breathlessly.

Lady Jersey laughed. "I gather it has been some time since you last saw your aunts?

"Not"—Constance blinked back quick tears—"since my mother died. Far too long, but I apologize for . . ."

"For loving them and being very glad to see them?" interrupted Sally Jersey, who was in a good humor that day. "I find nothing unladylike in that. Your father has chosen well when finding you chaperones for the Season." She turned her eyes toward Annabelle and back to Constance.

Constance, recalled to her manners, introduced her companion.

"Lord Fortesque's granddaughter?" asked her ladyship.

Annabelle rose from her curtsy and looked Lady Jersey in the eye. "I have been told it is so," she said politely.

Lady Jersey laughed a trifle uncertainly. *"Have* you then?"

Annabelle flushed but stood her ground. "Since I have never been introduced to the man, I cannot say, can I?"

"Impertinence," said Lady Jersey, but with a smile.

One could almost see the wheels turning in her ladyship's head. Annabelle was suddenly filled with dread at what schemes Silence Jersey, as she was known, might dream up!

"An earl's granddaughter, are you?" asked Miss Frederica Blackstone, eyeing Annabelle.

"I do not speak of it," said Annabelle stiffly. "I am not acknowledged, you see."

"Parents wed, weren't they?" asked Miss Josephina Blackstone gruffly. "Seem to remember an announcement . . . ?"

Annabelle flushed rosily. "Yes of course they were—

but my mother was supposed to have married her father's choice and he never forgave her."

"And now that we have washed your dirty linen quite thoroughly," responded Josephina, "we will forget it was ever said. Apologize for prying," she finished in her abrupt fashion and turned back to their guest. "Tell me, Sally, is what I hear of . . ."

While Josephina asked Lady Jersey for the details concerning some recent gossip, softhearted Frederica rose and led Constance and Annabelle to seats. A smile wreathed her plump cheeks as she poured them coffee, passed them the cake plate, and spoke to them about the rooms prepared for them. . . .

"—quite delightful and with a communicating door, my dears—"

. . . and, surreptitiously, watched to see that Annabelle recovered her equanimity.

While Constance and Annabelle settled into their new home, Lady Morlande fumed. She plotted several plots, swore roundly at her personal maid when the girl didn't dress her hair exactly as she liked, gave Bloom a piece of her mind for allowing Daisy—whom she'd been thinking of letting go without a character—to escape, and gave contradictory orders to her housekeeper and head housemaid, thereby sowing dissension between old enemies, before leaving home for a round of morning calls.

Each call proceeded in much the same manner. Complaints about her military son arriving with no warning, more serious complaints about the man refusing to go down to his estate, which—since he'd been gone forever and a day—must surely require his presence, and finally that he'd not only removed his daughter from her grandmother's house, but taken that Miss Adams along as well.

". . . I never approved of her, you know. Tried to get

rid of her when my daughter-in-law died, but that silly goose put it in her will that Miss Adams is to stay with Constance until my granddaughter weds. The Adams person's grandfather doesn't accept her, you know. Must be something wrong with her. And to go, unchaperoned, to my son's household! Well, one *knows,* does one not, what sort of young person . . ."

And on and on, here and there and elsewhere . . . discovering far too late that her son's sisters-in-law, the Miss Blackstones, had joined the colonel for the Season. Her attempt to blacken Annabelle Adams's reputation fallen into dust, Lady Morlande returned to her own house, where she proceeded to make life so difficult for her servants that Cook left her service without warning and the washerwoman the household had used for very nearly a decade told the housekeeper that, in the future, she must find someone else.

Lady Morlande had a new complaint. Having successfully separated her granddaughter from those dowdy Blackstone ladies, who were mere misses but had, by what means Lady Morlande had never discovered, far too much influence within the ton . . . *well,* to discover they were living under the same roof as Constance was very nearly unbearable.

Colonel Lord Cranston was a military man. Discipline had been his watchword for many years, so he did not turn around ten paces from his front door and return to it, but continued on to appointments he had made and now, whatever his druthers, would keep.

He kept them, yes, but it could not be denied that he was a trifle absentminded throughout his session with his solicitor; that, his mind elsewhere, he didn't see an old friend he passed in St. James Street; that he told Stultz, long-time tailor to the military, to use whichever cloth he wished rather than make that important decision himself, *and* that he excused himself more than a trifle abruptly from a conversation among his peers at his favorite club. Rath didn't attempt to deny he was preoccupied. At least, not to himself. Instead he strolled home earlier than expected, chiding himself for being a fool that he'd gone out in the first place.

My daughter needs me, he reminded himself—even as a mental picture of a very different woman, a quiet and intelligent woman, filled his head.

"My daughter," he muttered, startling a young lady walking with her maid into wondering if her mother had played her father false, herself the result! *I have returned home from India because of my daughter and I must not forget it.*

But no matter how he scolded, the vision of Miss Adams wouldn't go away. Not entirely. It did, however, shrink to a more reasonable size and tuck itself into a corner of his mind.

The next few days were delightful for both Constance and Annabelle.

Rather more for Constance than for Annabelle. Annabelle was forcibly reminded of the foolishness she'd endured each time the colonel visited his wife and daughter, the idiotic emotions roused by him in her maiden breast, emotions she had, each time she'd experienced them, fought down. Not only was the man her charge's father, he was husband to the woman for whom she worked. Annabelle had found it more than a trifle embarrassing that she had formed a *tendre* for Lady Cranston's husband.

Unfortunately the man was now a widower. There was no longer a deterrent in the form of a wife to put restraints on Annabelle's dreams—the only restraint, and that not exactly helpful, was her duty to the man's daughter when her dreams persisted in suggesting she could just as easily mother Constance as be the girl's mentor!

Worst of all, from Annabelle's point of view, Constance did nothing but talk about her wonderful father! It was, Annabelle found, very difficult to keep a proper perspective when the man she yearned to talk about, to see, to talk *to,* but whom, for her own peace of mind, she should avoid like the plague, was far too often talked about or brought to mind by his actual presence.

Constance's early suspicion that her beloved mentor was perfect for her much-loved father grew with each passing day. The more she saw the two together—at table or when drinking tea with the aunts or when discussing how best to forward Constance's Season—the more certain she became. Her desire to bring them together might have begun in the spirit of mischief—*nothing* would irritate her irritable and irritating grandmother so much as seeing Rath married to a woman deep in her black books—but time changed Constance's motives to more benign and positive ones. The two would suit. Her problem was how to make them see it.

Her plans were complicated by the fact that their days were filled to capacity with shopping and planning. The gowns Grandmother Morlande had had made up for Constance would not do. They were the wrong colors, the wrong fabrics, and badly styled. Both Constance and Annabelle had known they were wrong from the moment they were ordered, but neither had the authority to change Lady Morlande's decisions. Colonel Lord Cranston did. The newly ordered gowns were delightful—but choosing materials, designs, and standing for fittings took a great deal of time.

Constance fumed.

And then one day, during the aunts' regular at-home, Lord Tolbridge, leaning heavily on his silver-mounted cane, arrived on the scene. He came again the next day.

And the next—but never when Lord Cranston happened to be at home. The man, who appeared an ancient in Constance's eyes, was known to none of them, but Auntie Jo, an inveterate gossip, knew *of* him.

". . . buried three wives, you know, and still no heir. A flock of ewe lambs"—Josephina glanced toward her niece and grimaced—*"daughters,* I mean, some of whom are rather older than you, Constance, but not a boy among them. Freddy," she suddenly added, turning to her sister, "you don't think . . ."

"Surely not," said kindhearted Frederica, a worried look appearing on her usually happy features. "A young thing like Constance? No. He wouldn't be so foolish. What he wants is a nice widow who has proven she can bear sons."

"Ah! Someone like Mrs. Lambsworth?"

"Exactly."

"Surely you are not suggesting that any woman would be so foolish as to marry that . . . that . . . that roué!" When her aunts merely looked at her, their brows arched, she added, "You *are?"* Constance was aghast at the notion.

Annabelle cleared her throat.

Constance blushed in confusion, fearing she'd be reprimanded by her mentor for correctly using a word she should not have known existed. The throat clearing however was merely a prelude to wishing to speak, and when Freddy smiled at Miss Adams and nodded permission, Annabelle said, "You will recall, Constance, that the gentleman visited your grandmother on more than one occasion."

"A friend of my grandmother's?" asked Constance, doubtfully.

The man had smelled of the liqueur called maraschino, a subject on which her grandmother had once said more than a few treasonous words. That particular incident had occurred after they happened to meet the Prince Regent in the park and Prinny, noticing Constance, had deigned to say a few words to them. Maraschino was the Prince's favorite tipple and, that day, if one were near him, one was unavoidably reminded of that fact. Constance repeated all that.

"More than once, hmm?" said Josephina, ignoring Constance's anecdote. Josephina and Frederica exchanged a long look. "She wouldn't," added Jo in her gruffest voice and then sighed. "Yes she would."

"Oh dear," said Frederica softly. "Had you not better speak with our dear brother, Jo?"

"Yes," responded Josephina, "I believe I had."

"Then you think I have guessed correctly?" asked Annabelle.

Josephina nodded. Once. Firmly. "It is entirely possible."

"But we jested about it!" Constance, staring from one to the other and back again, felt a chill run up her spine. Annabelle shared with her charge a long look. "You *cannot* mean that my grandmother truly meant to marry me off to that awful old man!"

"Not all *that* old," objected Josephina, who knew these things. "Just excessively dissipated. He merely *looks* old. Not that *you* would think him young, of course."

"I think I'll just mention Mrs. Lambsworth to him if he comes around again," said Frederica thoughtfully and then firmly turned the subject.

Constance was too horrified to take the hint. "But what do I do? I won't . . . really, I refuse . . ."

"Shush, child. Your father would never accept that man's suit. You are quite safe." Josephina paused, significantly. "Now."

The implication that before her father came home she was *not* left Constance shaking at what might have been her fate. She shuddered. And, for the remainder of the afternoon, was unusually quiet. She knew her grandmother would go to extreme lengths to get her way. *Could* her father prevent her? Could anyone?

The next afternoon Annabelle strolled behind several young ladies, including Constance, of course, as the girls enjoyed the spring sun in the park. Constance had met the trio at a waltzing party only that morning, had found them congenial and, with the cooperation of the girls' mother and Annabelle, had made the current arrangement.

Annabelle smiled as she listened to the chatter concerning the difficulties of designing a presentation robe when the current style in gowns included an exceedingly high waist and slim skirt. One of Constance's new friends was rather tall and more than a trifle tart on the subject. . . .

". . . so I will look a veritable handbell!" said Miss Charles. "But there is nothing one can do when court etiquette requires those terrible hoops."

"I have never understood how our grandmothers managed them. Have you tried curtsying in yours?" asked a younger Charles girl.

"The hoops are a problem, but I also worry about getting into and out of a coach when not only must one wear hoops but those ridiculously tall plumes in one's hair," said Constance. "Have you . . ."

Annabelle stopped listening, her disobedient mind filling itself with thoughts of her charge's father instead of with her charge. It was harder and harder to remain properly reticent, properly in the background, when the gentleman would insist on drawing one into conversation. And each time he did so, then there would be another of those impossible daydreams that he spoke with her because he liked her, that he was *not* merely doing the polite, but that he *wished* to converse with her. . . .

Annabelle bit her lip. What must Constance's aunts think? Even though they spoke of nothing more intimate than his daughter's needs, still they did speak together often, the colonel requiring regular reports of how everything progressed and what more was needed in the way of clothes or pin money or, he'd suggested, a proper lady's mare for riding in the park. . . . which had included a discussion of a mare for Annabelle so that she, too, could ride.

"At least I had the sense to forbid him to do anything so quixotic!" she muttered.

The girls had stopped, a gentleman approaching them. Annabelle, chiding herself still again for daydreaming when she should not, hurried to catch them up. "Miss Charles? You know this gentleman?" she asked in her most governessy voice.

Miss Charles, the eldest of the three Charles girls, turned. "Oh, Miss Adams, do forgive me for being so impolite and allow me to present my cousin, Mr. Allen Charles. He has begged me to introduce him to Miss Moorhead. Allen, Miss Adams, Miss Moorhead's companion."

"And friend," said Constance, smiling.

Annabelle frankly studied the young man. Not *quite* so young as all that, perhaps? His mid twenties, she guessed, his slim build and light coloring no longer misleading her. "Mr. Charles?"

Mr. Charles smiled an understanding smile. "I am quite presentable, I assure you," he said softly.

"So I should hope!" said Annabelle, but she joined the group as it continued on down the path and finally, with the necessity of keeping a protective eye on Constance, had no difficulty at all keeping her mind on her responsibilities and off a certain gentleman who had the bad manners to creep into her thoughts far more frequently than was either suitable or comfortable.

The happy group approached Rotten Row, where, early as it was, several carriages had been brought out by the truly exceptional weather. One, an old-fashioned landau, pulled up and a gentleman lowered himself gingerly to the ground, and hurried to intercept the small party.

"Miss Moorhead," he said, bowing low. There was a smirk on his face, a greedy look in his eyes, when he straightened and stared at Constance. "Your grandmother requests that I escort you to her carriage," he said and, ignoring the rest of the party, held out his arm.

"Lord Tolbridge?" Annabelle stepped forward. "Lady Morlande wishes Constance to join her? Thank you," she said. "You need not put yourself to the bother of escorting us. I will take Constance. . . ."

Lord Tolbridge turned his head as far as his overly high shirt points would allow. "Miss . . . er . . . I do not believe you were invited," he said, sneering. "Come, Miss Moorhead. You do not wish to keep your grandmother waiting."

Annabelle sent a desperate look around and about and—as if he had appeared merely because she wished it so badly—her gaze met that of Colonel Lord Cranston. When he nodded, it seemed to her almost as if he read her mind.

Lord Cranston touched his roan's sides with his heels and approached the party. He dismounted. "Constance, my dear, do introduce your friends," he said.

"Go away, sirrah," said Tolbridge rudely.

His use of a word rarely heard these days and insulting in tone, had Lord Cranston stiffening even more than his usual military bearing made him appear. "Lord . . . Tolbridge, is it not?"

"I haven't a notion who you might be and I do not care to know. Leave us at once!"

"I think not. Constance? You have yet to introduce your friends." Colonel Lord Cranston smiled at the trio of subdued girls, nodded to the bristling young man, and nodded again to Annabelle.

Constance cleared her throat. "Miss Charles, Miss Mary Charles, and Miss Beth Charles. Oh, and Mr. Allen Charles, their cousin." She drew in a deep breath and, her gaze firmly on her father's face, added, "Father, Lord Tolbridge says that Grandmother wishes him to escort me to her carriage."

The older gentleman gritted his teeth. "Lady Morlande has not mentioned there is a *father!*"

"But there is," said Colonel Lord Cranston in a strangely soft voice. "*I* am Miss Moorhead's father and *I* will escort my daughter to my mother's carriage. You need not detain yourself further."

Tolbridge glared at the colonel, turned on his heel, and glared toward the carriage parked a distance along the Row and, turning back, he gave Constance one further hungry look before, finally, he took himself off.

"What a rude man," said Miss Charles.

"I . . . don't like him," said Constance in a small voice.

"He is not terribly likable," said Mr. Charles soothingly, "but he is gone now and you need not think of him again."

Colonel Lord Moorhead gave the young man a sharp look, caught Annabelle's eye, his brow arching in a question, and when she shrugged ever so slightly, he cleared his throat. "Constance, I know you are enjoying the company of your friends, but I have said I'll escort you to your grandmother and, having said so, I must do so. Make your adieus, my dear."

Constance chattered with the three girls for a moment

and Mr. Charles took the opportunity to ask Annabelle her young lady's address. Annabelle looked toward the colonel for direction. He nodded and Annabelle told Mr. Charles their address. "The Ladies Blackstone hold their at-homes on Wednesday afternoons," she added.

"Thank you. You are an angel in disguise," whispered Mr. Charles, bowing. He moved to Constance's side and said a few words before Constance accepted her father's arm and was led toward her grandmother's carriage. The others watched them go.

"Mr. Charles, I am in a quandary," said Miss Adams. "I have escorted your cousins to the park along with Miss Moorhead and I can safely leave Constance to her father, of course, but I must explain to him that I am responsible for Miss Charles and her sisters before I escort them home. Would you stay with them while I speak with Colonel Lord Cranston?"

"Why do I not escort them home in your place?" asked the young man. He smiled, his eyes twinkling. "It will give me an opportunity to ask them what they know of Miss Moorhead!"

"Allen, how you rattle on!" said Miss Charles. "Such a tease he is, Miss Adams." She smiled. "But we think him a very nice tease and merely ignore him when he becomes overly outrageous."

Miss Adams bit her lip.

"You are concerned that I am not approved by my aunt and uncle? You need have no worries on that score," said Mr. Charles, laughing—but with an understanding look in his eyes. "Come, let us join your Miss Moorhead and her father and you can decide then whether you must accompany us or not."

As the small party moved forward, Colonel Lord Moorhead bowed to his mother and Constance curtsied. They turned and rejoined the small group.

Constance, the girls, and Mr. Charles strolled on together and, hesitating only a moment, Miss Adams accepted the colonel's offered arm. "Do you know this, Mr. Charles?" she asked, glancing up at the man at her side. His well-behaved horse trailed along behind, his reins hanging over the colonel's shoulder.

"A second son, I am informed, and beneath contempt," said the colonel, chuckling. When she glanced up at him he smiled. "As am I, you see."

"Ah. I see." She nodded in a falsely judicious manner but then frowned slightly. "Should I ask the second son of whom?"

"Lord Avondale."

"Lord Avonda—!"

"Shush, my dear. You will embarrass the young man. Yes, a wealthy family. I doubt very much his lordship will leave any of his sons destitute. *My* only question concerns his character. Not that it is of concern at the moment, of course. Now tell me, Miss Adams, what do you think of this dance my daughter tells me is all the rage?"

"The waltz, sir? In the first instance I must support her statement. It *is* the rage. When done properly it is quite beautiful to watch and, I am told, wonderful to perform. There is always the possibility, as with any dance, of it turning into a romp. The problem, of course, is that, because the performers dance only with each other and in something which might be considered a sort of embrace, it can appear quite *improper* under such circumstances."

"Then you do not disapprove?"

Annabelle hesitated. "Shall I be frank?"

"Please."

She smiled. "I am, if you must know, exceedingly jealous! We had no such dancing when I was young!"

"Such an old cat as you are now!"

"My youth is long behind me, sir," she said repressively. "Now do be serious. I believe Constance must be allowed to waltz, once she is approved for it—" When he asked for an explanation of that, she explained the Almack's Patronesses' rules concerning the waltz. "—but I would suggest that we be careful to see that she dances it only with suitable partners. Sir," she added, thinking of one particularly ineligible partner, "if Lord Tolbridge were to ask her for a waltz, I am not entirely certain I would be capable of turning him off."

"He is something of a problem, is he not?" asked the colonel, his eyes on his daughter's laughing countenance as she listened to some tale Mr. Charles told the girls.

"Can you not simply tell him to stay away from Constance?"

"Unfortunately, until he makes clear his intentions, I've no reason for such rudeness."

Annabelle sighed. "No of course you cannot. I did not think."

"Let us discuss something of more interest than that not-so-fine gentleman. I have found a mare for Constance, but I truly do not wish her riding with no more than a groom in attendance. Do you *not* ride, Miss Adams, or is it that you think you *should* not?"

Annabelle felt heat in her throat and face. "I used to ride. But I have no habit and it has been many years since last I sat a horse."

"Oh if that is all!"

They had reached the gates and the subject was allowed to drop since, across the road, the Cranston carriage awaited the girls.

"I must see them home," said Annabelle and then, mentally, kicked herself for the regret she heard in her tone. "Will you, sir, discover what you can of the young man's character? I have been watching Constance and I fear that if she is allowed very much of his company she will soon find herself in deep water where he is concerned."

"Falling in love with him, you mean?"

"Yes. He is a very attractive young man and he makes no secret of the fact that, immediately upon seeing Constance, he developed a partiality for her."

"But he has known her for some time then?" asked a suddenly worried father.

Annabelle tipped up the tiny watch she wore pinned to her pelisse. "Approximately fifty minutes."

"Fif—" Colonel Lord Moorhead broke off. Half a moment later he barked a laugh. And then, another moment passing, he sobered. "But then it can take less than five when the right person appears, can it not?"

"I . . ." About to deny that she thought any such thing, she recalled, as if it were yesterday, her very first introduction to the colonel nearly a dozen years in the past. She found she could not contradict him as she wished to do. Her own partiality for a fine gentleman had begun in very few more minutes than five. "Perhaps. And now I must join the young ladies. Thank you for helping with Lord Tolbridge, sir. I hadn't a notion what to do."

"It was nothing more than coincidence that I was nearby. We must discuss this problem in greater detail, but not now." He snapped his fingers. "We will ask my dear sisters for advice. Ah, Charles," he added as they approached the others, "do you walk to your club in St. James?"

"No sir. I must return to Inns of Court. I am reading for the law and only the wonderful weather tempted me away from my study."

"Our way is still the same. Walk with me." The colonel very nearly laughed at the wry, knowing look the younger man cast first toward Constance and then toward him.

A few more words were spoken and Constance watched her new acquaintance walk off with her father. "He is a very handsome gentleman, is he not?" she asked no one in particular.

"He will be happy to hear you think so," teased Miss Charles. "It was obvious, was it not, that he fell in love with you the moment he set eyes on you?"

"Nonsense," said Constance, her cheeks rosy. "One does not fall in love in a moment!"

"Does one not?" asked Miss Charles slyly and laughed when Constance blushed still more rosily. "Not a word, Mary," she said to her sister, who was giving her killing looks. "I know I must not tease our new friend, but it is such fun, is it not? Watching them sigh and stare at each other and . . ." She put up a hand, laughing. "I will be good." Turning to Miss Adams, she said, "Do tell us how to manage one's hoops when getting into a carriage. I had not thought of that problem, which Miss Moorhead raised"—she glanced at Constance—"and, frankly, she gave me a fright!"

The conversation returned to a discussion of the fast-approaching Queen's Drawing Room and their presentation and Annabelle did her best to satisfy the girls, who had many questions—some of which she could actually answer!

Late that same evening Annabelle went to bed with heavy heart. She had returned home with Constance after attending to some errands only to be pounced on by Miss Frederica Blackstone.

"Just the one we need," that good kind lady had said, smiling gaily. "Come along now."

And having no choice, Annabelle had come, followed by Constance. They entered the back parlor to discover the furniture, excepting the pianoforte, had been removed. So had the carpet. Colonel Lord Cranston stood in the middle of the floor, looking like a small boy who has been up to mischief and is not quite certain how things would turn out.

Now, lying in her bed thinking about all that had followed, Annabelle sighed. Miss Frederica informed the girls that Constance's father wished to learn the waltz. He wished to discover for himself if it was a proper dance for his daughter. And Frederica had decided all by herself that he and Annabelle should learn together since both should understand the new dance.

"And I told him myself that I was jealous of the younger people!" Annabelle muttered into the darkness, half rueful, half distressed.

But it had been as wonderful as she'd expected and she had, once they'd both mastered the simple steps, enjoyed herself.

"Too much. I enjoyed it far too much," she scolded herself.

But she would never forget that hour in which she had danced with his arm around her waist, her hands, one on his shoulder and the other held firmly by his strong long-fingered hand. She had smelled the sandalwood of his soap, felt the warmth of his breath on her forehead, the firm pressure of that hand at her waist as he'd guided her around their barely adequate dance floor.

"Perhaps I do not wish to forget," she murmured and sighed.

It was wrong, so very wrong, to indulge dreams of what could never be. *She* was merely the daughter of a sea captain. It was more than likely that, one day, *he* would be Lord Morlande. The match was far too unbalanced. Colonel Lord Cranston would remarry, certainly . . . but not someone so far below himself in the social order as his daughter's companion—even if she *was* the granddaughter of an earl. Being an earl's granddaughter didn't count when the earl did not acknowledge one.

"I am a fool," she whispered into the dark room. "A fool. I should leave here. Tomorrow. *Now.*"

But she made no move. Even knowing the heartache she would suffer, she could not bring herself to leave the house in which he lived, forego those moments when he might speak to her or smile at her as he'd done as they'd danced.

"Besides, I promised Lady Cranston. . . ."

True enough that she had promised to remain with Constance until her marriage, do what she could to protect the girl . . . but that was a specious argument, was it not? She was no longer needed. Constance's father would protect Constance far more adequately than she herself could ever do!

"But it was a promise. Promises should not be broken."

And with that Annabelle satisfied her better self enough she was able to slip into sleep—where she dreamed of Colonel Lord Cranston as they waltzed the night through.

After all, one could not blame oneself for one's dreams.

Colonel Lord Cranston dreamed as well—and if his dreams involved a trifle more than mere dancing, well he was a man, was he not? Unfair, perhaps, but men have more freedom than women. Even in their dreaming.

Constance's presentation before the queen went very well. She did not require aid from the equerries, stationed there for the purpose, to rise from her curtsy. Nor did she stutter or stammer when one of the princesses drew her aside for a few words. Colonel Lord Cranston was proud of his daughter and gave credit where credit was

due. "You have done very well by Constance, Miss
Adams," he said when he and Miss Josephina returned
to Cranston House with Constance, where Miss
Frederica Blackstone and Miss Adams awaited them.

There had been only one brief incident. Upon hearing
her name, a gentleman, garbed, as required, in the wig
and formal dress of the last century, had glanced around.
He had stared. Constance had glared back until he looked
away. She had glared again when the gentleman appeared
at the Misses Blackstones' next at-home.

"He is so *rude,* Annabelle," said Constance, who had
not heard the gentleman's name. "He stared at me at my
presentation and now he stares at you."

Annabelle colored up. "Shush, my dear," she said,
turning back to listen to the eldest Miss Charles tease
her younger sisters, all of whom had been presented together, about their presentation. But Annabelle could not,
no matter how she tried, ignore the presence of her
grandfather, who was who the rude man was, nor stop
herself from wondering why he had come.

Happily, for her curiosity was very near to overcoming
her, she heard Miss Josephina's deep voice call her name.
Annabelle excused herself from the group of young girls
and moved gracefully across the salon to join the group
seated by the fireplace, where a small fire made a cheery
note although was not really needed.

"Yes, Miss Blackstone? May I do something for
you?"

"You may be seated," said Josephina in her blunt way.
"This is your grandfather, Lord Fortesque, come to make
your acquaintance."

The elderly gentleman reddened up to his ears. "My
dear Miss Josephina!"

"Well? Is there another reason you are here?"

He harrumphed, but admitted there was not.

"I am one who calls a spade a spade and never a

shovel," said Miss Josephina and then changed her mind concerning the two. "Miss Adams, do *not* sit. The two of you will get on far better without me. Or anyone. I suggest you take Lord Fortesque to the library, Miss Adams."

Annabelle blushed still more furiously than her grandfather. She cast him a look, rolled her eyes, and politely asked, "We appear to have been given our orders, sir. Will you accompany me?"

He harrumphed again, bowed to the two Blackstone ladies, and followed Miss Adams from the room. When they arrived in the library, he stared at her from under bristly brows. "So like her."

"Like my mother? Am I?" asked Annabelle wistfully.

"Very." Lord Fortesque grimaced. "I was a fool, my dear. Will you forgive me and give me an opportunity to become acquainted with you? I cannot ask that you love me as I wish you could. I was too mean-spirited, too stubbornly demanding of my own way, and do not expect to be forgiven to the extent that you will love me." He held up his hand when she would have responded. "Please tell me how my daughter fared before you tell me you never wish to see my face again."

Annabelle, who had been about to say no such thing, smiled. "She and my father loved each other very much. It saddened her when she thought of you, sir, of the estrangement between you, but her joy in my father's company made up for a great deal."

"But he, a sea captain, must have been gone most of their life together. How could she bear it?"

Annabelle's brows rose. "You did not know? She sailed with him, of course. I, too, when the voyage was not a long one."

"Ah. I see." He was silent for a moment. "Knew she died at sea."

"They died together as they would have wished to do."

"And you?"

"I was with my grandparents. They did their best for me."

He nodded and sighed. "One Season"—he smiled—"I was convinced you would have Hobart and lost a bet to that effect."

Annabelle bit back sarcastic words. That he had known of her Season and not come forward was bad enough. That he had actually bet on her decision to wed or not wed the rotund bore, the only man to offer hand and hearth but not his heart, was disgusting. An unworthy glee that he'd lost salved her wounded pride. When she was sure she could control of her voice, she said, "I was unaware you knew of my Season, sir."

He sighed again. "My exceedingly ridiculous stubbornness."

She could not keep back a chuckle at his self-deriding expression. "You have had a change of heart, my lord?"

He nodded. "Perhaps it is that I gain wisdom in my old age. I want you to come live with me, Annabelle, if you can bring yourself to forgive me to that extent. I do not entertain a great deal, but I am not an utter recluse. You will have pin money for your fripperies and may buy your gowns from the very best modistes and . . ."

Annabelle held up a hand. "Sir, I hold no animosity toward you. Mother would not allow it, even when I said you had been unfair to her. Which you were!"

He tried to speak but she shook her head.

"I would come to you now if I could but I am bound."

His brows rose, forming high arches. "Bound!"

"By a promise to Lady Cranston, who died worrying about her child. I cannot leave Constance until she is wed. I will not." She paused, and forced herself to make the only sensible decision. "But, if you will have me then . . . ?"

"I will wait impatiently for word of your charge's nuptials!"

She nodded. "There is one thing, sir . . ."

"Can you not bring yourself to call me Grandfather?" he interrupted.

Annabelle stiffened slightly. "I will try. As I was about to say, Grandfather"—the appellation came with obvious difficulty—"I must stipulate one thing."

"Stipulations, is it?"

"Yes. I can, you see, be quite as stubborn as you." She smiled to take some of the sting from that. "I will *not* have you attempting to marry me off to the man of your choice! I am fully adult and you cannot force me. If you've any plans in that direction, then we will forget the whole business and I will find another position once this one is ended."

He barked a laugh. "Don't want me throwing you out on your ear as I did your mother, hmm? Well, no fear. Not only is that a lesson well learned, but"—he sobered—"my dear, you are not merely legally an adult."

"You would say I am firmly on the shelf." She nodded. "Very likely true, sir . . . Grandfather," she amended when his brows rose, "but you must be aware that no woman gives up all hope even when at her last prayers!"

They laughed together and it was thus that Constance found them when she tapped at the door and entered the library.

"Ah! How very wonderful. Lady Jersey is here and she asked after you, Annabelle, wishing to know how you go on."

Lord Fortesque growled. "That busybody! Cannot leave a man in peace!"

"Had she a hand in your coming today?" asked Annabelle, stiffening once again.

He, too, straightened. "Not until *after* I had decided all on my own I wished to know you!"

"Then that is all right," said Annabelle. "I would not wish you to feel you'd a duty to me and that you must, whatever your own feelings, do that duty."

"I made my decision when I saw your charge at the Queen's Drawing Room. So you see, it is not merely wishing to do my duty. I like you," he added in some surprise. "I thought I would," he added a trifle complacently.

"Lady Jersey?" asked Constance, looking from one to the other.

"Shall we allow her to believe she played a winning hand and brought us together, sir?" Annabelle cast her grandfather a mischievous look.

" 'Twon't matter if we do or don't," he grumbled. "Her interfering ladyship will take the credit willy-nilly!"

Again they laughed.

Once again Constance gestured toward the door and began to speak, but his lordship waved her to silence.

"We are agreed then?"

Annabelle nodded. "When my work here is done, I will come."

Constance felt instant alarm. Annabelle meant to leave her? Go to her grandfather? *Not if I can bring my father up to scratch,* she thought.

But his lordship, knowing nothing of Constance's plans, merely nodded and rose to his feet, holding his hand to help Annabelle rise. He offered his arm, she took it, and Constance, wishing to observe the faces in the salon when the two entered, followed closely on their heels. The expressions, she noted, were quite as interesting as expected. And perhaps the very best of all was

Lady Morlande's. Her grandmother's jaw dropped in shock, followed by a touch of horror. "No . . ."

"Everyone," said Lord Fortesque blandly, "I would like to introduce to you my granddaughter, Miss Annabelle Adams, friend and companion to my old friends' niece." He cast a smile at the Ladies Blackstone as he drew Constance forward. "Today it has been my privilege to meet two very nice young ladies." He bowed first to Annabelle and then to Constance.

The despised servant had been acknowledged by the earl! Lady Morlande didn't quite faint, but she came very near to doing so.

Colonel Lord Cranston joined his small family before dinner as had become his custom. He stood near the fireplace, tall and straight, in the best military style, and, seemingly, listened to Miss Frederica. Really, he had an ear cocked to the serious conversation between his daughter and her mentor. A tiny smile touched his mouth, tipping his lips only the least little bit, when he heard Constance ask, rather breathlessly, he thought, how one knew one was in love. He put up a finger when Freddy attempted to draw his attention, and, listening further, was not merely pleased, but filled with admiration at Miss Adam's sensible response.

Love. It was not an emotion he'd known to any great degree. Certainly there had been no maternal love from his mother. For Constance? Yes, of course, his child was loved and loving, but the tender feeling had *not* been a part of his marriage. That was arranged for him and his wife by his mother and her father. Neither had had a say in it. And, although they had never been estranged—unlike his brother and his wife—their early relationship had begun with no more than mutual respect. Only as time passed and their letters crossed in long-delayed posts, had a sort of friendship developed.

But nothing beyond it. No more than that quiet warmth one had for a friend. Rath found he felt a trifle forlorn over all the wasted years. He sighed softly, wishing things might have been otherwise.

But not so softly that kindhearted Miss Frederica did not hear. "What is it, Brother?" she asked her dead sister's widower.

Her words caught his wandering thoughts, pulling them up short. He blinked, bringing his full attention to the plump little lady seated before him. "What is what, Freddy?"

"What is bothering you?"

His eyes jumped to where Annabelle and Constance, heads together, continued their discussion. He looked down at Miss Frederica. "It is a huge responsibility, is it not? Seeing to a daughter's future?"

"It should be," said Frederica. For her, the words were spoken tartly.

"You are thinking of my mother."

She nodded. She did *not* speak the unfilial thought, *And my father.*

"She firmly believes she did her best for my sisters."

"But Morningside! She *must have known* his character! And Shirebourn. If she'd asked only a few questions she'd have known he drank to excess. And Thurston of all men. That utter bore! How could she not consider her daughter's lives with such men?"

Rath sighed. "To my mother's way of thinking, status and income are everything. You know that. Think of my own bride," he added a trifle mischievously.

"A huge dowry, yes, but no particular status," said Frederica, her voice taking on a touch of her sister's gruffness.

"Ah! But I am only a second son and Mother could

not have predicted that my brother and his wife would take each other in such abhorrence they would separate before the wedding visits were complete! Actually, I was the luckiest of all of us, was I not? Your sister, Frederica, was a very nice woman."

"But not the love of your life." Again there was a touch of that gruffness one expected from Josephina rather than Frederica.

Rath sighed, his eyes trailing to where the two younger ladies had joined Miss Josephina. "No," he agreed, "but then, I was never the love of her life either."

Frederica was not so certain of that as was Rath, but she did not attempt to say so. If her sister had truly loved her husband, would she not have followed him and lived near to where his orders took him? She had never done so, so perhaps the notion her sister's feelings for Rath were warmer than his for her was wrong.

Dinner was announced and their discussion was, perforce, ended. Frederica, noticing how warmly he looked at Miss Adams, vowed she would do her best to arrange *two* weddings during this spring Season. Constance would be made safe from her grandmother's plots and Rath would, finally, wed for love rather than advantage.

Frederica, before going to her bed that night, said as much to her sister, who did not, as Frederica had expected, scoff at the notion.

"I am surprised at you, Freddy," said Josephina mildly.

"Surprised?"

"That you have come up with such a sensible notion. Miss Adams has discovered her grandfather, but they can, at this late date, never be particularly close. There is too much bad history. Far better she wed the colonel. Yes, a very good notion, indeed. We must think how to bring it about."

"You mean, Jo, that we should scheme as did his mother and once again marry him off willy-nilly?"

Josephina looked down her nose at her sister. "Your sense of humor has once again led you into error, Frederica!"

Frederica grinned in a manner well known to her family. "You must admit we think, as did she, to Know What Is Best."

Josephina snorted in an exceedingly unladylike fashion. "There is a difference, Freddy. We *do* know best."

Frederica put her hands over her mouth to hold back giggles and even Josephina smiled.

"Well," she amended, still smiling at Frederica, "I *hope* we do. I hope very much that we do!"

While Josephina and Frederica laid a few preliminary plots, Rath himself lay on his back and stared at the ceiling, which the new gas lamps in the street outside his open window painted a mellow yellow. Not that he saw the ceiling, of course. What he saw was a vision of Miss Adams, her new gown revealing her form in a manner the dresses Lady Morlande demanded she wear had not. A surprisingly pleasing form, he mused. In fact, Miss Adams was a surprising woman in many ways.

There was that quick intelligence. He had always admired intelligent women—perhaps in contrast to his mother whom he could *not* admire. A sadness touched him at the thought but he put it aside for the far more pleasing dreams of a youngish woman who, he thought, would fit into his arms with wonderful comfort. Dancing with her had only emphasized that she was just the right height, just the right shape. . . .

The waltz! They had danced so that they could determine if it was a proper dance for Constance, and Rath was suddenly certain it was not. *Not if my thoughts are anything like those that other men think when dancing the waltz!*

He made a mental note to discuss the problem with Josephina and returned to happier notions. Once Constance was married, then Miss Adams would be free to . . . to do other things. Would she . . . ? Might he . . . ? Was it at all possible that they . . . ?

Reluctantly, Rath decided it would be far better if he did not think of Miss Adams in those delightfully intimate terms. Nothing could be arranged until after Constance stepped into Parson's Mousetrap. And there was her grandfather. *Almost* Rath regretted the rapprochement between Miss Adams and Lord Fortesque. And then he berated himself for selfishness. Miss Adams had had no one but herself on whom she could depend for a very long time. It was good she had reconciled with her grandfather—at least Rath tried very hard to convince himself it was so!

And yet—a neat little house? In Chelsea, perhaps? Complete with discreet staff? A quiet neighborhood and an adequate trust in which she'd hold a life interest? Would she perhaps . . . ? He sighed and scolded himself still again. He really *must* stop thinking of Miss Adams in such terms. She was a *lady*.

Not that ladies did not . . . Rath gave himself a further lecture, firmly turned his thoughts to his daughter, and soon drifted off to sleep . . . to dream of a small house in Chelsea occupied by an intelligent lady who welcomed his company whenever he came to her!

Constance sighed happily and looked over at the small boat beside theirs in which a guitarist, a flautist, and a rather old-fashioned lute in the hands of experts, produced one newly popular waltz after another. Then she turned back to the others. "Is it not glorious?" she asked.

"I hoped you would enjoy it." Mr. Charles smiled. He sat across from her, his cousin, Miss Charles beside him.

Constance looked around. In still another boat her father and Annabelle were rowed across the Thames with Mr. Charles's parents. Constance felt an inward shudder—a not totally uncomfortable sensation, although one might think such should be.

This particular sort of shudder was composed of such elements as anticipation of the pleasures of Vauxhall Gardens, a faintly fearsome concern that Mr. Charles's parents, the earl and countess, might not like her, and a touch of confusion that Annabelle had tried very hard to beg off when she learned that Colonel Lord Cranston would accompany his daughter.

Luckily Auntie Jo had overheard and pooh-poohed Annabelle's suggestion she would not be needed.

Constance turned a smile back toward Mr. Charles. So handsome. So very nice. So attentive to her comfort . . . And he seemed to like her, which was quite wonderful when Constance was already certain she liked him a great deal more than she ought.

In the other boat taking the party across the Thames to the Gardens' water gate the colonel found sitting so near Miss Adams more than a trifle distracting, but he had a duty to do as a guest and did his best to ignore the warmth of her arm where it rested against his and the distinctive scent that drifted from her and which could, thanks to their proximity, occasionally be experienced even though the river's pungent odor did its best to thwart him in that respect. But his *duty*. He replied to an innocuous comment by his hostess but was interrupted by Lord Avondale.

"Pooh, Sarah! The colonel is not interested in your new gown! Sir," barked his lordship, "do tell me what you think of the government's latest idiocy! What can they be thinking?" He harrumphed—half disgust and half a laugh. "More than likely they are *not* thinking!"

"Which particular idiocy have you in mind?" asked

the colonel and hoped the reading he'd done since his return to England was sufficient to allow him to hold up his end of a political conversation.

"Do you refer to the iniquitous import duties on grain, my lord?" asked Annabelle softly. "I am exceedingly concerned that the poor will starve this coming winter if our government does not relent."

"Not that." Another harrumph. "But it *will* be hard on many. Ah! But the debts! We must pay off the war debts, you know. Money has to come from somewhere!"

Annabelle looked at the jewels gracing Lady Avondale's neck and then down at her own hands.

"I myself," continued his lordship, "am encouraging my neighbors to hold back some of their crops for distribution this winter. I've a granary set aside for that purpose. If you've not yet thought of it, Lord Cranston, perhaps you might wish to order your agent to do likewise."

Lord Cranston, who had thought of little but his daughter—except when his mind was occupied with Miss Adams—since arriving in England, nodded. It was a good notion. "I'll send orders to that effect tomorrow. Thank you for suggesting it. I have a great deal to learn now I am home again. My"—he hesitated only a moment—"wife was very good at such things and I did not worry about the estate when I was away. I knew it was in good hands, but now . . ."

"Ah yes," said Lady Avondale, a quiet sympathy to be heard in her tone. "She died last year, did she not?"

The colonel nodded. "Yes. I was in India and by the time I'd word she was ill it was too late to return before she succumbed." They were silent for a moment and then Rath smiled. "But such melancholy thoughts must have no part in tonight's festivities. I met your son in the park one day recently and walked with him as far as St. James. A very sensible young man I thought."

Lord Avondale frowned and his wife chuckled. "My husband wished him to go into the Church, but he has had no interest but the law ever since he first began helping his father with his work. Avondale is the magistrate in our district, you see."

"He says he will soon be finished with his studies and means to take up the silk."

"Harrumph. Not certain I approve. Never been a Charles in the law," said his lordship a trifle pettishly. "Been many in the Church."

"I am the first military man in my family. I suspect there is often a twig that bends away from the family tree's pattern and perhaps it is for the best. One has a foot in many camps that way."

Lord Avondale's eyebrows arched, then lowered, and for a moment he was silent. "Something," he said, although with obvious reluctance, "in what you say."

Rath glanced toward the other boat, which was nearing the landing. He frowned slightly, a trifle worried that there might be difficulty getting four young ladies ashore when only one gentleman attended them, and then found himself impressed by young Charles's handling of the difficult situation. Was this the young man his daughter would accept for her husband? Rath had had several hints that that was what *Mr. Charles* hoped! Allen Charles was not a man to allow grass to grow under his feet but had spoken like a sensible man—and a caring one.

The evening progressed as such evenings do progress. Quiet, keeping herself in the background except when Rath or Lady Avondale brought her into the conversation, Annabelle tried very hard not to wish she were truly the colonel's partner for the evening. There was also the problem of keeping an eye on Constance without seeming to play propriety with too heavy a hand. It was some time before she realized that young Mr. Charles was tactfully keeping just as firm an eye on his cousins.

One potentially bad situation occurred when his middle cousin attempted to pull the other young ladies into the Dark Walk, a notorious path down which a man might lead his *chère amie* for a bit of slap and tickle, behavior a young and innocent girl should know nothing about. Annabelle was amused but also impressed by Mr. Charles's handling of the contretemps. She said as much to him. He cast her a rueful look.

"Not quite the evening to which you looked forward?" she teased.

The rue deepened. "I thought Miss Moorhead might find it more relaxing if my cousins were present. I must remember to be less shortsighted in future."

"I suspect your first thoughts were the best. She is enjoying herself more than she expected when she learned Lord and Lady Avondale were to be among your guests. I noticed your mother talking to her when you went to request that particular song from the orchestra."

"Ah. I didn't know anyone was aware," he said, coloring. "I know it is a favorite with Miss Moorhead."

"Buying the ladies posies was also a very nice thought. I have noticed Constance touching hers and looking at it more often than she might such a token bought her by her father, for instance!"

"You, I believe, are my friend," he said, eyeing her. "Will not Lord Cranston wish to look higher than my poor self for her husband? Not," he added, "that she does not deserve the very highest in the land!"

"No, you are wrong," said Annabelle, jesting. "She deserves far better than the *highest* in the land!"

Rath, overhearing the last of this exchange, cast a quick look around to see if anyone had heard Annabelle's near-treasonous comment concerning the royal dukes. He breathed a sigh of relief as he joined the pair. "I see the young ladies are impatient to see the lady walking the tightrope, Mr. Charles. Perhaps you could tell them her history?"

When Allen Charles excused himself to Annabelle and moved to join the young ladies, Rath warned Annabelle to watch her tongue. "No one was near, so you will not find yourself clapped into the Tower, but that might not be the case in the future."

Annabelle blushed furiously. " 'Twas but a jest, but a thoughtless one. The sort of thing one may say among friends. Close friends. Mr. Charles is so very easy to talk to that I relaxed my guard too far."

"You approve of him? For Constance, I mean?"

She drew in a deep breath, wondering if she dared be frank with him. Since Constance's future happiness was involved, she decided to chance it. "Yes," she said. "He is just the sort of upright young man her mother and I hoped she'd meet. He is intelligent without being priggish. His humor is never hurtful of another. He is thoughtful. You noticed how he ordered a footstool for his mother when he saw she found her chair too high for comfort? I think that a good indication of how he'd treat a wife."

"Well . . . it is early days, of course. Altogether too soon in fact! I admit," said Rath pensively, "that I find myself a trifle selfish. I have just returned to·discover I've a delightful daughter and, simultaneously discover I must lose her to another before I've any time with her." He glanced down at Miss Adams. "I have done my duty over the years, but I have lost a great deal by doing so, have I not?"

"You have." A trifle diffidently, she added, "Surely you have given enough of your life to the Crown?" She drew a deep breath. "Can you not retire from the army and enjoy a home life now?" Fearing that might have been too forward, too suggestive of her dreams, she quickly added, "You may lose a daughter, but you may gain grandchildren and I cannot think you will wish to be a stranger to them!"

"No, I would not! But grandchildren! She is still a child herself!" Then he smiled ruefully. "I am a bit of a fool, am I not, to have such thoughts when she has reached an age to wed? Shall I tell you a secret, Miss Adams? I have given in my resignation at the Horse Guards, but please do not speak of it. My mother, who hated my taking up colors, will now be just as hateful about my abandoning them! I wish to avoid that scene as long as possible!"

Annabelle chuckled. "She is a perverse lady, is she not?"

Rath grinned. "What an exceedingly deft manner of speaking of her *difficult* nature. What a shame it is that women are not allowed a place in our diplomatic corps. You would immediately rise to ambassadorial rank, I am sure!"

Annabelle blushed. "I am not always so tactful, my lord," she replied and then, as Lord and Lady Avondale, who had crossed the green to another box to speak to friends, rejoined them, she once again effaced herself. It was not proper for a mere companion to put herself forward! Which thought reminded Annabelle of Constance. She craned her neck, located the young people talking and laughing with some friends of Mr. Charles's, and kept her eye on them all, watching that mere high spirits did not lead to them into going beyond the line.

After the fireworks the party returned to their boats, recrossed the river, and after they had given appropriate thanks to Mr. Charles for arranging such a delightful entertainment, Rath closed the carriage door on Annabelle and Constance. He walked along Parliament Street toward Whitehall, where he would find a hack to take him to his club and wasn't at all surprised when Mr. Charles joined him.

"Well, cub?" asked the colonel.

"I hope it went well. Do you think she enjoyed it?"

"I believe everyone enjoyed themselves," answered the father.

Allen sighed. "Very tactful but hardly helpful. Sir," he asked straight out, "do you object to my courting your daughter?"

Rath chuckled but inside felt a sadness he didn't entirely understand. "I doubt you've been taught to be so frank when dealing with legal matters. I always find anything a solicitor has a hand in complicated beyond belief," he said, evading an immediate response.

Allen laughed. "Ah! But I mean to be a barrister. Not that that too can not involve obfuscation! Muddling the waters is what keeps us in work, is it not? But you have not answered. Would you prefer to know me better before making up your mind?"

"No," said Rath, slowly. "That isn't the problem." He explained much of what he'd said earlier to Annabelle.

Allen nodded. "Yes. I see. Can you not think of it as gaining a son rather than losing a daughter?" he asked with patently false innocence.

Rath smiled but the sensitive would have noticed it was not wholehearted. "I will not make difficulties if you are Constance's choice, young Charles. I have long experience of judging newly arrived subalterns. However ambivalent I feel about losing my daughter, I admit I would rate you highly if you were one of them."

"Thank you," said Allen quietly, knowing it a high compliment indeed.

They soon went their separate directions, Rath to his club and Allen to his rooms in the Albany, the identical set of rooms leased by Beau Brummel before scandal and debts forced him to flee England. Rath, arriving at his club, was asked to join a table playing whist, one of the gentlemen taking his leave just then. He did so and very soon wished he had not. He found what he really wanted was to return home, join the family for a last cup of tea, and take himself up to bed.

"Getting old," he muttered.

"Hmm?" asked the man to his left.

"Nothing. Nothing at all—I believe that is *my* trick," he added, when the man to his right began to gather it in.

The next morning Constance dallied over her breakfast until her father appeared. "Well, puss," he said, "this is nice. Did you enjoy Vauxhall Gardens as much as you thought to do?"

She nodded. "Oh yes, it was delightful, was it not?" The faintest of frowns remained to mar her usually serene brow.

"Something bothers you, my sweet." All sorts of notions ran through Rath's mind, including the thought that Allen Charles had, somehow, managed to insult his daughter—but common sense soon told him there was no time during the preceding evening when the two had not been thoroughly chaperoned and that the notion was idiotic. When she didn't respond to his hint that he was willing to listen, he asked, "Can you not tell me?"

She sighed. "It is silly, I suppose."

"Nonsense. Couldn't possibly be! I've a most practical daughter!"

She smiled at his jesting tone but it wasn't her usual merry expression and it quickly faded. "It is Mother's birthday," she said after a moment.

Rath's brows arched. "Why . . . so it is." He waited. When she said nothing, he asked, "Are you merely sad, thinking about your mother?"

She drew in a long breath, let it out, glanced at him,

and then sighed again. "I would like to take flowers to her grave."

Rath set down the teacup he'd held in both hands. "But, my dear! You must know it is too far a drive to Landon Hall," he said, naming his brother's estate.

"Oh, but she is not there," said Constance, her eyes glistening. "Grandmother said it was all nonsense and had her buried here in London. Those last months we lived here, you see, so as to be near her doctor."

For a moment Rath stilled. Something in him boiled up and his disgust and anger with his mother very nearly overcame his control. Then, seeing his daughter's eyes widen, he very carefully forced himself to relax—first his fists and then, bit by bit, the rest of him. "Of course we will take flowers to her grave, Constance, if that is what you wish. Will Miss Adams wish to accompany us?"

"Would it be very bad of me to want just us?" she asked in a small voice.

Rath smiled. "Not at all, child. Can you be prepared to leave in"—he calculated what must be done—"half an hour?"

An hour later Rath looked down at the paltry stone his mother had had set at the head of his wife's grave and anger once again rose to choke him. His wife. For a long moment grief swept through him. Sorrow for the woman. Perhaps a trifling bit of pity for himself. He remained silent as Constance knelt for a long moment, her hand on the stone. Then his daughter looked up. He offered his hand and she took it, rising to stand beside him.

"My dear," he said softly, "she should not be here. I will arrange that she rests with our family where she belongs."

Constance seemed to relax something inside her he'd not known was wound up. She smiled one of her glorious smiles. "Thank you. I had hoped . . . I wasn't certain it could be done. . . ."

"It can and will be done," he said, determined to see to it the instant he returned Constance to Miss Adams's care. "I will consult my solicitor to see how it may be managed."

A few days later Rath stood by while the grave was opened. He stared down at the box the diggers revealed and something inside him stilled.

"My wife," he muttered. "My wife is *dead*," he said slowly.

For the very first time it was real for him. They had been separated throughout most of their marriage and, even though he had known in his mind that she was dead, *emotionally* it was very much as if, as usual, she was merely elsewhere. Rath could not deeply grieve for the woman he'd known mostly through letters, but he was filled with a sudden sense of loss, an unexpected feeling of loneliness.

Rath was very nearly silent throughout the journey into Sussex to his brother's estate, where, Lord Morlande at his side, he watched the casket reinterred, his brother's vicar saying the proper words and offering up a prayer for Lady Cranston.

Rath stayed a few precious days with his brother and discovered he actually liked the man. They had been so different in their youth and there had been their mother to set them at odds whenever it seemed possible they might actually become friends.

His brother's last words to him, coming as they did from nothing at all, stayed with him the whole of his journey back to London. "This is not the time to say it, but, Rath, you must remarry." Rupert lay a hand on Rath's arm. "The succession must be seen to."

Marry? he asked himself. For the first time it occurred to him he was free to do so.

He arrived back in London in time to change into evening gear in order to escort the ladies under his protection to Almack's for Constance's first appearance there. "Excited, child?" he asked—and thought that she looked anything but a child in the pearl-embroidered gown with the neckline down to *there*. He frowned slightly, wondering if he should object, order her to change into a more modest evening dress.

Reading his mind, Miss Josephina barked a rough laugh. "She is all the crack, Rath, as the children say these days."

"What," asked Constance, a mischievous smile twitching at her lips, "did they say in other days?"

Josephina allowed her brows to arch.

"In our day," said her father, "we claimed to be dressed to the nines."

"And we would add," said Miss Frederica, "that one looked rich as Midas. From where," she continued, "do these expressions come?"

Josephina chuckled her deep laugh. "I will remind you that this began when I suggested our Constance looks like an angel and that her appearance is perfect." She caught her brother-in-law's eye. "It is true, you know."

"But . . ."

"She looks just as every other young lady will look," said Annabelle softly and then, her pride in Constance speaking, added, "only *better.*"

Constance blushed. "Father?"

"I have been away from London too many years," he said only a trifle plaintively. "To my fond eyes you look exceedingly lovely, my dear, but a trifle . . . er . . . underdressed?"

They all laughed. Even Colonel Lord Cranston.

They were not among the first arrivals that evening, but climbed the stairs and entered the long low room well before the doors were closed against all comers. A cotillion was in progress and, after a few words to Lady Sefton and Mrs. Drummond Burrell, who were greeting guests that evening, they found a place along the wall, saw a few friends to whom they nodded, but were soon surrounded by young men who had made their way to where Constance stood between her father and Miss Josephina.

The first gentleman to reach them asked for the next dance and Josephina was about to nod when Rath said no. "I mean to have my daughter's first dance at Almack's, young sir. You must wait your turn!"

The gentleman looked a trifle chagrined, but, perforce, gave way gracefully and agreed to the country dance following the quadrille that would follow the cotillion currently in progress. All too soon Constance had given away all her dances but the waltzes, which she was content to forbid as was demanded of a young lady not yet approved by the patronesses as suitably well behaved and mature and therefore allowed to indulge in that dangerous dance.

And then she paled.

"What is it?" asked Annabelle, noticing.

"Mr. Charles! He just followed my grandmother into the room."

"Are you surprised to see him? He has come with his cousins, has he not?"

"Oh no, it is not that, but, Annabelle, I've no more dances!"

"Ah. Then he will offer to sit with you during one of the waltzes."

Constance smiled gratefully at her mentor. "I had not thought of that."

"I think I should warn you, since you've no eyes for anyone but your friends"—Annabelle very slightly emphasized the word "friends," subtly warning Constance she was making a cake of herself by staring at the young man—"that your grandmother has Mrs. Lambsworth and Lord Tolbridge with her. And they are coming this way." When Constance still didn't look away from the Charles's party, Annabelle pinched the girl's arm. "Take care, child!"

Constance's gaze drifted and she saw her grandmother. "Oh!" She moved closer to her father, who, when she took his arm, looked around. He saw his mother approaching, the much-married Lord Tolbridge escorting her, another unknown lady on his lordship's other arm. Lady Morlande looked particularly smug and Rath, knowing that expression, straightened his already military-trained straight-backed stance.

"Good evening, Mother," he said politely. "I suspect the patronesses were surprised to see you. *Unsurprised,* however, to see that gown. I recall it from before I left for India."

"An excellent fabric and years more wear in it," said Lady Morlande with pride. She hadn't a notion she'd been insulted since she firmly believed the current practice of filling one's wardrobe with gown after gown was ridiculous. One chose a fabric that would wear, could be worked into the simplest of styles, and could be worn to a variety of kinds of parties. That should be quite sufficient for anyone, in her ladyship's opinion. "Constance, you will give Lord Tolbridge two of your dances. Three would be better."

Three? Announce to the world that she and Lord Tolbridge were engaged? Feeling both panic that she could not obey her grandmother and *relief* that she could not, she said, "I've none left!"

"None?" Lady Morlande got that look that meant she could easily throw a tantrum, something dreaded by all. "When you knew very well you must save your most important suitor his dances?" She drew in a deep breath, controlling her temper with difficulty. "Very well, then, it is quite simple. You will simply tell two partners that you forgot you'd already given their dances to his lordship."

"She will do no such thing, Mother," said Colonel Lord Cranston firmly. "In the first place, Lord Tolbridge is not a suitor." He was in charity with his mother for the moment since she'd offered an opportunity to make that clear. "Constance is far too young for such as he. Besides, I've no wish to marry her off any time in the immediate future." He cast a quick look toward Tolbridge, who bridled, two spots of color appearing to stain his cheekbones. "You have another guest this evening?" continued Rath when he was certain Tolbridge had understood his message even if his mother would pretend she had not.

For a moment her ladyship's reaction hung in the balance, but this was Almack's and Lady Morlande was forced to swallow her ire that her son played the marplot when any idiot could see that Tolbridge was the very best catch available that Season. She gritted her teeth and then recalled the second string to her bow. "Mrs. Lambsworth." She clutched the lady's arm and pulled her forward to stand before Rath. The woman looked up at the colonel, blushed rosily, and batted her short stubby eyelashes at him. "Well, looby? Ask her to dance!"

"I dance only with my daughter," said Rath quickly, angry that he must forego dancing with Annabelle as he had hoped to do after his dance with Constance.

His mother, he realized, meant to foist another bride on him but he'd have none of her choosing! His more beneficent mood toward her faded. A bride he needed. A bride he *wanted*. But she would be *his* choice.

He drew his mother aside and told her just that. "And do not make a scene, my lady mother, or . . ."

"Or what? You will forbid me the pleasure of Constance's company? Or something equally ridiculous that will make the family a laughingstock before all the world?"

"I don't know exactly what I'll do, but you will cease your matchmaking for the both of us or it is likely to be something regrettable."

She scowled. "Very likely you will wed to disoblige the family," she said sourly. "Make a complete cake of yourself by choosing a young chit with no dowry and very few looks and no status in the ton at all. Merely to spite me!"

"Since you have never understood the tenderer emotions, you think they do not exist. And you judge everyone by their blood and how well their pockets are lined. By doing so, you have made each of your children miserable. But I am fully adult now and not under your thumb. You have no justification for interfering in my life. You will cease attempting to do so. Good evening, Mother. It is time for my dance with my daughter."

Rath bowed to her and moved back to where Constance and Annabelle were in stilted conversation with Mrs. Lambsworth while the Misses Josephina and Frederica spoke in hushed tones to Lord Tolbridge, who frowned down at them—but nevertheless listened to all they had to say and, at one point, cast a speculative glance toward Mrs. Lambsworth.

Constance had not expected to enjoy the set with her father, but found he was an accomplished dancer who never put a foot wrong. Better yet, he led her through the complicated figures with a confidence lacking in many a younger partner with whom she'd danced at the two ton balls she'd attended. At the end they curtsied and bowed and Rath offered his arm.

"There," he said. "Not so bad as you expected, was it?"

She laughed. "No. In fact I am of the opinion I should

tell all my partners that I only dance with my father. I will monopolize all your dances from now on!"

"Even if Mr. Charles asks for a dance?" asked Rath, teasing her.

Constance blushed, looked to where the Charles party had joined their own, and blushed more furiously.

"Ah," said her father softly, "I have discomposed you. I am sorry. Should we walk around the floor until you feel more collected?"

She smiled up at him gratefully. "Am I so ill-bred that everyone will see how much I . . . *admire* Mr. Charles?"

"Likely no one will notice. It is just that I am particularly noticing where you are concerned, my dear. May I ask that you carefully consider more than the fact the young man is presentable as to looks and smoothly conversable?"

"His parents?" She frowned. "But surely he comes from a good family?"

"Oh yes. Even my mother cannot object to his family. She might cavil at his having an older brother, but I do not. My dear, it is his character and his interests you must determine. In *any* man you think you might wish to wed."

She nodded. "Yes. Mother said it is a good thing if one can be a friend to one's spouse. That friendship lasts longer than that first hot feeling a girl is likely to experience when she meets certain men. She said that is a feeling that is likely to fade as one becomes acquainted and knows more of the man's character."

"And did you experience that, er, hot feeling for Mr. Charles?"

Constance frowned. "Not exactly. Not if I understood Mother. But I am so very comfortable with him. He does not frighten me as some men do but makes me feel protected and happy." She looked up at her father. "Is that a good thing, Father?"

Rath felt as if his cravat were far too tight and wished Miss Adams were walking on his daughter's other side. He had not felt embarrassed up to that point, but now he was uncertain as to what he should respond. It seemed to him that what Constance felt was the prelude to falling in love with Allen Charles. Deeply and earnestly in love, rather than into the far shallower emotion of an infatuation. He sighed.

"Father?"

"Most certainly it is not a bad thing, child. But do not hurry into any decisions. Time will tell you if Mr. Charles is the man for you."

She nodded again. "Yes, that is what Mother said. She said I must not make too quick a decision since my whole life rested on the outcome."

Rath glanced at the top of his daughter's head. "Your mother was an exceedingly wise woman, Constance. Do not forget her words."

Constance glanced up. It was her mischievous look and gave a gentleman watching her palpitations along with a desire for an immediate introduction. "Yes," said Constance, "but she also said that Grandmother would do her best to see that I'd no chance to make any decisions at all. I am so glad you arrived home, Father. So very glad!"

"Harrumph. So am I my dear. And now I believe we must return to your chaperones so that your next partner will not despair of finding you."

"Father?"

"Hmm?"

"Will you too keep in mind that when you choose a new wife you must think about *her* character and interests?"

He stopped her. Very softly he asked, "You do not think it disloyal that I might take a bride, setting another woman in your mother's place?"

"Not at all," replied Constance promptly. "Your mother and her father made that marriage. Mother said you would make your own this time and she wished you nothing but happiness in your choice."

Rath blinked rapidly, experiencing a sudden desire to cry, shedding tears he was unsure were sad or happy. Perhaps both? "As I have already said, your mother was wise and wonderful. A very special woman." He put her hand on his arm and led her back to where the others awaited them.

Except for the two waltzes she sat out with Mr. Charles, the rest of the evening passed for Constance in something of a blur. She feared she'd been terribly impertinent when talking to her father about the possibility of his taking a second wife, and she had certainly chosen an exceedingly dangerous place for such a conversation. Still, so far as she could determine, no one had overheard her words, and her father had not seemed to mind. Still, she should not have done it—and so she told Miss Josephina when, later that evening, her blunt aunt asked in her blunt manner what had happened to overset her.

"I think you are wrong to be perturbed," said her aunt slowly. "It was a good thing you did. Perhaps not at Almack's," she added, "but your father will be glad to know that our sister hoped he'd remarry and hoped he would do so quickly. He need not feel guilty, you see. Felicity truly wished for his happiness and that he'd have good fortune in choosing a bride who would love him and whom he could love."

"May I tell you a secret?"

"I'll never stain," promised Josephina, using still another cant phrase from among those she should not have admitted to knowing—but which she loved sprinkling through her conversations. At least, such as would not shock her friends *too* badly.

"I hope very much Father will have Miss Adams."

"Now I will tell *you* a secret."

Constance nodded, her expression one of anticipation.

"Your Aunt Freddy and I hope for the very same thing!"

They laughed and, arm in arm, went up the stairs, each to her own bed.

The very next day an exceedingly nervous Allen Charles asked for an interview with Colonel Lord Cranston. "I fear two things," admitted the young man.

"And those are?" asked Rath when it seemed Allen had fallen into a brown study.

"Hmm? Oh! That it is exceedingly impertinent of me to ask for Miss Moorhead's hand in marriage when it is so obvious she might match herself with a man of far higher status and far more wealth than I can command. Not," added the young man quickly, "that I cannot keep your daughter in the elegancies of life!" He proceeded to lay before his love's father an outline of his holdings and added that, until he actually began garnering an income from his choice of profession, his father would continue his allowance. "He has told me he will increase it if I wed before-times." Allen grinned, his eyes twinkling. "My father is a great believer in marriage, my lord. He believes it steadies a young man!"

"So it does," said Rath, nodding. "I will tell you frankly I've no objections to you on the grounds of your being a second son, nor do I worry that you cannot support a wife."

"I believe I hear a caveat?" Fearing what it might be, Mr. Charles quickly added, "May I finish before you go on?"

"Certainly."

"The second problem is that I know I am rushing my fences! We have known each other for such a brief period. I promised myself I would give her time to know her own mind. And yet, when I watched her last night"— his ears turned bright red—"I found myself jealous of every man who looked at her. My feelings toward those who actually spoke to her and those who danced with her! Well, you can imagine, I am sure."

Rath chuckled. "Oh yes. I have known those same emotions on occasion."

Such, he thought, *as last evening when my Annabelle was accosted by more than one man!* He blinked. *My Annabelle?* He forced his mind from a sudden and inescapable realization that his emotions for Miss Adams had grown a trifle more complicated than he'd realized. This was not the time for such revelations—not when he must think only of Constance, so he'd best get rid of young Charles quickly. *Then* he could think his own thoughts!

"You have come to ask if you may speak with her immediately?" he asked.

Mr. Charles nodded. "Yes. I have."

Rath, too, nodded and smiled to see the young man relax. "One moment please before we have her sent for. I've a pair of caveats—to use your word." Allen tensed up all over again. "You yourself pointed out that you and Constance have known each other only briefly. I will not permit the taking of vows until . . . oh, shall we say after Christmas? Early in January, perhaps?" Allen looked disappointed but nodded. "It will give you time to finish your studies, as well as time for the two of you to become better acquainted. Which brings me to my second point."

When he didn't immediately continue, Allen fidgeted, and then forced himself to stillness.

"Allen . . . May I call you that?" Allen nodded. *"If* Constance agrees to this engagement, then I mean to have a serious discussion with her. I want her to know that if, at any time, she decides she cannot, for any reason, go through with the marriage, then I will support her decision to jilt you."

"But . . . !"

"Yes, I know. A young woman does not lightly do such a thing, but"—he cast a sharp look toward Allen—"do you by chance know any of my sisters?" Allen frowned, unsure that he did, and Rath told him about their marriages. ". . . so you see I will not have my daughter suffering as they have. I do not think you've any hidden vices, but if it becomes evident that, under that very charming exterior, you are a beast, I will not force her to wed you even if the banns have been read!"

"Then," said Allen, relaxing all over again, "since I am not an ogre, I will not concern myself!"

Rath smiled a trifle grimly. "I just wished you to know my feelings on this."

"Understandable emotions." The younger man frowned. "If you had not returned to London just now, would Lady Morlande have had a hand in choosing my Constance's husband?"

"She had already done so," said Rath dryly. "She is exceedingly angry that I have returned. Her insistence on having her own way and her tendency to interfere are, frankly, the reasons I am willing to permit an engagement between you far sooner than I feel reasonable. An official notice will stop her plotting and scheming to have her way in this."

"Lord Tolbridge?" Rath nodded. Allen whooshed out a breath. "May I speak with Constance immediately? We cannot chance something happening to bring about *that* alliance."

Constance was called to her father's study. Her brows arched when she saw who was with him and then she smiled. And *then*, her eyes widening in sudden suspicion, she blushed.

"My dear," said Rath, turning suspicion to reality, "Mr. Charles has asked permission to speak to you on a very serious subject. Are you agreeable? Do not say yes," he added hurriedly when she began to nod, "unless you are certain."

She grinned, approached her father, and rising on tiptoes, kissed his cheek. "I had a dream in which I was certain almost before I knew his name, but that is nonsense, of course." She held her hand toward Allen who approached and clasped it. "I have not been rash. Instead I have thought long and carefully before deciding I can not live without him!" And having spoken from the heart she blushed furiously. "Oh dear. What if he has come only to ask us if we would care to see the maze at Richmond!"

Rath laughed. "You would be in the basket for certain, my child!"

"Oh no," said Allen, keeping a sober visage with difficulty. "I am so much the complete gentleman that I will instantly forget all plans for a picnic at Richmond and offer hand and heart so that you need not feel embarrassed!" Then he sobered for real. Grasping her other hand so that he held both firmly, he added, "My dear, will you? Do you know how much I have come to love you? Will you accept me for your husband?"

Constance smiled mistily. "You can love me no more than I love you, Allen. And of course I will wed you. When and where you will."

Rath, who had meant to leave the two alone, was impressed with Allen's savoir faire, that he could say such things before the chit's sire! Now it was too late and his daughter's last comment could not be allowed to stand without comment.

"As to that," he interrupted hurriedly, "I have decreed the *when* must not be until the New Year arrives. I have more to say to you, my child, but it will wait until later.

Allen, you will see to inserting the announcement into the papers as soon as you've apprised your parents of your change of status?"

Allen nodded, his eyes never leaving Constance's. "Yes sir. I will go to them when I leave here and send in the notices immediately after."

"Then I will allow the two of you a moment's privacy. Fifteen minutes only. You will come then to the salon and face the company," he finished and grinned, suddenly looking very much like Constance in a mischievous mood. "As I recall that is the most difficult part of marrying. The fending off of the curious both before and immediately after!"

Two days later, upon reading the notice of her granddaughter's coming nuptials, Lady Morlande threw such a tantrum even Bloom thought seriously of leaving her service.

For nearly a month, as the Season continued, the Cranston House household was occupied from morning to very late at night. Annabelle was so tired she almost wished Lord Cranston had allowed Constance to wed her Allen immediately.

If only, she thought, *I had not fallen in love with him. If only I did not have to hide it from everyone.*

But hide it she did. In fact she hid it so well Rath could not nerve himself to approach her as he wished to do. Keeping himself well in line, he continued to carry on as if nothing had changed, but he knew himself well and worried that he could do so for very little longer.

In fact, the time came when he entered the back parlor one afternoon and discovered Annabelle curled up sound asleep in one of the large comfortable chairs he'd bought for his own comfort. He'd not been allowed to put them in the formal salon, of course, but everyone liked them for reading, which, he saw, Annabelle had been doing. He eyed her and knew he should leave her.

Instantly.

Before he did something truly stupid. Miss Adams had not given him the least bit of encouragement that she would welcome his advances . . . but advance he would if he did not put himself on the other side of the door.

Still he didn't move.

He could neither leave nor approach her. His legs had mutinied and refused his orders. He looked down at them and scowled. He still held the crop he'd taken with him when he'd ridden out an hour earlier and he used it, giving a sharp crack to the side of his boot.

The boot didn't react. Miss Adams did. "Oh!"

He looked across the room. Blinking sleepily, Annabelle smiled at him, a sweet welcoming smile. Then, shaking her head, the smile faded, and she straightened her limbs, sitting more primly.

"Lord Cranston."

Her voice was no more than polite and there was a faintly wary questioning look in her eyes—but there had been that first sweet reaction to seeing him. . . .

"You wished something?" she continued.

"Wished something?" Rath felt his lips twitch at the corners and knew from the warmth that his ears had turned bright red. "Oh yes. I very definitely do wish—" He strolled nearer. Perhaps an observer would have said he prowled. "—something."

Alarm replaced polite inquiry and Annabelle grasped the arms of the chair, her knuckles rather yellow from the tightness of her grip. "My lord?"

He realized what he was doing and turned away. "I apologize." He swung back. "No I don't. Miss

Adams . . . Annabelle . . . have you any notion at all of my feelings for you?"

She swallowed. Hard. "Sir?"

"You are an attractive woman. An intelligent woman. You . . ."

When he didn't continue, the hopes his first words roused faded and she turned pale from the disappointment. "Thank you?"

He groaned. "I am doing this all wrong," he said.

"This?" she asked, her hopes once again wiggling around and calling attention to themselves.

"Miss Adams, I've the temerity"—he straightened to military erectness—"to hope that you . . ."

The door swung open and Constance rushed in. "Father! Annabelle! Do come! Quickly!" She ran back out.

Annabelle and Rath stared at each other. He swallowed, sighed, and holding out his hand to her, said, "Obviously this is not the proper time for this. Shall we go?"

Annabelle, for the first time ever, gnashed her teeth. Had he or had he not been about to ask for her hand? Or had he merely been about to—the dreadful thought was *not* so *unacceptable* as it should have been—give her what was called a slip on the shoulder?

"Do come!" she heard Constance's voice drifting back from the front of the house.

They came.

Rath's older brother, Rupert Moorhead, Lord Morlande, stood in the hall, smiling down at Frederica, who fluttered and twittered. Constance, who had met her uncle only twice before, also smiled. "See who has come for a visit!" she exclaimed when Rath, seeing his brother, hurried forward.

"Rupert! You took my advice and came to town!"

"It occurred to me I'd not have to stay with Mother since you had opened up Cranston House. Miss Freddy has been telling me a room will be prepared for me instantly and that I may stay as long as I like. May I?" he finished whimsically. His eye lit up on Annabelle and he smiled. "Hello there. Miss Adams is it not? Delighted to see you again. Ah! Miss Blackstone!" he added, as Miss Josephina joined them. "And how are you?"

Upset that, when he'd finally nerved himself to ask Miss Adams to wed him, he not been allowed time to do so, Rath could, even so, *not* be *unhappy* that his brother had come. Even if totally unexpectedly and at the least auspicious moment.

While Annabelle's possessions were transferred to Constance's room and Miss Frederica's to Annabelle's, he took Rupert off to their club, where many were surprised and delighted to see their old friend, who had become something of a recluse.

Lord Morlande admitted to Rath that the fact his wife had left England and gone to Paris, as had many others now that it was open to English visitors, had been the deciding factor in his coming to London.

Everyone knew the two were estranged and were aware that Lady Morlande had made for herself a reputation no one would envy. And since Lord Morlande was well liked, no one mentioned her name. Lord Morlande set about enjoying himself as he'd not done for many a year.

On any number of occasions over the next week, Rath sent a rueful glance toward Annabelle. Annabelle, still uncertain just what her love had been about to offer her—if anything—grew still more exhausted as she attempted to control all her ridiculous emotions when others were near. With Lord Morlande's arrival, she did not even have a room of her own into which she could retire at night. Life had become exceedingly difficult.

One fine day the party from Cranston House along with several Charleses, drove out to Richmond Park for a picnic. Once everyone had eaten their fill, the party broke up into small groups. Rupert walked off with Miss Josephina. Miss Frederica, Constance and Allen strolled off in another direction. Allen's cousins joined Lord and Lady Avondale, who were determined to add a new butterfly to her ladyship's collection. And Miss Adams, feeling more than a trifle de trop, settled herself on the rug in the shade and opened the book she'd brought for just such a situation.

Rath, who had started off with his brother and Miss Jo, soon concluded he was unnecessary to either and turned back. When he saw Annabelle sitting by herself, he grinned and hurried his pace a trifle.

"Miss Adams," he said softly.

But soft as it was, his voice startled her. She dropped her book.

Rath stooped to pick it up, glanced at the title, and handed it to her. "By a lady? Is it good?" He settled himself beside her.

"Have you not read Miss Austen's tales? She writes about real people and real situations and with a great deal of humor. If you have not tried one, I will loan you this," she said and offered it to him.

He took it, but laid it aside. "Miss Adams . . ." His voice trailed off and he felt his ears heat up. *Why*, he wondered, *is it so difficult to ask a woman to be your wife?*

Annabelle, not quite certain she wished to hear what he was about to say, just in case it was not the words she most wished to hear, asked him if he was satisfied with the settlements made by Lord Avondale on behalf of his son.

"His lordship was all that was generous. Miss Adams . . ."

Once again he was not allowed to speak the words he'd practiced over and over in the privacy of his room. This time it was Miss Mary Charles running up and demanding that Miss Adams and Rath look at the lovely butterfly carefully saved in Lady Avondale's killing jar. "Isn't it lovely?" asked the young woman. "Do come help us. We've extra nets you know." She ran back toward the meadow area, where one could see Lady Avondale, bent over, raising her feet high for each careful step, the net held at just the proper angle, stalking still another of the lovely insects.

Rath sighed. He rose. "Shall we, Miss Adams? It appears there is no privacy even here in a park so large as Richmond's!"

Privacy. How he wished for a bit of privacy.

The word and the implication circled in Annabelle's brain until she wondered if she might not be better off moving, immediately, to live under her grandfather's roof . . . but she didn't want to. Whatever Rath—she changed that to Lord Cranston—had in mind, he had not yet said it. Time enough to leave once she knew all he wanted of her was what she could not, with propriety, give.

Even if she wanted to!

Twice more Rath attempted to be private with Annabelle. Once Rupert interrupted when he wished to consult his brother about an estate matter that would, someday, affect Rath. The second time Miss Josephina walked in on them.

Josephina was not a stupid woman and guessed what was going forward. She whisked herself back out of the room. Once she was alone, she gave herself a terrible scold for interrupting a tender scene that would very likely have ended just the way she wanted it to end.

The *next* time Rath happened upon her when no one else was around, Annabelle lost her nerve and invented an excuse to leave him before he could open his mouth.

Rath, watching her leave the room in something of a
rush, frowned. Was she telling him she didn't wish him
to speak? A lady could not, after all, tell a gentleman he
should not court her. She was only allowed to say no if
and when he actually proposed. Miss Adams had no one
she could ask to hint him away . . . so what to do?
Should he continue to hope? Or should he accept she
had no interest in him and leave her in peace? . . .

But she does like me, he told himself. *I am very nearly
certain she does.*

While Rath struggled to understand and attempted to
determine how to proceed, Miss Frederica entered the
salon.

"Ah," he said, "just the one I need. Freddy, I am at
my wits' end."

"What troubles you?" she asked, coming immediately
to his side and looking up at him with sympathy and
that willingness to listen that made her one of the kindest
women gracing the ton.

"It is Miss Adams, Freddy. I have been trying ever
since Constance agreed to wed Allen to ask her to marry
me, but we've been interrupted every time . . . until today when she made a ridiculous excuse and left me before I could do more than ask if she'd had a pleasant
day!"

"What would you have me do, Rath?"

He felt his ears burn. "Could you, perhaps . . ." His
voice died away.

"Talk to her? Discover if she wishes you to the
devil?"

He smiled but it was a rather wry smile. "You sound
just like Josephina, Freddy!"

She smiled. "Nonsense. No one can sound like Jo!
But you do not say if I should talk to Miss Adams for
you."

"Please?"

Her smile broadened. "Since you ask so nicely, I'll do it." Inside she was gloating. All was working out just as she had hoped. "I'll do it right now."

She left him and, knowing he'd pace the salon until she returned, hurried to find Miss Adams. "Ah. There you are, Annabelle. May I speak with you for a minute?"

Annabelle turned on the piano bench. "Yes, Miss Frederica? Can I help you?"

"Actually, I am hoping to help you. I have just come from Rath. He is terribly upset."

"Upset?"

"He cannot seem to find a single moment when he can discuss something of importance with you," said Frederica in a teasing tone. Then she sobered. "Is it that you do not wish him to speak?"

Annabelle bit her lip. Then she blurted, "It is that I haven't a notion what he will say!"

Frederica's eyes widened. "Ah! You feared a . . . a *dishonorable* proposal? Surely not!"

Annabelle hung her head and fiddled with the hand-kerchief she had not realized she'd pulled from her sleeve. "But I am . . . Surely you do not suggest it *might* be . . ." She raised wide desperate eyes to meet Frederica's kindly gaze.

"Honorable. Of course he means to ask you to wed him. Would he insult you by any other sort of question? Nonsense. You cannot have been so foolish as to think such a thing!"

"Foolish? But, Frederica, think! I am so firmly on the shelf! I am thirty-two, an ape-leader who will lead apes in hell! Far too old and far too much a nobody! How can he possibly . . ."

"Perhaps because he has fallen in love with you?" Frederica smiled to see Annabelle blush. "Mind you, I am not quite certain he knows it himself, but I've watched it happening. He was attracted to you from the

first, you know. And the more he came to know you"—
Frederica's smile widened—"the less he wished to lose
you. When Constance agreed to wed her Allen, he decided he was free to ask you to wed him, but even though
he has nerved himself to the point on several occasions,
he has yet to speak the words!"

"He loves me?" asked Annabelle. "Me?"

"You, my dear, are a very special lady—as our sister
knew. She told me—oh perhaps a month before she
died—that she rather hoped you and Rath might discover
your mutual appreciation of each other."

Annabelle felt her face flame. And then the blood
rushed from her head and embarrassment was followed
by a feeling she might faint. "Lady Cranston knew I felt
a silly *tendre* for Lord Cranston?"

"Not silly. Not at all silly!"

"I am so embarrassed. I thought I had hidden it from
everyone." Her hands went to hide her cheeks, which
reddened all over again.

"There is no reason for you to feel embarrassed." Silence followed and Frederica waited patiently for Annabelle to absorb what she'd learned and feel ready for the
next step. When Miss Adams was again composed and
her usual contained self, Frederica asked, "Shall I put
poor Rath out of his misery and tell him you await him
here?"

Although more than a trifle disconcerted at the
thought her heart's desire was about to be fulfilled, Annabelle managed to nod.

Frederica left the room and went to the salon, where,
as she'd expected, Rath paced from end to end and back
again. She smiled. "Rath."

He turned on his heel and came to her. "Tell me!"

"She awaits you in the little parlor and"—Frederica
grasped his coat sleeve as he passed her and hung on—
"lock the door when you go in!"

He turned, still backing toward the salon door. "Excellent advice, oh you best of ladies!"

Ten minutes later he drew his fiancée into his arms and, if she hadn't been so very agreeable as to want it, the passion of his kiss might have frightened her into running from him once again! When he finally broke away from her, Rath stared down into her bemused face. "Annabelle," he said, the shock of his discovery plain in his voice, "I have fallen in love with you! I wonder when that happened!"

She chuckled. "I haven't a notion, Rath, but it cannot have been so long ago as I fell in love with you."

"Can it not?"

"It has been nearly a decade since I first knew I loved you."

He blinked. "So long ago?"

She nodded. "At first I thought it merely a silly and unsuitable infatuation, but it would not go away. Finally I had to admit I loved you."

That was such agreeable news that Rath had to have another kiss, which turned into two and then three and, if someone had not knocked on the door just then, might have turned into something much more than a kiss—and neither would have objected for a moment.

"Quick," he whispered, "say you'll wed me as soon as the settlements may be drawn up and I acquire a special license!"

"Yes."

He grinned. "Excellent lady!"

Opening the door wide, he was unsurprised to find his whole household waiting in the hall. He bowed them into the small parlor. A footman, who carried a tray on which rested a bottle of champagne and glasses, followed them in. As soon as the toasts had been made, Rath excused himself. "I've much to do. Merely for politeness's sake I must inform Lord Fortesque. Then I'll see my solicitor, and after that I must ride out to Lambeth Palace to visit the archbishop. Rup?" He turned to his brother. "Will you come with me?"

Rupert did so gladly.

Lord Fortesque, when told, sighed. He nodded. "I feared it. I had hoped . . . ah, but she will be happy with you, Lord Cranston. I will have my solicitor meet with yours and have the papers drawn up. They should be ready for signing by the end of the week. May I make one request?" When Rath, a trifle fearful of what the reclusive earl might say, nodded, his lordship continued. "I would like it if she were married from this house and if I was allowed to give her away."

"Is that all!" Rath wasn't certain what he'd feared. "Of course. Annabelle will be pleased to have it so."

He wasn't as certain as he sounded, but he knew the ton would be far less likely to make rude comments about his Annabelle if her grandfather made it clear he approved their marriage, so he would, if necessary, convince her it was for the best. And then, deciding a further possibility of embarrassment would be avoided if they did things in the traditional manner, he put aside all thought of a special license. He would bide his soul in patience until the banns could be called rather than make of their nuptials a hurried thing.

"I would not have the least word whispered to her disadvantage," he said to Rupert as they rode toward the City and Rath's solicitor's office, where Rath gave his orders as to Annabelle's rights when the settlements were written up and how a new will should be drawn up.

Rath was pleased to discover Annabelle was happy with Lord Fortesque's notion and, now that they were officially engaged, she made a further suggestion. "Perhaps," she said, "it would be best if I removed to my grandfather's until the wedding. I know it is only a couple of weeks, but the instant the notice appears, the gossips will find all sorts of reasons why I should not be here."

It had not occurred to Rath she'd be the object of gossip for *that* particular reason, but since he'd no wish to make her uncomfortable, he reluctantly agreed it was the proper thing to do . . . but asked if she objected to having the first reading of the banns that very Sunday.

Three Sundays in a row the banns were read and then Annabelle and Rath were married. An exceedingly happy and, it must be admitted, rather smug Constance stood up with Annabelle. Rupert supported his brother. Lord Fortesque somehow managed a miracle, and although the wedding itself included only close family and very close friends, the wedding breakfast was the most elaborate and best-attended function held that spring. Everyone enjoyed themselves immensely . . .

. . . excepting, of course, the dowager.

Lady Morlande predicted disaster of all sorts—particularly that the necessary heir would not be forthcoming—but, secretly, she felt a deal of relief upon discovering Lord Fortesque had not only given his granddaughter the dowry that should have been her mother's, but had added a small estate in the Lake District and another—unfortunately smaller still, but one could not have everything—situated in Kent not far from Canterbury.

The next morning the Misses Blackstones and Constance waved Rath and Annabelle off as they started on their wedding journey. Allen Charles arrived just too late to see them before they left, but was invited in for breakfast so did not feel he'd wasted his time getting up early and rushing to Cranston House.

Lord and the new Lady Cranston enjoyed their travels

and bride visits immensely, but both were imbued with a rather difficult sense of duty and less than a month after they set off they returned to London.

"There is a great deal to do to prepare Constance for her wedding, you know," said Annabelle earnestly. "A trousseau to begin with . . ."

"Yes, there is that and I really must go up to Colemere Hills for a few days to see what needs doing to ready it for our eventual return there. I'll not plan any great changes, my Bella, for you will wish to do that yourself, but I can check that all is clean and the servants are up to snuff."

"I can make a *few* suggestions," she said a trifle diffidently, and did so, citing the need for new hangings in Rath's bedroom, and the need to replace the drugget covering the upper hall and the floor of the butler's pantry along with a number of other things of a similar nature that needed doing but which did not require her personal decision to accomplish.

"—Oh, and Cook has been demanding one of the new closed stoves. Your nearest neighbor, Mrs. Bronston, installed one for her cook and Cook has been jealous ever since!"

They spoke of practical things, but both knew their return was really that they could not bear to be away from Constance a moment longer. All too soon they would lose her and they wished to enjoy her presence in their home for as long as possible!

They had been back in London only a few days when Rath's solicitor requested a meeting with the two of them. Rath, curious, agreed, and the two sat in the small back parlor, awaiting the man's arrival.

The usual politenesses were exchanged, refreshment offered and refused, and then the solicitor opened a leather folder and took from it a sealed letter. He held it a tantalizingly few inches from Rath's hand. "I was

requested by your first wife to give you this if it chanced
the two of you married each other." He extended the
missive and then drew it back. "I nearly forgot that I
am to tell you it was her greatest hope." Again he held
out the letter and this time allowed Rath to take it. Then
he stood, said all that was proper, ending with, ". . . I
know you will wish privacy in which to read it so I will
leave you now." He smiled, bowed, and when Rath offered to see him out, shook his head. "I know the way,
my lord. Good day." He bowed again and was gone.

Rath and Annabelle looked at each other. Rath noticed
his hand trembled slightly and laughed weakly. "Why,
when I have faced Napoleon's troops in the Spanish high-
lands, and rebellious Marathas in India, do I feel far
more nervous at this moment?"

"Words from beyond the grave?" Annabelle smiled
weakly. "He did say Lady Cranston wished us well, did
he not?"

"The *first* Lady Cranston." Rath nodded but still could
not bring himself to put a finger under the wax seal and
lift it. Finally he handed it to Annabelle. "It is addressed
to the both of us. Will you read it to me, my dear?"

Annabelle nodded. She opened the stiff folds and
pressed them back and then, turning the missive the right
end up, she quickly perused the brief message. She
smiled. "My Dears," she read and lifted her eyes to meet
Rath's. "My Dears," she began again, "if you are reading
this then my hopes have become reality. It has been a
comforting thought in my head these last months that
you two will suit each other very well. The two people
who most love our Constance will continue to look after
her and see to her welfare and then, when she weds, will
be a comfort and a joy to each other. I wish you both
all the best. You will have a long and loving life together
and that thought pleases me. All my love to both of you,

Felicity Moorhead." Again Annabelle lifted her gaze to meet Rath's. Tears made her eyes glisten.

Rath, too, felt he might cry. "It is a lovely and loving letter," he said quietly. "I don't know what to say."

"We are a very lucky pair, are we not? Not only do we have Felicity's blessing, but Constance's as well."

"And my brother's. Yes. I believe there is only one who does not wholeheartedly approve our marriage, my dear, but that is only because she did not organize and manage the whole. My mother cannot bear that she not control everyone and everything."

"Your mother, Rath, is a very unhappy woman. I am sorry for her."

"Hmm. Yes. Perhaps." Rath and the whole of his family had suffered too much from the dowager's interference in their lives to find it easy to try to understand her. "Shall we join the others and allow them to read this?" He flicked the page his wife still held.

Constance did cry, but they were happy tears. "Isn't it wonderful?" She grasped Allen's hand and held it tightly. "We may *all* be happy!"

The only one who was not was the Dowager Lady Morlande. She was neither a happy lady nor so healthy as of yore. Whenever any of three particular weddings celebrated that year crossed her mind, the poor lady would experience one spasm after another!

Since she could never see anyone's point of view but her own, knew she was right about everything, and always found it intolerable when others did *not* do as she demanded, she could never admit that Rath and Annabelle, or that Constance and Allen, or, for that matter, that Lord Tolbridge and Mrs. Lambsworth, had made proper decisions and done what was best for themselves.

"My idiotic son spent far too long in foreign parts,"

confided Lady Morlande to anyone who would listen.
"Very obviously the hot sun baked his head and he returned to us quite out of his mind! I am thinking seriously of having him incarcerated in a bedlam!"

But of course she did not. Her solicitor of many years
looked her in the eye when she suggested it, told her not
to be more of a crackbrain than she must and, before
she could dismiss him, also told her she could find herself another man of business. He had had enough.

The only time Rath himself thought he might go out
of his mind was very nearly a year later. His son and
his grandson were born within hours of each other, and
when everyone survived the ordeal in good health, both
mothers and sons *and* the fathers—who had paced par-
allel paths in a carpet at Colemore Hills while waiting
for the news—he thought he might very well go mad
for the joy of it!

More Zebra Regency Romances